CLOSING THE DISTANCE

LA WOLVES BOOK SEVEN

CADENCE KEYS

Editors: Happily Editing Anns

Cover Design: Kate Farlow, Y'all. That Graphic

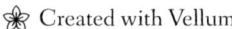 Created with Vellum

For every woman who's ever felt unwanted or unlovable. You are worthy of the deepest love in the world.

CLOSING THE DISTANCE

LA WOLVES FOOTBALL
BOOK 7

CADENCE KEYS

ONE

Lexi

This is not how I usually spend a Friday night. Actually, this isn't how I'd choose to spend *any* night, but when your best friend calls you and begs you to go out with her so she can get over her shitty ex, you put aside your personal desires and put on the sluttiest dress you own—which is arguably not that slutty at all—and join her in a night of debauchery.

As I toss back another shot of liquid courage, I decide to say "fuck it" and throw caution to the wind. Maybe it's good for me to do something out of my norm.

Blaire tosses her hands up in the air as she smiles at me. "Hell yeah. Lexi is finally letting loose."

I give her a wan smile as I fight the urge to cough from the burning sensation working its way through my chest into the pit of my stomach.

I can barely hear her over the pounding bass in the fancy Hollywood club she chose. I take a sip of lemon water, hoping it'll cool the burning of the shot, and remind myself I'm doing this for her. It doesn't matter if I'd much rather be curled up at home in the oversized beanbag I got on sale at Target with the latest romance pulled up on my tablet that I bought just to try to reduce my book buying.

Books are my happy place, and I'm much more comfortable getting lost in a book than fighting against the overly loud music blaring through this club just to have a conversation with my friend.

God, I sound like I'm eighty-seven instead of twenty-seven.

Blaire tosses back her own shot and then grabs my hand and pulls me away from the bar into the throng of people. She lets her body move to the beat of the music, and I stand there trying to find my rhythm, but I've not had nearly enough alcohol. She squints at me when she notices my lame moves, and I offer her a shrug.

"You are too hot to dance this badly," she shouts.

"I like to be unique!" I shout back with a smile.

She rolls her eyes, but her lips pull into a wide grin as she grabs my hands and tries to guide me to dance like her. I'd tell her it's useless, but I know she won't give up. She's stubborn like that. I'm convinced it's the only reason she refused to let me push her away. She decided we were going to be friends, and no matter how many times I brushed off hanging out or made excuses, she inserted herself until I finally caved. It helped that I couldn't get away from her even if I'd wanted to since we're the only eighth-grade English teachers in our building and team up often to talk about how to support our students.

She's the first real friend I've ever had, and most days, I'm grateful she was stubborn enough not to let me hide in my shell like I usually do.

Although, now is not one of those times. I'd still definitely rather be home reading.

We dance—and by dance, I mean, she dances and I look like I'm a robot that needs some WD-40—for another half hour before I gesture back to the bar. Not only are these heels killing my feet, but I'm desperate for another drink if we're going to keep dancing. I'm too sober not to be totally mortified by how bad my moves are.

She nods her head, and we move back to the bar which is only slightly less crowded than the dance floor. In the hour we've been here, this place seems to have exploded with people.

"Isn't this way better than sitting at home on a Friday night grading papers?"

"You grade on Fridays?" I shout and try to get the bartender's attention.

"Don't even pretend you don't."

I shake my head. "Fridays are my night off." Saturdays on the other hand...I definitely spend too many weekend hours grading papers. But Fridays are mine to decompress from the long week. I just prefer to decompress in fuzzy socks, yoga pants, an oversized sweater, and no bra.

Her expression sobers. "Are you really not having fun?"

My anxiety flares, but I push it down. I may have fought against Blaire's friendship in the beginning, but now that I have her in my life, I don't want to do anything that might push her away. I can sacrifice one night for her.

"I'll have more fun after I have another drink. Promise," I say, squeezing her hand.

The bartender starts making his way toward us when Blaire grabs my arm tight. "Oh my God, the sexiest man I've ever seen is walking this way, and he's staring at us."

I spin around trying to see. "Are you sure?"

She roughly forces me to stay facing her. "Don't look! Play it cool."

She smiles, her eyes scanning down a man behind me, and there's no way to miss the way her smile widens and she gets all flirty. Her hands fall from my arms, one going to her hip and one resting along the bar. I fight back my grin at her pose.

"Hey ladies. My cousin and I were wondering if we could buy you drinks?"

"We'd love that," Blaire says.

I spin around to check out these guys that apparently have Blaire all twitterpated and nearly forget to breathe when my gaze connects with golden-brown eyes. They light up and then I manage to actually see the man attached. He's tall—like, really tall, easily six foot four if I had to guess—and built. His black button-down shirt is snug across his toned chest and thick biceps, but hangs loose down his torso, no doubt hiding a drool-worthy set of abs. The sleeves are rolled up slightly, showing off his toned forearms covered in tattoos. His sandy-brown hair is a little unruly on top, but trimmed short along the sides. A piece falls on his forehead, and my fingers itch to brush it aside.

A tingle starts deep in my core, nearly startling me. It's been a long time since a man made me feel anything besides minor curiosity. No one has ever made my skin feel tight and my stomach fluttery, let alone made my lady bits waken with a fierce awareness and my nipples bead in arousal.

This man is sex personified.

A voice next to him catches my attention, and I barely manage to rip my gaze away to focus on the dark-haired man beside him whose gaze is locked on Blaire. He's the one who spoke to us.

I glance back at brown eyes wondering what his voice sounds like and find him still staring at me. There's an expression on his face I can't quite name—curiosity maybe, but also a hint of trepidation, like he's waiting for something.

"I'm Blaire and this is my bestie, Lexi."

The dark-haired man who looks to be about our age puts his hand out, taking Blaire's hand but holding it seductively instead of a typical handshake. "Blaire, that's a lovely name. I'm Devon. This is my cousin—"

"Ty," my brown-eyed man speaks, his voice deep and sexy and making that fluttery awareness in my belly pulse harder. Wait, no. He's not *mine*. But his gaze is still locked on me like I'm the only woman in the room, and I can't deny that I suddenly want him to be.

At least for tonight.

For the first time in my life, I consider the benefits of a one-night stand. The man standing in front of me could easily have any woman here, so I have no misconceptions that he's likely a one-and-done kind of guy. Could I do it? Could I actually let my guard down enough to let him give me all the pleasure his eyes promise?

Maybe tonight I don't have to be a wingwoman. Maybe tonight I can be the one who gets the attention of a man better than she ever could've imagined. And if that man just so happens to be this sexy Adonis in front of me, then sign me the hell up.

TWO

Ty

She has no idea who I am.

An excitement I haven't felt in a long-ass time fires up inside me. This woman is absolutely gorgeous with her dark blue eyes, long black hair, and hourglass figure. Thank God Devon went for the blonde or I'd have to fight him.

I put my hand out. "Nice to meet you."

"Lexi," she says, her voice a little breathy, her eyes wide yet heated. But she's missing the one thing I always look out for now that the Fierce Four have become so well-known. Women—jersey chasers specifically—have a particular glint in their eye when they know exactly who I am. While there's a gorgeous sparkle in Lexi's eyes, it's not one of recognition.

Just pure, old-fashioned attraction.

I hold her hand and give her a genuine smile. I don't think she realizes that her friend already gave her name, but I think it's cute she said it again. "Lexi, you wanna dance?"

As soon as the words leave my mouth, I start to worry. If we go out on the dance floor, someone might recognize me. Why did I ask her to dance? I should've had her and her friend come up to the VIP booth, which is where Devon and I were on our way to when he saw the blonde.

Lexi nibbles her lip, and her upper body sags slightly, and now my worry is about something else entirely. Is she about to shut me down? I can't remember the last time that happened.

"Um, I'm not very good." There's a hint of vulnerability in her admission that makes something tighten in my gut. I want to soothe her, not make her feel bad.

I also can't deny I'm grateful for the out she gave me so I can fix my error. "What about just grabbing some drinks and heading upstairs?"

"Oh, those are reserved for high rollers and VIPs," her friend—Blaire—says.

Devon claps me on the back with a shit-eating grin on his face, and I know exactly what he's about to say, and there's no way I can let him expose who I am.

I can't remember the last time I met a woman who didn't recognize me and see instant dollar signs. I'm dying to see how this night goes with someone who thinks I'm just an average Joe, albeit a rich one—there's no way to hide that, but she doesn't need to know I'm famous—out for a night on the town.

So before Devon can open his big mouth, I say, "I'm friends with the owner of the club, so he got us a booth. You ladies want to join us?" It's not a lie.

Lexi looks to Blaire and then back to me, that plush lip still trapped between her teeth. But whatever reservations she may have are completely shut down when Blaire says, "We'd love to."

"After you, ladies," I say, gesturing toward the stairs. Blaire wraps her arm around Lexi's, leaning her head close, and I'm sure they're talking about us, but it gives me the perfect opportunity to get Devon on board so he doesn't ruin what's turning out to be a way more interesting night than I imagined it would be.

"Dude," he starts, but I give him a look that shuts him up. "They don't know me. Let's keep it that way."

"Do you know how easily you could get that chick to agree to go back to your place if you told her who you are?"

I let out a heavy sigh. He doesn't get it. Of course he doesn't; no one does unless they live this life. Fame and fortune come with many perks and privileges, but unfortunately they also come with a lot of distrust for new people, especially when they know who I am. I can never guarantee that they want me for me. I didn't think about it much when I was a rookie. Hell, I tossed around my status as an NFL player to every woman I met. It wasn't until I got traded to the Wolves and found my big-time career success as a member of the Fierce Four that I realized how desperately I craved finding a woman who didn't know I was famous. Who wanted *me* and not the publicity that comes with being attached to me.

Unfortunately, every woman I've dated since getting drafted has had an agenda, and I was always just a means to an end. And despite what my cousin says, I've been dealing with this a lot longer than he has, and there are certain types of women who are not drawn to celebrities. I get a sinking feeling that Lexi might be one of those. She seems a bit skittish, and skittish women don't tend to want to date a guy whose face is plastered in the media every weekend during the season, which will start in a couple of weeks. Preseason games have already begun, which means my time to lie low is about to be up. Once the season kicks off, my face, along with the other three members of the Fierce Four, will be all over the city for promotion.

I'm not willing to risk losing the first woman who appears to show genuine interest in me on the off chance she might think it's cool that I'm famous.

"I want to see how this plays out without her knowing who I

really am, okay? Can you play it cool and keep that to yourself?" I ask Devon, hoping he can be a decent wingman. Normally, I would go out with one of the other members of the Fierce Four —Gabe Romero, Dominic Smith, and Romel Watson—but Gabe and Dom both have their own women now, and Romel has his three-year-old daughter who he prefers to spend time with, especially before the craziness of the season starts. I didn't even think I'd be going out tonight until Devon called to let me know he was in town for the weekend on a business trip and wanted to go out.

As we get closer to the booth where the women were directed, I'm suddenly grateful he reached out, or else I might not have gotten this opportunity.

We settle in the horseshoe shaped booth—Devon sitting next to Blaire, Lexi next to her, and me on Lexi's other side— and Devon immediately starts asking questions.

"So what do you two ladies do for work?"

"We're teachers," Blaire says, leaning into Devon and clearly feeling what he's feeling.

I focus my attention on the beauty next to me—Lexi. Even her name is sexy. "What do you teach?"

She takes a sip of her drink before focusing those mesmerizing dark-blue eyes on me. "Eighth grade English."

"Do you like it?"

Her smile grows, and any nervousness disappears as she tells me about her job. Each word out of her mouth makes me want to lean in and learn everything about her. She's passionate about what she does—that's obvious—and that passion is insanely attractive.

"What do you do?" she asks.

Fuck. I should've thought this through better. "Uh, I'm in risk management." Yeah, that works.

She cocks her head to the side, looking utterly adorable. "What does that entail?"

"I assess a given situation and coordinate with my partners on how best to deal with it so that everything plays out in our favor." Not a total lie. I just haven't said I do it on the football field.

She squints. "That's vague. Is this for marketing? Or..." She lets her sentence trail off, and I know what she's thinking. She's thinking I'm into something illegal. God, I'm fucking this up, but I don't want her to know what I do. It'll ruin everything.

But I also don't love the idea of outright lying to her. "Do you watch sports?"

She frowns. "No, sorry."

Thank fuck my instincts were right. "I do risk management for a local team. To protect the players and their goals."

Again, it's not an outright lie. I definitely do that in a sense in my position as safety. Except the players I protect are my own, and I'm not actively protecting them, but defending them so our quarterback can get back out on the field faster and our offense can score some points. But those are minor details.

She stares at me for a moment, an expression on her face that tells me she's not buying what I'm putting down. And then she sets down her glass, and my hope starts to fade.

Shit.

But she surprises me. She leans forward. "Listen, I teach eighth graders, and while they can be sweet, they also often test boundaries and push the truth, so I know when someone's not telling me the full story." She glances over at Blaire who's already making out with Devon—good for him—and then refocuses on me. "But I promised myself I would let loose tonight. It's been a rough first couple of weeks at work, and Blaire dragged me out because we both needed a night to let our hair down. So what if we just enjoy the night, see where it goes, and keep things casual?"

Is she saying what I think she's saying? And if she is, why does that make me feel cheap?

"I don't like talking about my job." Not a lie. "But I do want to get to know you. I gotta be honest with you, Lexi, it's been a long time since I've been this drawn to a woman I just met."

Her face morphs, and before I know it she's giggling into her hand. She places her other hand on my leg, and my brain short-circuits as the blood starts to flow south. "Does that line usually work on women?"

I can't help but laugh with her and shake my head. Who is this woman? "It wasn't a line, but yeah, most women tend not to give me such a hard time." Most women also already know who I am and want something from me.

She smiles brighter than she has all night, and my gut tightens with need. "I'm not most women."

I give her my own smile as my interest in her skyrockets. "No, you most certainly are not."

THREE

Lexi

As soon as the elevator doors close in his fancy apartment building, my body is crowded against the wall, and Ty's lips crash down on mine. My whole body melts against his while heat licks across every nerve ending, setting my skin on fire with a lust I've never felt before. I've never wanted a man this badly, but after hours of flirting, all I want is for him to keep kissing me like he needs me to breathe.

All night long, there have been small touches between the two of us, steamy looks, and a growing tension like someone was pulling a rubber band taut until it was about to snap. But unlike Devon and Blaire, he didn't kiss me at the club, which honestly, only made me want him more.

My hands grip his hips and pull him against me, grinding on his thigh while his hard bulge rubs against my belly.

"Fuck, Lexi," he curses before his hands slide into my hair, holding me exactly how he wants me, and his tongue licks across my lips. I grant him entry, wanting nothing more than to feel his tongue against mine. My hips have a mind of their own and grind against him, seeking some kind of reprieve from the out-of-control desire coursing through my body.

The ding of the elevator breaks through my lust fog and he pulls away, clearly reluctant if the heavy sigh is any indication. "God, I can't wait to get you naked."

Same. But my brain is hazy and blissed-out from his drugging kiss, and no words come out of my mouth.

He grabs my hand, and I follow him out of the elevator, barely aware of our surroundings because I'm so distracted by him. His hair is disheveled and his clothes a little less perfect than they were when we met at the club, but he's still sexy as hell with his strong jaw peppered with some scruff, and those tattoos that I want to trace with my tongue. And goddamn, can the man kiss.

He opens the door in front of us and allows me to walk inside. I already texted Blaire the address just as a precaution, but now that I'm walking in front of him and not distracted by how hot he is and how badly I want him, I'm suddenly very aware of how high-end his place is.

It looks like a professional did the interior design. It certainly doesn't have the typical bachelor pad look I was expecting. Everything is white, black, and stainless steel. It's modern, but perfectly placed rugs make it also feel comfortable. It looks like something I'd see in a magazine featuring a rich bachelor pad, and in this part of LA, given the sheer size of his place, there's no doubt this guy is loaded.

The door shuts and I spin around to face him. He's gripping his neck and staring around his place as if he's embarrassed or something. I'm not sure what he could possibly be embarrassed about. It's not even messy like I would've expected from a bachelor pad.

And then a horrible thought hits me, and I want to puke.

"You're not married, are you?"

His brown eyes widen. "What?! No. Why would you think that?"

I glance around his relatively spotless apartment. "Because I've never met a man who keeps a place this clean unless he was married or in a very serious relationship."

His shoulders drop and a small smile lifts his lips. "No relationship. Not for over a year now. But my mom would kill me if she discovered she raised a slob. I hire a cleaning service to come over once a week, and I maintain it the rest of the time."

"Oh." The frantic beating of my heart settles again.

"Oh? Nothing else?" he asks, walking forward, his heated gaze locked on mine and trapping me in my spot.

"No," I whisper as he gets within a foot of me, staring down at me like he finds me endlessly fascinating.

And beautiful.

It's there in his gaze, his attraction to me. It's a type of focus I can honestly say I've never had from a man before. He's been attentive to me all night, even when the waitress in the VIP lounge tried to flirt and show off her cleavage every time she dropped off drinks or food. He never once wavered in giving me every ounce of his attention. It made me feel special in a way that also makes me nervous.

This is supposed to be casual. He's not supposed to make me feel anything besides sexual attraction. But there's a weight to his stare that is definitely more than casual, and it's right there on the tip of my tongue to ask him about his life. The desire to learn more about this man who came out of nowhere is strong, and it's making me rethink my stance on how this night is supposed to go.

No.

One night only. I'm letting loose. That's all. I don't have time for a relationship anyway.

I ignore the pang of disappointment that follows that lie. Blaire's the first person in a long time who put in the effort to climb over my steel walls and get to know me. I don't let people in, but there's a big part of me that wants to let *this guy* in, and that's so terrifying, I banish the thought immediately.

This night with him has been perfect. Anything more and he'll probably show his true colors like every other man from my past. And none of those colors were ever pretty. I don't want to learn that Ty is like all the rest. So, one night is all we'll have, and I'll be able to cherish the memory instead of letting him taint it.

"Kiss me," I plead.

"Gladly," he murmurs before his lips are back on mine and he's plundering my mouth with his tongue like he wants to learn every inch of it. I moan against him and sag into his body. His hands swoop me up into a bridal carry as he walks us somewhere farther into his apartment. I hope it's his bedroom because I need to feel his naked body on mine more than I need my next breath.

He pushes open a door at the end of the hall and then sets me down on his bed. I frantically go for his shirt buttons, but he grabs my hands, stopping me. "Not so fast there, sweetheart. I plan to take my time with you, unless you're in a rush to leave?"

"No," I say, but it's not the entire truth. I'm worried the longer I stay, the more the lines of tonight will blur and I'll want so much more than he can give me. This doesn't seem like a man who settles down with a teacher who had a bad upbringing and no family roots whatsoever. This looks like a man who ends up with some model or celebrity and has his wedding splashed all over the pages of *People* magazine. He's so far out of my league, it's not even funny. I'm just grateful he doesn't seem to have figured that out yet.

"Good," he says. "Now take your clothes off nice and slow for me."

"What about you?"

He smiles, his hands already reaching for the buttons on his shirt. "I'll be doing the same thing."

"Why don't you take my clothes off for me?" I ask, trying to be a little sexy when really I just want his hands on me.

He leans over me on the bed, caging me in with his thick arms, and slides his nose along my jaw before nipping at my ear. A zing of desire shoots straight to my clit, and my stomach clenches. "Because if I touch you, I won't be able to control myself and take this as slowly as I want to. God, you have no idea how desperate I am for you, to be inside you, how much restraint it's taking not to ravage you right now."

A needy moan escapes. "Please," I beg. God, I want him to do exactly that. I can't remember the last time I was ravaged. If I'm honest, the answer is probably never, at least not the way I imagine this man will. I'll be hugely disappointed if he turns out to be a dud in bed.

He groans and quickly stands back up, putting distance between us. "Lexi, you're fucking killing me."

But he still doesn't touch me. If I want him to, then I need to entice him with something he can't say no to. I stand up and spin around. "Can you unzip me?"

I hear him take a ragged breath before the heat of his body is at my back, and he grips the zipper in his big hands, pulling it down slowly. When he gets to the bottom, he pushes aside the upper half of my dress and drops a kiss at the top of my spine. "Where on earth did you come from?" he whispers so quietly, I'm not sure he meant for me to hear.

But I did, and those words affect me nearly as much as his touch. Not just the words themselves, but *how* he says them. Like I'm a gift—someone who's wanted.

I've never been wanted by anyone, not for anything real at least. Emotion sweeps through me, but I have lots of practice pushing it down, so that's what I do—shove it down as far as I can until I'm certain it won't threaten to ruin tonight for me.

When I'm sure my emotions won't show on my face, I spin around and slip out of my dress until it pools in a pile at my feet.

His eyes darken and smolder. "God, you are fucking gorgeous."

Nerves swirl and swoop in my belly as I laugh it off. "I'm sure you say that to all the girls."

His serious gaze pierces me and forces the lighthearted smile right off my face. "Not at all." He slides his hands into my hair again, holding me close and searing my soul with his intense gaze. "Lexi, I haven't felt like this about someone I just met. Ever."

I swallow thickly. No. That can't possibly be true. He's just playing me. That's what obviously rich guys do when they're with a girl from the wrong side of the tracks. Right?

"I don't care. Kiss me," I mutter, pushing up on my toes in an attempt to close the distance between our mouths.

He holds me just far enough away that I can't get what I want. "Not until you tell me you understand. You're special." He says it so softly and tenderly my heart aches.

"You don't know me," I say, hating how low and shaky my voice has gotten.

"I know enough. I know you're passionate about your students. You care about your friend—I heard you making sure she would be safe with Devon. You are respectful and kind. You thanked the waitress even though she kept trying to throw herself at me. You wished the bouncers a good night, and our driver a safe drive home. Do you know how many women have done that when I'm around?"

I shake my head.

"None. You are special, and I know we're just getting to

know each other, but I can't wait to learn everything I can, and not just how to make you scream my name," he adds with a soft smile, but there's still an intensity in his eyes that makes my stomach clench with nerves.

I can't give him what he thinks I can. I can give him this— sex and a night together. But this man has his life together, and I'm broken. He doesn't need my baggage. If he really knew me, he'd discover what a mess my life has been and that I'm nothing but ordinary. There's never been anything remotely special about me.

"Do you understand?" he asks again, his eyes pleading.

"Yes," I say. I understand that he's going to make it difficult for me to leave him. Already my heart aches, wanting to believe his words, even when I have a lifetime of examples proving them wrong.

Words are pretty things that are often empty and meaningless. Actions never fail to tell the truth.

I'll give him my body, but that's all I can give him.

He stares at me for another minute, and then because I need to move this along before I fall any deeper, I run my hands over his bare chest where his shirt gapes and slide my hands up and over his pecs until I reach his shoulders and push his shirt off. He lets me, his eyes never leaving mine but growing heavy-lidded the longer I touch him.

Once his shirt hits the floor, I move my hands to his belt, but he grabs them to stop me. "If you touch me there right now, this will be over embarrassingly fast. It's...it's been a while." He says it like he's self-conscious, but I'm curious what his definition of a while is.

"How long?"

"Six months."

That's longer than I would expect from a man as hot as he is who's clearly loaded.

A look crosses his face. "How long's it been for you?"

"Longer than that. Now take those pants off and fuck me."

His smile returns. "You're pretty pushy when you're horny, aren't you?"

"I was promised earth-shattering sex. Most men would've already started by now. Hell, most men would probably be done by now."

He undoes his belt and his pants as he talks. "I'm not most men," he says, spinning my own words from earlier in the evening back to me.

"No, you most certainly are not," I agree, and that's what's so terrifying. I'm used to knowing what men expect from me. It's why it's been so easy not to have sex for the last year and a half.

Ty is unlike any man I've ever met, and I wish he wasn't so heart-wrenchingly handsome or sweet so I could pretend this was just sex. But already, I can feel my walls crumbling and my need for him morphing into something deeper. Something I shouldn't feel for him after only a few hours in his company.

Then his pants fall, along with his boxer briefs, and he's standing before me completely naked while I'm still in my bra and underwear. His hot gaze slides over my breasts and then down to that space between my legs.

"Seems you're a bit overdressed."

I scan his insanely sculpted body, my mouth watering with each defined line I see and the assortment of tattoos covering his arms, torso, and upper thighs. This man has never skipped gym day in his life. That or God really does pick favorites, and Ty is definitely His. No man should be this perfect.

"Lexi?"

I rip my gaze away from the hard dick that's already leaking a bit of precum and force myself to meet his eyes. One brow is arched as he smiles knowingly at me.

"Do you need a hand?" he asks as he steps closer.

All I can do is nod. Yes, hands. I need his hands on me. He slides them up my sides and then to my back, unhooking my bra within seconds and discarding it on the floor. His hungry mouth finds mine, and all thoughts are obliterated as he moves us to the bed, slips my underwear off, and then works his mouth down my heaving chest, over my stomach, until he reaches that magical place between my legs that I was convinced men didn't know existed.

Oh, but Ty finds it. Because of course this sexy-as-hell man knows how to find a clitoris.

My fingers dig into his hair as he shows me how skilled that mouth of his is, taking me right over the edge of oblivion within minutes. My body has barely recovered when he grabs a condom and thrusts deep inside me.

"Oh fuck, you feel so good," he murmurs, his voice tight like it's taking all his strength not to give in to the pleasure.

"Don't stop," I beg, my nails digging into his ass while I tilt my hips, eager to keep this pleasure going. God, this man is going to ruin sex for me. No one will ever be able to live up to this.

"Fuck," he curses, then slides his hand between us, rubbing tantalizing circles on my clit while his cock thrusts hard into my pussy, hitting a spot deep inside I didn't know existed.

My back arches as a scream rips from my throat, the pleasure rushing through me so intensely I can hardly catch my breath. Two more thrusts and he follows me over with a deep groan.

"Give me ten minutes and then we definitely need to do that again," he says as he collapses next to me, his body lax.

Four hours and three rounds later, my body is deliciously sore, and I can barely keep my eyes open, but I know I can't fall asleep like Ty already has. It's time to go. I put my clothes back on as silently as I can and then move toward the door of his bedroom.

I glance back one last time, memorizing how relaxed and peaceful he looks asleep. Ty. A man I'll remember for the rest of my life, even if he was only mine for one night.

With an aching heart, I sneak out of his fancy apartment and take a cab back home.

FOUR

Ty

"Please tell me you're not doing what I think you're doing—again?"

I press the side button to darken the screen of my phone and look up at Dom. Romel and Gabe put their stuff in the cubbies we're using while we're visiting Seattle and come over to join us.

"Are you still trying to find her? I thought you gave up on that weeks ago?" Gabe asks, his brow furrowed with worry. He's a beast of a man, huge and scary looking on the field, but he's the biggest softie of us all. Since he found love, he's gotten even softer, which I wasn't sure was possible.

I toss my phone into my cubby and scrub my face. "I can't stop thinking about her."

It's been almost a month since my night with Lexi, and not a single day goes by where she doesn't cross my mind. I spent days after our night together searching for her online. I've searched so frequently all I have to do is type the letter L and my phone's suggested word spits out her name. I even went back to the club multiple nights in a row hoping she'd come back. Every time, I left alone and disappointed.

It's like she was a figment of my imagination, and it's driving me crazy. The bitterness of waking up to find her gone dissipated quickly, leaving a hollow ache and an endless desire to find her. That night was the best night of my life. There's no way she didn't feel the connection between us, the spark of chemistry I'd seen my friends find but wasn't sure I ever would —only to find it in the woman who left without so much as a note or her last name.

The only thing I haven't tried is hiring a private investigator, and that's only because I mentioned the idea to the guys and they all looked at me like I was certifiable.

They're probably right. Hiring a PI to find a one-night stand is a little creepy.

Clearly she doesn't want anything to do with me, and that idea is the most disappointing of all. I thought our connection was stronger than that, undeniable even, but I guess it was one-sided.

Now if only I could figure out how to stop thinking about her all the damn time.

Romel sits down next to me and claps me on the back. "Listen, man, I know you liked this girl, but it's clear she's not interested. You need to respect that and let her go."

My heart sinks, but I know he's right.

"I really thought she was different."

"We know," they say in unison, and I look up at them, all their expressions sympathetic.

"I've been talking about her too much, haven't I?"

Dom laughs. "Dude, every time I look at you when we aren't on the field, you're on your damn phone searching for her."

Truthfully, I didn't think she'd be so hard to find, but I'm not even sure she has a social media profile at all. I've scrolled through thousands of Lexis in Los Angeles, and not a single one was her. I even Googled "Lexi Teacher Los Angeles" and still couldn't find her.

I stare at my phone in the locker as resignation washes over me.

"It's time, man," Gabe says.

"I know." There's no way to miss the disappointment in my voice. I don't want to stop searching for her. I've never had a connection with anyone like I had with her, but I can't deny they're right. If she wanted to see me, she would've left a note with her number or something. How would she even respond if I did find her and reach out? Would she be upset? The idea makes my stomach clench. The last thing I want to do is make Lexi uncomfortable.

I swallow thickly. "It's time to let her go."

They nod and pat me on the back before going back to their lockers and getting ready for the game. I suit up in silence while the rest of the room is filled with the guys talking and laughing. I've always been good about compartmentalizing and keeping my head focused on football when I'm on the field, but today it's especially hard to get into that mental state.

The loss of her the morning after was hard enough, but the idea of really letting go of her is so painful it makes my chest ache. I've been through breakups with girlfriends that I didn't feel as viscerally as I feel the loss of giving up on Lexi.

By the time we rush out onto the field, my head is still not as focused as it should be. A hand grips my pads, and I look up to find Romel looking at me, concern clear in his dark-brown eyes. "Put all that emotion you're feeling and let it loose on the field. Every tackle, let a little bit of it go. Leave it all out there, but channel it. Don't let it bring you down. Use it to drive your every move. Got it?"

I stare at him for a second and then truly absorb what he's telling me. Is that how he got through losing his wife? I think back to what a wreck he was when she died. It was the offseason, but when preseason started he was still a mess. Yet I can't think of a single time when he didn't perform on the field. As I stare into the eyes of one of my closest friends, I see something I haven't noticed in a long time. All the pain and grief he must still feel over her death.

"Is that what you do?" I ask, even though I already know the answer.

"Every single time," he says.

I nod and he lets me go. I let my gaze wander over the full seats, the sea of green and blue, the low buzz of thousands of voices as people fill the stadium. I close my eyes, take a deep inhale, and then let the breath out slowly, the sound disappearing as my usual focus takes over.

The game starts, and our defense is on the field first. I get into position, letting every ounce of disappointment, regret, frustration, anger, and hurt build in my body until every muscle feels like it's humming with it. The ball snaps and I move, my gaze focused on my target, even as I'm aware of the other players scattering around me. The quarterback throws the ball straight to the guy I'm supposed to be covering, and the ball is barely in his grasp when I tackle him, bringing him down to the ground hard, my body jolting from the force of hitting the unforgiving ground. I get up and walk away, shaking off some excess energy as my focus sharpens even further.

The next play is the same. Until finally, the quarterback stops throwing the ball anywhere near me. It doesn't matter. Our defense is solid, and every player is in the zone today. We shut them down at every turn, and by the end of the game, it's clear they're exhausted while we're feeling on top of the world.

The locker room is chaotic after we pull off the win, but I can't feel the same level of joy because all that's left after putting all my emotions on the field is an exhausted and empty feeling permeating every inch of my body. I sit on the bench in front of my cubby, letting my head hang, my chin nearly tucked to my chest as I try to remember what I felt like before I met Lexi. One night with a woman should not fuck my head up this badly.

Romel stops beside me. "You did good out there."

"Thanks."

He watches me for a moment and then pats me on the back again, his voice dropping so no one else can hear. "The hollow feeling gets easier after a while." And then he walks away and heads over to the showers while I'm left sitting with a whole new respect for one of my closest friends.

I had no idea this is what he deals with every game, and I can't help but think he's stronger than I ever gave him credit for. Because this feeling?

It fucking sucks.

FIVE

Lexi

This cannot be happening. I grip my fingers curled in my lap, while my thumbnails scrape across each other, hoping I'll wake up and this will be a dream. Or that my doctor will come through that door and tell me I was mistaken.

I shake my head, trying to banish the negative thoughts. I can't think that way because if that test is positive, I never want my child to think they weren't wanted. I know too painfully what that feels like.

The door opens and I sit up, trying to remain calm and steady on the outside, even though there's a raging storm of whirling emotions happening inside me right now. Not to mention the insane nausea.

"Well, Lexi. Your urine test was positive, so the one you took at home definitely wasn't a false positive."

I took three, but I'm not about to confess that to her because I already feel a little panicked.

"We'll do a blood draw today to check your HCG level, and if everything is normal then we can refer you to an OB-GYN."

"So, I'm…" *Say it. Say the words.* "I'm really pregnant."

The doctor nods and offers me a tender smile. "You're really pregnant. I'm guessing this wasn't planned…"

"No," I confirm, my gaze dropping to the floor. "This definitely wasn't planned. He wore a condom. I…I just don't understand how this happened."

She shrugs. "Condoms aren't foolproof. They're only 98% effective. There could've been a tear in the condom, or there are any number of causes for accidents to happen, even when you take preventive measures. Do you want to talk about your options?"

My gaze snaps to hers. "I'm keeping it."

The words are out of my mouth without thinking. Maybe it's stupid, but I can't get rid of it. I'll be a single mom if I have to, but it'll haunt my nightmares if I don't follow this through. My baby isn't unwanted. Unplanned, yes. Unwanted, never.

I'm fortunate enough to be in a position where I can afford a child. I spend very little on myself, and I have a reliable job. The only thing truly terrifying about being pregnant is having to do everything on my own.

The doctor nods in understanding and then moves back toward the door. "Then once the nurse does your bloodwork, you'll be free to go. I'll get the referral to an OB-GYN sent off."

"Thank you," I say and wait for her to leave before I let my whole body sag on the table.

By the time I get out of there and back to my apartment, exhaustion and reality are hitting me hard.

I'm pregnant.

After my one and only one-night stand with a man who made me feel things he was never supposed to. And now I have to figure out what I'm going to do.

I place my hand on my still-flat belly, emotions bubbling up until my vision blurs and tears spill down my cheeks. I can admit that I'm scared—really scared—but I'm feeling something else too.

Hope.

For the first time in as long as I can remember, I won't be alone. I'm *not* alone. He or she is in there right now, and yeah, maybe it's just a cluster of cells right now, but it's mine.

Tears cascade down my cheeks as I cave and walk to my bedroom, opening the closet and digging out the small shoebox I keep hidden. It's too painful to pull out very often, but every once in a while, I need to remember, as best I can, what it felt like to be loved.

I was only five when my adoptive parents died in a car accident. I barely remember them anymore, but sometimes I think I remember what it felt like to be loved unconditionally, like I was a gift instead of a burden or another mouth to feed, but it's like a wisp of air so light you're not really sure if you felt it or not.

I have one picture of them. The three of us are smiling at the camera, their arms wrapped around me, and we sit in front of a Christmas tree with bright, multicolored lights. It was our last Christmas together. I wish I could still remember their voices, their laughs. Sometimes I dream of her telling me bedtime stories and dropping a kiss to my forehead like I was precious. But so often those memories are shoved aside for all the painful moments that came after they were gone.

No one in their families wanted me—not that they had big families to begin with. Since there were no relatives willing to take me in, I was put in foster care and moved from one home to another pretty regularly. Some homes were better than others. Some were living nightmares.

Not a single one ever felt like home. There was no foster parent like you might see in the movies who believed in me. I came with a check, and that was more important than I was.

I wish my memories weren't filled with those homes. I wish

I could remember my adoptive parents more than all the horrible foster parents that came later. I wish I could understand why my birth parents didn't want me. I don't know how many times I've looked in the mirror, wondering if there's something I can't see that tells everyone else that I'm unlovable.

I place my hand back over my stomach as the tears fall silently down my cheeks, and I stare at the picture of the only two people in the world who ever loved me. This may not be how I planned for things to go, but I will love this baby so much. I never want him or her to know what it feels like to be unloved, unwanted, alone.

I lean back against my closet wall and close my eyes, trying to even my breathing as another bout of nausea sweeps through me. It's always worse this time of day, and I'm glad I took the day off even though it's often more work having a sub in my classroom than just pushing through and doing it myself. But that's a problem for Monday.

Today I'm going to accept that my life is changing and it's not a bad thing. Scary—terrifying—but not bad. I drop my head back against the wall, my hand resting on my belly protectively.

"I love you already," I whisper, hoping my baby can feel how much I mean those words. "I'll give you everything I can, okay? We're a team, you and I."

Even as the words leave my lips, I know they aren't the whole truth. There's one more person who deserves to know. Whether he wants to be involved or not is up to him, but he still deserves to know.

I have to tell Ty, which means going back to the apartment building I snuck out of six weeks ago and hoping he still remembers me.

The building seems more intimidating in the full light of day. The sun was barely starting to light up the sky when I snuck out a month and a half ago, but I'm sure this is the right place. I take a fortifying breath and then walk inside. The security guard/doorman is standing behind a small desk set to the right of the door and politely smiles at me.

"Can I help you, miss?"

"I'm here to speak with Ty. Is he available?"

His smile falls, and his look can only be described as a mix between disappointment and condescension. "He doesn't have anyone on his list for today. You'll need to come back another time when you're on the list, *if* he wants to see you."

It's the way he enunciates the "if" that has my shoulders tightening. "Can you call up and ask him? It's important that we talk."

His gaze gets hard. "You need to leave. If you think you're the first woman who's come here trying to get something from that young man, you're mistaken. I know your games, and you should be ashamed of yourself. Now, can you leave on your own, or do I need to forcibly remove you from the premises?"

The burning sensation of tears building behind my eyes is the first sign that his words hit their mark. My heart sinking to my stomach is the second. The third is the emotion which clogs my throat so completely I can't even work up a reply. Before the tears have a chance to fall, I spin around on my toes and exit the way I entered. I make it half a block away before I duck into an alley just out of sight of passersby so I can get myself under control. The tears fall silently down my cheeks, and I brush them away as quickly as I can, but they're relentless. I don't know what to do. We never exchanged numbers. I don't even know his last name.

I bang my head back against the wall and then close my

eyes. I'm going to figure this out. I always do, and this time will be no different.

But I'm not going back there today. My emotions are too all over the place—thanks, hormones—and now that I know what I'm up against, I have a better idea of how I need to proceed next time.

I walk around the block to where I left my car, get in, and then place my hand back on my belly, centering myself and reminding myself that I'm a mom now. I have to be strong, and my baby deserves to know that I did everything in my power to tell their father about his or her existence.

Whether he wants to be involved or not.

SIX

Ty

I exit the private penthouse elevator and greet the doorman. "Hey Lewis. How's your day going?"

He gives me a warm smile, but there's something in his eyes that has my steps pausing. "It's going good, Mr. Russell. Thanks for asking."

"Everything okay?"

His smile dims a bit. "I know you value your privacy, but I thought I should warn you that a young woman tried to get in to see you today."

Now he has my complete attention. "A woman? Did she give her name? Was it Lexi?"

His eyes widen at my rapid-fire questions. "Uh, she didn't that I recall."

My brows furrow. "Did she say why she was here?"

"Just that she needed to speak with you."

I glance up at the cameras in the lobby and then back to Lewis. "Can you pull up the security footage?" I need to know. If it was Lexi, then maybe I'm not the only one who hasn't been able to stop thinking about our night together. I can't imagine it would be anyone else—I haven't hooked up with anyone since her—but I have to know for sure.

I may have put my search for her on hold after my talk with the guys a couple of weeks ago, but if she sought me out, then I'll do whatever it takes to find her. To see if our chemistry is still as explosive as it was that night.

He quickly focuses on his security system, and I round the desk so I can see what he sees. He pauses the video, and my heart starts racing as an energy I haven't felt in a long time pulses through me. I couldn't stop the smile that forms on my face even if I tried.

It's her. Lexi came back.

Hope and excitement fills my chest so completely, but then like a leaky balloon, it disappears the longer I watch the tape. Her expression falters while she stares at Lewis. His back is to the camera and there's no sound, but it's clear that something happened—that he said something that bothered her—when her mouth turns down into a frown and her shoulders sag with defeat. Even from the slightly grainy video, the heartache is written all over her beautiful face.

"What happened? Why does she look so upset?"

"Uh…" His hesitancy turns any excitement I feel into pure dread and anger.

"Lewis," I say, my tone sterner than I knew I was capable of. "What did you say to her?"

He licks his lips, not making eye contact with me as he stumbles over his words. "I…uh, I might've told her not to come back."

"You *what*?!" I shout. It's impossible to stop the way my body is itching for a fight in this moment. She was *here*. She was so close, while I was right upstairs, and he sent her away.

"Why would you do that without consulting me?"

His only saving grace is the remorse that's clear as day on his face. "I'm sorry, Mr. Russell. I thought she was another of those jersey-chaser women that have come here over the years trying to get to you. You always give me a heads-up if you're planning for company. You didn't have anyone on your list, so I figured you weren't expecting her. I thought she was just an overeager female fan. I'm so sorry, sir."

I don't look away from him as I point to the screen. "If she ever comes back, you let her up, no questions asked. Do you understand me? She is never to be turned away again."

"Yes, sir."

My phone beeps, and I pull it out of my pocket more force-fully than it deserves, but I'm seething and barely keeping my anger restrained.

"I gotta go, but I mean it, Lewis. If she's given any more trouble, you'll be out of a job. Am I clear?"

I don't know that I can actually get him fired, and I've never thrown my weight around like that in the years I've lived here, but the look on her face is already haunting me, and I refuse to let her feel like she doesn't belong here.

"Crystal, sir."

Jaw clenched, I move back around the desk and out the side doors leading to the garage. By the time I get to Gabe's house for our family barbecue, I'm still riled up and righteously pissed off.

She was *there*. Right there. I was in the building. I could've talked to her, slid my hands through her silken black hair I've dreamt about since our night together. I could've asked her to come to this get-together and meet the guys and their women. They might not be family by blood, but they're my family all the same. I'm as close to Gabe, Dom, and Romel as I am my own brothers, Tanner and Taron.

Fuck. I wouldn't blame her if she never wanted to come back again. The stricken look on her face from today is seared into my memory just as clearly as the feel of her body underneath me and the way she cried out my name as she squeezed my dick so tight I saw stars.

No woman's memory has stayed with me as long as she has. Not even my ex, and I thought I could be falling in love with her. But maybe subconsciously I always knew she was just using me.

But Lexi wasn't.

Maybe that's why it seems so easy to feel this way after one incredible night. I was real with her in a way I haven't been able to be with other women since I got drafted.

There's a loud banging on my driver's side window that nearly sends me into cardiac arrest, and I glance out to see Dom, bent over laughing his ass off. I open my door and get out.

"Hardy har har, asshole. Hey Alayna," I say to his wife.

God, that's fucking weird. Never in a million years would I have expected that Dom, of all people, would get married before me, but sure enough, the fucker realized his best friend was the love of his life—about damn time—and they didn't want to wait. I was honored to be invited to their small beach wedding they had this summer before preseason started.

"Hey Ty. How's it going?" she asks. She's too sweet for Dom, but it's clear they love each other. And I can't deny she's brought out a softer side to him. I have to admit, I like this version of him a lot better than the party boy he was before.

"Could be better," I admit, and that stops Dom's laughter instantly.

"Everything okay?"

And this is why he's one of my best friends—my brother from another mother. He might be an asshole sometimes and a jokester, but I know when shit goes down, he always has my back.

"Let's head in. I don't want to have to keep telling this story over and over cause it'll just piss me off more, and I know Gabe and Romel will want to hear it."

We enter the house without knocking because Gabe always leaves the door unlocked when we're coming over. It was only awkward once when we walked in probably less than a minute after he and Danae had clearly had sex because her hair was a mess, their clothes were in disarray, and they were both still panting. None of us asked any questions, but we all gave him high fives later because that's the kind of supportive friends we are.

"Yo, anybody home?" Dom calls out.

"Out back," comes the reply, so we head through the vast living room out to Gabe's back patio. It's surrounded by tall trees and thick, well-manicured green shrubbery which gives it a very private feel.

Gabe and Dom give each other a quick handshake and then a pat on the back before Gabe moves to me and offers the same. Alayna and Danae, Gabe's wife, curl up on the lounge chairs by the pool and start chatting away.

"Where's Romel?" I ask.

"He should be here any—"

"I'm here," Gabe's cut off by Romel's voice behind me, and I spin around to find him carrying a half-asleep Kaylee in his arms.

"Want to put her in the guest room?" Danae asks, standing from the lounge chair and walking over. She's got a soft spot for Kay. All the women do. So do all the men for that matter.

She may have lost her mother before she ever got to know her, but she'll never lack for female role models in her life. Or men willing to go to battle for her if necessary. Her future boyfriends will piss themselves when they come to meet her dad and see the four of us ready and waiting to interrogate them. Poor kid.

Romel shakes his head. "Thanks, though. She's been pretty needy for daddy time since the season kicked off. This last away stretch was rough on her."

His voice is rougher than usual, and he's made it no secret that every season gets harder now that his wife is gone and he's Kaylee's sole provider. I think all of us are just holding our breath and waiting for him to announce his retirement. It would be the end of an era—no more Fierce Four—and I'm not sure any of us are ready for that.

We all take a seat at the round table set up near the barbecue while Gabe grills up some burgers.

"Okay, time to talk," Dom says to me.

"Talk about what?" Gabe asks.

"Something's up, and he didn't want to spill it all in your driveway, so now he needs to share. I suspect it's about a woman."

Gabe shakes his head. "Not unless it's about that one from... what, a couple of months ago now? I'm pretty sure he's still hung up on her."

"It has been a long time for you, hasn't it?" Romel adds. "Normally you go out when we're in other cities, but you've called it a night like the rest of us."

"It's no fun going out without my guys, but yes, she's been a big reason." I lean my elbows on the table. "I found out she came back to my place today, and my doorman sent her away."

"Why the hell would he do that?" Gabe asks.

"Because he thought she might be a jersey chaser just trying to get to me. Don't worry, I chewed him out for not checking with me first. But you're missing the point. She came back. Maybe that means she hasn't been able to stop thinking about me either. Maybe I shouldn't have stopped looking for her."

"Damn. Do you think she figured out who you are?"

I chew the inside of my lip. I hadn't considered that. I was so excited to see her on that security camera, I hadn't thought what the driving factor was for her coming back. "I don't think so," I say slowly. "But I suppose it's possible."

"She's not like your ex, right?"

"She's nothing like Emily," I state. My ex was a piece of work. She was shallow but hid it well for the first six months we were together. Over the last six, her cracks started to show, and then when I found out she just wanted to marry me so she could be a trophy wife and spend my money, that was the deal-breaker. My brother Tanner told me the first sign that it wasn't going to last should've been when I refused to bring her home for the holidays because I was ninety percent certain my mom wasn't going to like her.

He's not wrong.

I want a partnership like my parents have. I want a woman who can be my best friend and my lover. Emily was never going to be that partner for me, but ever since her, I'd started to wonder if I'd ever find a woman who wanted me just for me instead of what I could provide for her.

And then I met Lexi.

Maybe it would've been better not to sleep with her that first night, but there was no going back after that first kiss. I craved her the way I've never craved another person.

I still do.

"Is it too stalkerish if I hire a private investigator to find her now? I'm worried after what happened with my doorman, she won't come back on her own."

The guys all look around at each other before Dom and Gabe say no while Romel says yes.

Well, that's helpful.

SEVEN

Lexi

I'm three bites into a pint of ice cream while stupid tears fall down my cheeks when there's a knock on my door. Checking the clock, I can guess who it is and put my ice cream down on my coffee table before going to the door. Sure enough, standing on the other side is Blaire.

As soon as she sees my tearstained cheeks, her worried expression shifts to one of pure rage. "I'm going to kick his ass. What did he say to you?"

She doesn't ask for an invitation as she moves past me into my apartment. I close my door and then go back to the couch, settling in the corner and pulling my favorite super-soft throw blanket over my legs before I grab my pint of ice cream and bury my spoon in it.

"I didn't talk to him. His doorman wouldn't let me up."

Her mouth parts in indignation. "What the hell? Shouldn't that be up to the tenant?"

I shrug and nibble my lip, tears of frustration brimming in my eyes again and my appetite completely vanishing. Goddamn, I'm sick of crying. I'm stronger than this, but for the last two weeks I've been crazy emotional. It was one of the first things that tipped me off that my late period might be more than just stress related. I am not normally someone who cries at the drop of a hat. Before being pregnant, I barely cried at all. I learned at a young age that tears didn't solve anything, so they didn't seem worth my time. And now I can't stop the damn things from streaming out of my eyes at the slightest inconvenience.

"Oh, Lexi. I'm so sorry." She moves to the couch, snuggling next to me and wrapping her arms around me. The second she squeezes me, the dam bursts and the tears come pouring out in heaving sobs. She doesn't try to tell me it'll be okay, and I'm grateful for that.

Blaire's the only person I've been brave enough to tell. I don't really have anyone else anyway. When the time comes, I'm not sure how I'm going to explain to my principal—or my students—that I'm pregnant. I'm not ready for the deluge of questions I'll get about the baby's father. My students are already way too invested in finding out if I'm dating someone, even when I do everything in my power to maintain boundaries and never talk about my personal life. The gossips in the staff room will have a field day at lunches when it comes out. I can already hear the murmurs and judgment now.

There's a reason Blaire and I tend to eat lunch together in one of our classrooms instead of going to the staff lounge.

The sobs start to slow, and Blaire grabs a tissue for me from the box on my coffee table.

"Thanks," I mumble before blowing my nose. I look over at her to find her staring at me with her bottom lip between her teeth. "What?"

"I think you should go back," she says.

"Really?" I was thinking I'd avoid him for another week or

two—or ten—and maybe leave it up to fate. If we're supposed to see each other again, we will.

"Yeah, I mean, if it was the doorman that kept you from going up and not him, then maybe he'd want to see you. But you won't know if you don't go back and try again."

I drop my head to the back of the couch and let out a heavy sigh. "I know you're right, but I also really hate that you're right. It was embarrassing." My voice cracks and I take a minute to get my emotions under control before I continue. "I've never felt more like trash than I did in that moment, and that's really saying something."

"But Ty didn't make you feel that way."

"No," I say, staring at the ceiling. "I've wondered a lot about what would've happened if I had stayed."

"The next morning?"

"Yeah," I say.

"Why didn't you?"

I shrug and then look at her. "He was perfect."

"No one is perfect, hon."

"You don't understand. He wasn't pushy. He wasn't controlling. He wasn't mean or selfish. He was giving and complimentary. He made me feel like I was a gift. Do you know how many men have made me feel that way in my life? None. Not a single one has made me feel anything but used after sex. I was simply a body that helped them get off. It wasn't like that with Ty, and maybe I wanted to sneak away before he could ruin that for me. I want that memory of the guy who put my pleasure first. The guy who made me feel cherished while still being a fucking animal in bed. I mean, he's a freaking unicorn. Why would I stay so he could ruin the image and show me he's just a horse with a horn superglued to his head?"

Blaire's serious expression breaks as she bursts into laughter, which only causes me to also start giggling. "What a visual," she says between fits of laughter.

I slap her arm. "Well, you asked."

She sags back against the couch, her pose mirroring mine. "I still think you should go back and try again. I could go with you if you need backup."

I grab her hand and squeeze it once. "Thanks, but I think I should do this on my own."

I've done everything else on my own up to this point. If I'm about to be a mom then I need to do hard things without help, especially if Ty decides he doesn't want anything to do with me or the baby.

The building seems taller and even more intimidating when I show up the next day. I stay in my car parked just down the street and chew on my lip while my heart races chaotically in my chest. This has to work. If it doesn't, I don't know what I'll do. I'm not putting myself through a third round of humiliation, that's for sure. Twisting my keys out of the ignition, I grab my purse and open my door, forcing myself to get out of the car.

Each step closer to the building adds a weight to my chest, but I keep trudging forward. When I reach the doors, the same doorman from yesterday stands at his station inside, his head down. Pushing my shoulders back, I lift my head high and hope I give off an air of confidence even if I'm trembling on the inside.

When I pull the door open, the doorman looks up, and I swear relief seems to cross his face before he holds his finger up and picks up a phone. I stand just inside the door, waiting for him to get off the phone so I can ask him about seeing Ty, all while nerves tangle like knots in my stomach. He mumbles as he talks so I can't hear what he's saying. I try not to let my shoulders drop and keep a confident air that is one hundred percent fake. I need to act like I belong here and have a right to see Ty or else this man will kick me out just like he did yesterday, and I'll be out of options. I have no other way to tell him about the baby if this doesn't work.

He sets the phone down and focuses his attention on me. I step forward, opening my mouth to tell him why I'm here when he speaks. "You can go on up. He's expecting you."

That takes me aback, and I swallow down the words that were right on the tip of my tongue. "Ty?" I clarify.

The doorman's expression narrows. "Were you here to see someone else?" The judgment from yesterday is back in his tone, and I try not to bristle.

"No."

He nods, but his jaw clenches, and I know exactly what this man thinks of me. "Go on up."

Nerves swirl in my belly as my shame skyrockets. I was in such a rush to leave the next morning—my exhaustion so heavy, I barely remember leaving—and too enamored with Ty the night we were together that I didn't pay attention to his apartment number. And now I feel exactly like the type of woman this doorman thinks I am.

"Can you tell me his apartment number?" I try to push strength and authority into my voice, but I fail spectacularly when it comes out weak.

"The penthouse, miss."

The penthouse. No wonder he's looking at me like I'm a gold digger. I could tell Ty was wealthy from his apartment, but I didn't realize it was the damn penthouse. Suddenly new doubts start to rise. Who is this guy? What if he fights me for custody?

Oh my God, would he take my baby from me?

New fears slither in between all the existing fears I already carry as I take unsteady steps to the elevators. When I get in and spin around to press the giant P at the top of the panel, I catch the doorman watching me carefully, and I'm wondering if it's too late to run out of here and live my life without Ty ever knowing I had his kid.

But then the doors slide closed and the elevator rises swiftly, taking any chance of escape away.

EIGHT

Ty

I'm pacing back and forth, waiting for the knock on the door while I also try to tell myself to chill the fuck out. But damn, I'm so excited.

She came back.

When I got the call from Lewis, I couldn't believe my luck. I thought I was going to have to hunt her down after the way I saw her face fall in that security video yesterday.

But she's here.

I check my watch. How long has it been since Lewis called? Shouldn't she be up here by now?

The knock on my door has my heart in my throat, and before she can knock a second time, I'm already pulling it open. All my breath whooshes from my lungs as I finally get a good look at her for the first time in a month and a half. God, she's even more beautiful than I remembered. Her cheeks are pink with a flush, and her silky skin practically glows.

"Hi," I say, my voice a little deeper than normal because of how much this woman affects me.

"Hi," she whispers, her gaze tracing mine and her lush lips parted. Fuck, I remember what it felt like to have those lips wrapped around my cock, and I'm suddenly hyperaware that it's been six weeks since I had sex. With that thought, blood rushes south, and I know I'm dangerously close to popping a boner, which I refuse to do the first time I see her again.

Hopefully, we'll get to have another round, but I'd prefer to take her out on a real date first. My gaze slides down her frame, loving the way her dark wash denim jeans hug the curves of her hips. Her long hair falls in soft curls over her shoulders and to her breasts that are covered by a loose black top.

She looks as gorgeous as I remember.

"Please come in," I say, opening the door wider and gesturing inside. She walks in and looks around the space, but her silence is getting to me. "I'm so glad you came back. I was pissed when I found out Lewis made you leave yesterday."

She turns so she's facing me, her face puckering in the cutest little frown. "Lewis?"

"The doorman."

She still looks confused. "You were mad he made me leave?"

I step forward because I can't stand the distance between us. I've been aching to hold this woman for what feels like forever. I'm dying to kiss her, but being near her will have to be enough for now. She has a skittish look on her face—worse than anything I remember from that night at the club—and I'm not about to do anything that will cause her to run from me again. I brush a loose strand of hair away from her cheek because I can't *not* touch her. "Yeah. I wanted to see you again. I hated that you left without giving me your full name or your number. I tried to find you, but you're a hard woman to track down."

"You did?" she asks, looking completely surprised, and once again I'm taken aback by how much gratitude I feel now that she's here. She's the breath of fresh air I've been aching for. Most of the women in my past would've thrown out some snarky line about how lucky I was they came back, and here's this goddess who has absolutely no idea what a gift she is.

"Are you hungry? Thirsty? I can get us something to eat while we talk. Or better yet, can I take you out, on a proper date this time?" I ask with a smile tugging at my lips. I'm too happy to hold it back any longer.

Her mouth parts while her dark-blue eyes stare up at me. I can't quite place the look on her face. "You want to take me on a date?" she asks, her voice a little hoarse.

I step closer, my body thrumming with an excited buzz at being this close to her finally. I love how I feel when she's near. "I would *love* to take you out on a date." I smile. "In fact, I've got the perfect place in mind. Are you down?"

She stares at me for another moment, her gaze unsure, and then looks down at her outfit. "Um, am I dressed okay for what you have in mind?"

I use the excuse to peruse her body once more. It takes everything in me not to close the distance, pull her body against mine, and kiss her with nearly six weeks' worth of pent-up desire. Her lush lips are a temptation I'm all too willing to give in to. I focus on her face, memorizing how her long, dark lashes highlight her deep-blue eyes. Her cheeks look like they have a natural flush, and there's a smattering of freckles along the bridge of her nose.

All minor details I missed during our night together because of the lack of lighting, but now I'll picture whenever I think of her.

Which, if the last several weeks are anything to go by, will be often.

"You're perfect," I say, meaning every word.

I don't usually have to work to impress women, but it's clear by her narrowed eyes and puckered lips she thinks I'm full of shit. Somehow that only endears her to me more.

"Shall we?" I ask.

She nibbles on her lip and then nods.

"Are you okay if I drive us?"

"Yeah, that's fine," she replies, but there's a slight wobble in her voice, almost like she's nervous or distracted. If anyone should be nervous here, it's me. This woman is clearly unimpressed by my typical swagger, which means I need to step up my game so she doesn't bail on me like she did before.

I take her to Alberto's, my favorite pizza joint. It's just after the lunch rush, so I should be in the clear, but I put on a baseball cap I pull low, hoping it'll help me stay incognito until I can tell her the truth about me. I know I should do it soon, but a bigger part of me wants to wait. If I wasn't in the middle of my season, I'd definitely wait, but there's no way I can explain how frequently I go out of town without her getting suspicious. And the last thing I want is for her to think there's another woman.

Because there's not.

And if I have my way after this date, there won't be anyone else until she's done with me.

She's quiet during the short drive and lets me take the lead in ordering our pizza before finding us a table tucked in the back. There are only a few patrons here, but I'd still rather not risk it.

She stares down at her hands in her lap, and my gut clenches at the idea that she's not comfortable with me.

"You okay?"

She looks up, her eyes wide and darting between mine. She opens her mouth and then snaps it shut. Her attention drops back to her hands, and my brows furrow in concern.

"Maybe this was a bad idea," she murmurs.

I lean forward, moving my hand across the table, palm up, hoping she'll take it. Hoping she'll use me as a lifeline and realize I want her with a desperation that's completely out of character for me. I've never wanted a woman this way—never been so consumed I couldn't stop thinking about her.

"I'm really glad you came back."

Her gaze shoots up to mine, but she nibbles her lip and doesn't say a word.

"Like I said, I tried to find you," I say, willing to put it all on the line if it will get her to smile at me the way she did the night we were together. I don't know what's got her so uncomfortable, but I'm willing to work to ease her concerns the best I can. "Don't ever Google 'Lexi-Los Angeles' because you'll get all kinds of crazy results, and not a single one was the one I was looking for."

She stares into my eyes, and a feeling passes between us— one I can't name that makes me feel both soothed and yet on the edge of my seat, unsure of what's coming.

"I have to tell you something," she whispers.

"Okay," I say, sure that nothing she could say would deter me from pursuing this—unless she's married, but considering she nearly freaked out the night we were together because she was worried I wasn't single, I doubt that's the case.

She closes her eyes, and her throat bobs as she swallows and then opens them, the dark blues swirling with fear and worry that makes my heart ache for her.

"I'm pregnant."

Everything freezes.

I gape at her, not sure I heard her correctly. "W-what?"

"I'm pregnant," she whispers.

I sit back, my heart dropping to my stomach as I stare at her in complete shock. And then the shock morphs to burning disappointment tainted with anger. She was supposed to be different. She wasn't supposed to be a jersey chaser trying to nab herself a baby daddy and a guaranteed eighteen years of checks. All the excitement I felt at seeing her disappears in a haze of red as anger slithers through the disappointment like a quick-acting poison in my veins.

My jaw tics as I stare at her, my eyes narrowed. I know this game. She's not the first to try to play it on me, and I won't be manipulated.

But I wish she still didn't make me feel things for her so I could focus on my anger instead of oscillating between that and the crushing disappointment. Instead, I focus on getting to the root of the issue.

"When did you find out?" I spit out. I have to know. Did she know I was a famous football player that night, or did she find out after? If she knew then, she's one hell of an actress.

And that only pisses me off more because I never saw it coming. She seemed so real, so down to earth, so genuine.

Fuck, this hurts.

She flinches and drops her gaze. "It was confirmed by my doctor yesterday. I tried to find you right away after my appointment."

I shake my head. "I mean, when did you find out about me?"

Her brows furrow, and I refuse to let myself find it cute. "You? W-what do you mean?"

"Cut the bull, Lexi. When did you find out I was famous? Did you know I played for the Wolves that night? Or did you find out after? I deserve to know the truth if you're carrying my kid. If it's even mine," I spit out.

She blinks at me, and then a mask falls over her face, and she shakes her head like she doesn't recognize me at all. I hate the sheen of tears filling her eyes, and disgust—at myself—fills my gut.

She swallows once, then twice like she's trying to find the strength to speak but can't. And it's the way she's trying so hard to hold herself together while her body cracks right before me that has my anger dissolving as quickly as it came.

This isn't right.

She's not responding the way I've seen others react. She's certainly not responding anything like my ex when we broke up and I called her out on her bullshit—on the way she used me and manipulated me for months.

Lexi isn't acting like that at all. I'm questioning if this is an act, or if I've once again let my past relationships get in my way.

Did she really not know?

She drops her gaze to the floor and practically whispers, "This was a mistake."

Then she gets out of her chair and walks out.

NINE

Lexi

He thinks I'm making it up. Or that I tricked him.

I rub at my chest as I walk away from him. The second I'm out the door, I pull up my phone to get an Uber. I just need to get back to my car and then go home and forget this day ever happened.

I never should've gone back to his place. I should've taken my first rejection from his doorman as a sign from the universe. Because now he's done the one thing I was so afraid of—he's tainted the memory of our night together.

The look he just gave me in there...

My heart clenches, and I lean against the side of the building, trying to focus on my breaths and not burst into tears like I really want to. How the hell am I going to explain this to my baby one day when he or she asks about their dad?

And what the hell was he talking about with the Wolves? I'm not completely ignorant that I don't recognize the name of the local NFL team because my students talk about it all the time, but I've never watched sports.

I blink and a tear falls. I'm about two seconds from letting the sob rip through my throat, and at this point I'm just praying

I can hold it together long enough to get to my car. My hands shake as I pull up the Uber app.

The door I walked out of only moments ago opens, and on instinct, I glance up to find Ty looking the opposite direction. I quickly brush away the evidence of my tears before he looks this way because I refuse to let him see me fall apart when he clearly thinks I'm nothing but a manipulative gold digger.

His worried gaze finds mine, and he rushes over, closing the distance between us in the blink of an eye. "Lexi, wait."

I steel my expression. I've had a lifetime of practice that not even my whacked-out hormones should be able to overcome. I don't want him to know how close I am to falling apart. He'll know he got to me. He's not the first person to make me feel worthless, but after our night together when he made me feel so treasured, so cherished, it's a much harsher blow than anyone from my past who made me feel this way.

At least those assholes always looked at me like I was worthless, so it was no surprise when they treated me like trash. But Ty was supposed to be different. I'm mentally kicking myself for doing the right thing. I should've kept the memory of him sacred for all my lonely nights. Now I won't even have that.

"Lexi, I'm so sorry." His voice has softened, and it's the kind, sweet voice that had me melting for him during our night together.

I don't speak. I can't. What is there to say at this point? I told him why I came back, but I want nothing to do with him—and certainly none of his money—if he's going to look at me like I did this on purpose as some kind of trap.

He bends down so his face is right in front of mine, both his hands on my arms. His brown eyes that were so warm before are filled with panic.

"I'm sorry," he repeats. "I shouldn't have reacted that way." He closes his eyes as if he's in pain, then opens them and I'm surprised to see the remorse in his gaze. "I've...I've had women in the past try to use me and take advantage of me. I didn't think you were like that. I *don't*," he adds quickly. "I want to hear you out. Please come back inside."

I *am* hungry. I'm always hungry at this time of day. I nibble my lip, torn between escaping for self-preservation and sitting through what is likely to be a disaster of a meal to tell him what little I know about our growing child.

"Please," he says again, pleading with me.

And even though it makes me feel weak, I give in. "Okay," I say, my voice whisper soft.

"Okay," he says, nodding as if he's reassuring himself that I actually said the word.

He takes my hand, and my stomach swoops from the touch, but I ignore the feeling and let him lead me back to our table. My stomach growls as we approach and find our pizza waiting for us. Ty grabs the back of my seat, and I avoid his gaze as I sit down. He rounds the table and starts dishing us each a slice, handing me my plate before he takes his own. We both take a bite as the silence thickens until it feels like an actual weight sitting on top of us.

He clears his throat. "How far along are you?" There's none of the heat to his words like there was before I walked out, but my defenses still rise.

I scowl at him. "I promise it's yours. I haven't been with anyone else in nearly two years."

His shoulders drop, and he puts his pizza slice down on his plate. "I didn't mean it that way. I don't know anything about pregnancy except for what I've seen in movies."

"I'm eight weeks along, which I know seems like too much, but that's the way pregnancies are dated—back to two weeks before conception." I take another bite to give myself an excuse not to say anymore.

He watches me. "How have you been feeling?"

"Fine." Another bite.

He lets out a huff and then lifts his ball cap, sliding his hand through his brown hair before putting the cap in place and leaning his elbows on the table. "Let me in. I know I don't deserve it after the way I just reacted, but I'm asking, nonetheless. We're having a kid together. I want to know how you're doing with all this, because frankly, I'm freaking the fuck out a little bit over here."

I set my half-eaten slice down. He's right. We're in this together, and if he wants to be involved then there's no point making this awkward for the both of us. It doesn't mean we have to date or anything, but we do need to be civil to each other in order to co-parent.

"I get nauseous throughout the day, but I'm always hungry around this time. I'm exhausted all the freaking time, and I cry at the drop of a hat which I hate because I'm not typically so emotional." I decide to give him more, even if I'm not convinced he deserves this much honesty, but I can't quite look at him, so I stare at my plate instead. "And I'm scared. I didn't plan this, but I'm not getting rid of my baby. I understand if this doesn't fit into your plans. If you don't want to be involved, just tell me now and we can go our separate ways."

When I look up at him, his jaw is slack like I slapped him across the face, his warm eyes filled with hurt. "I want to be involved. I'm sorry if my reaction earlier gave you the impression that I'm the kind of guy who doesn't want his own kid, but that's not the case. I want this baby, even if it wasn't planned. I'm still wrapping my head around all this." If possible, his expression gets even more serious. "I want you too, Lexi."

I no longer believe that. "All I can give you right now is the chance to co-parent."

His sharp jaw clenches, but his gaze never wavers from

mine. "I think there's something you should know about me."
He leans forward, and I brace myself for the worst. "I'm not a
guy who gives up, even when the odds are stacked against me.
And I may have massively fumbled this date, but I'm not giving
up on you—on us. I lost you once when you snuck out after the
best night of my life, and trust me, I learned my lesson. I'm not
letting you go so easily this time. So if you need me to work for it
to prove myself, then I will, but I'm not going anywhere. I'm not
leaving you, or our baby."

I hate the way my heart rate speeds up when he calls it
our baby. But more than anything, I hate how desperately I
want him to mean every single word.

TEN

Ty

The phone rings twice before my older brother, Tanner, picks up.

"Hey, don't you have a game today?" he asks.

"Yeah, I'm driving there now for our pregame meeting, but I needed to call you and..." My voice trails off as I figure out how to share the news.

My brothers and I have been close our whole lives. Tanner is eighteen months older than I am at twenty-nine and Taron is two years younger at twenty-five, but most of our childhoods we acted like three peas in a pod. I should've called him last night, but I was still reeling from Lexi's announcement.

And how epically I fucked up our date.

"And what? You okay, Ty?"

Tanner also plays professional football, but his team doesn't play until tomorrow, and I know he understands the caution I've had with women. But I have no idea how he's going to take this news.

"Do you remember that woman I told you about back during the preseason?"

"The one who bailed on you the next morning?"

"Yeah."

"Sure. What about her?"

I open my mouth to speak when I realize there might be an issue with my brothers and I being so close. Will he jump to the same—wrong—conclusion I did about Lexi?

"She's pregnant," I blurt, choosing to just rip off the Band-Aid.

There's sputtering and choking on the other end of the line before my brother's hoarse voice comes through my car's speakers. "What the fuck? Give a guy some warning before you drop a bomb like that. I'd just taken a sip of water thinking you were going to tell me you ran into her again and finally got her number. I was *not* expecting you to tell me she's pregnant. Damn, she moved on fast. Maybe you dodged a bullet."

I rub my jaw, waiting for him to figure it out. It doesn't take him long.

"Wait...are you telling me she's pregnant with *your* kid?"

"Yep."

"Fuck, man. Please let me be there when you tell Mom."

"Fuck you." I'm not even close to ready to tell my mom about Lexi and the baby. She's going to have a million questions I likely can't answer, especially with Lexi freezing me out since our date yesterday. I can't even be mad about her doing that considering it's my own fault.

"Are you sure it's yours?" he asks, his voice low and skeptical. A guy on his team just recently went through a paternity scandal, and I have no doubt that's what he's thinking about right now.

And I get it, I do. It's not uncommon in our industry, but I'm choosing to believe Lexi—to trust that she's not manipulating me, even if that might be stupid.

"I'm sure."

"You should get a paternity test done. It wouldn't be the first time a woman tried to con a pro athlete into eighteen years of payments." He's got his big brother voice on, and I fight against an eye roll.

"Lexi's not like that."

"I've heard you say that about a woman before. I'm sure Lexi is nice and everything, but I'm sorry if I don't trust your judgment right off the bat. I don't want to see you get hurt."

"I don't want that either," I admit and then tap the back of my head on the headrest of the driver's seat while I sit at a red light. "I just found out yesterday, so we're still sorting everything out, but I needed to tell someone."

"I'm not trying to rain on your news, but I think you need to be smart about this. You know I'm always here for you, little brother."

"You know you're not that much older than me, right? And I'm two inches taller, so I'm not really that little."

He huffs a laugh. "You'll always be my lil bro no matter how tall or old we get. Deal with it. So, when are you going to tell Mom?"

"I don't know."

He hums. "Better do it before the news spreads."

"You're the only one I've told so far."

"Yeah, but you're on your way to your game where you'll see the guys, and you four are like the weirdest married quartet I've ever met. You don't keep secrets from each other. Hell, they plaster your bromance on billboards."

"You're just jealous," I say with a laugh before saying goodbye and hanging up.

He's not wrong about us though. We're a tight-knit group. You have to be if you want to be the best, and we've worked our asses off to get to this point in our careers.

I think about my conversation with Tanner the whole way to the stadium. I know he's right about the paternity test; it's the smart thing to do. But I abhor the idea of asking Lexi for one, especially after how I fumbled things yesterday. I'm still haunted by the broken look on her face when I got mad at her, and I'd like to avoid ever seeing it again.

Even if a tiny part of me is wondering if maybe he's right and I'm trusting her too easily.

When I get to the locker room, the guys are already there as other members of our team trickle in. I go straight to my locker and toss in my keys and wallet. Romel glances over at me from his locker right next to mine. I've always considered him the dad of our foursome—maybe because he actually is a dad, but he's also always so steady and put together compared to the rest of us.

"You okay?" he asks.

And apparently he can read minds. Or maybe yesterday's events are written all over my face. When I focus my attention on him, I notice Gabe and Dom are also looking at me with little furrows on their brows. These guys may be intimidating as hell on the field, but they're big softies who I know will always have my back.

Romel puts down the socks he'd been about to put on and stares at me. "Okay, what's up? You're too quiet, and you're not smiling."

That gets a small smile out of me. I grip the back of my neck. "I got some news yesterday."

Gabe and Dom crowd my other side, essentially blocking us from the rest of our teammates and allowing me to keep my voice low—and this news relatively private. "Lexi came back."

"Why do I get the feeling that's not a good thing like you hoped it would be?" Dom asks.

I grip the back of my neck tighter, mentally replaying every moment with her yesterday. "It is a good thing. You know how badly I wanted to see her again, but she's also pregnant."

They all stare at me, their jaws dropped. That's a fair reaction. If anyone was expected to accidentally knock up a chick, it was going to be Dom, not me.

"You're shitting us," Gabe says.

I shake my head.

"Fuck, man. That's huge. I thought you always wrapped up?" Dom says, shock filling his features.

"I did. Accidents happen, I guess."

"Well, that's fucking terrifying. Thank God that didn't happen to me. Before Laney, the thought of kids was a literal nightmare."

"How are you feeling about it?" Romel asks me, his gaze boring into me like he's trying to gauge if the words I'm about to say are true or not.

My body relaxes as I let down my guard with my closest friends. "Honestly, I'm fucking overwhelmed. When she came to see me, this was the last thing I expected." Maybe it shouldn't have been. The timing was there right in front of me. Why wait so long unless you're about to drop a bomb on someone?

A part of me hates that she didn't come back because she wanted to, but because she felt she had to. Has she thought about me at all since we were together? I haven't had sex since that night because I haven't been able to get her out of my damn mind.

Now I'm being hit with insecurity after insecurity. I don't think Lexi is a gold digger; she's never shown any of the indicators we've all learned to look out for, and it was dumb to jump to that conclusion yesterday. If she was, she would've come back a lot sooner. My penthouse makes it obvious I make a lot of money. But that still doesn't mean that she might not have some ulterior motives, as much as I hate doubting her.

I look down at my feet, processing the mix of emotions I'm feeling. "This might sound crazy, but even as overwhelmed as I am and disappointed this is the reason she's back in my life, I'm glad she is. I'm glad I have another chance to see if what I felt for her that first night was a one-off or the start of something deeper. Is that crazy?"

Romel's lips lift in a kind smile. "Not at all, man. Sometimes when you know, you know. That said, maybe slow things down a bit and get to know her so you can gauge if she's being real with you. We all know how easy it is to get taken advantage of in this profession, and I'd hate to see her crush you worse than she did when she left the first time."

The coaches come into the locker room for our pregame talk, disrupting our conversation, which might be for the best because I definitely need more than a few minutes to tell them about how I messed up with her yesterday and get their advice on how to fix it. Gabe's woman was skittish when they got together, so he might have some good tips for me, and we all know Dom put his foot in his mouth a time or two—or twenty. Combined, we should be able to come up with a plan to get me back on the right foot with Lexi. Because Romel is right; I need to get to know her, really *know* her, and I can't do that if she's freezing me out.

The game is an easy win, and I'm thankful it didn't require too much mental focus because I can admit my head wasn't in the game the way it should've been.

As we run off the field and back to the locker rooms, Romel pulls me aside. "I know you said you're glad she's back, but you should know, pregnant women are a completely different type of woman. Syd was a ticking time bomb of crying or being angry or being totally in love with me the entire time she was pregnant with Kaylee. It's a wild roller coaster you're boarding, so I just want to make sure you're prepared."

"You got some advice?"

He pats me on the back. "A ton. First and foremost, the first trimester can be a nightmare as far as sensitivity to smells and food goes. She could be crazy nauseous or not have any morning sickness at all, but you should figure out quick what her triggers are and do everything in your power to banish them from your life immediately."

"Got it. What else?"

He rubs his jaw. "Have ginger ale and saltines on hand for her. Give her foot rubs and massage her lower back if she'll let you. Those were Syd's two places, especially at the end, that always gave her the most pain, but after a little rubdown, she'd melt into the bed and sleep great. Oh!" He grips my shoulder. "If you manage to get her to live with you during the pregnancy, invest in some ear plugs. Syd slept like an angel until about halfway through the second trimester, and then she snored like some deranged, feral monster in one of the mythical books she loved to read. It was terrifying—almost as terrifying as the fact that she could sleep through it most of the time. Just a fair warning."

I laugh. "I appreciate that."

"Anytime. Seriously. We dads gotta stick together. Call me anytime, and I'll help out best I can."

We dads. My chest expands as his words hit me square in the heart. I'm going to be a dad.

"Thanks, man." It's not lost on me that this is the most I've heard him talk about Sydney since she died from cancer when Kaylee was just a baby. "You know, there is something I was hoping you and the guys could help me with."

Romel calls out to Gabe and Dom who are ahead of us as we walk into the locker room.

"What's up?" Dom asks.

I put my hands on my hips and quickly tell them what happened with Lexi yesterday—after she dropped the pregnancy bomb on me.

Romel closes his eyes and shakes his head. "Damn. I really thought you were smoother than that."

I drop my chin to my chest before taking a deep breath and looking back at them. "I know. I'm well aware that was not my finest moment, and I'm paying for it. So how do I fix it?"

The guys look at each other and then back at me. Romel puts a hand on my shoulder. "You said she's a teacher?"

"Yeah."

A smile grows on his face. "I've got an idea."

ELEVEN

Lexi

I'm in the middle of my lesson on imagery when there's a knock on my classroom door. I glance up in time to see my principal, Mrs. O'Dell, walk in with a huge smile on her face, her eyes wide, and her cheeks a little flushed.

I tilt my head. "Everything okay, Mrs. O'Dell?"

And that's when I see the man walk in behind her, and my heart races in my chest even as I feel my own cheeks heat. What the hell is Ty doing here?

And then three more guys follow him in, and my students erupt in squeals and cheers.

"Oh shit, it's the Fierce Four!"

"Don't curse," I tell my student, Marcus, but my voice sounds hollow and lacks the authority it normally carries.

Who the hell are the Fierce Four? It sounds like a character group from a comic book or something.

Mrs. O'Dell turns to my class and raises her hands in a signal for them to settle down. They do, albeit reluctantly. As it is, several of them, boys and girls alike, are squirming in their seats with giant grins plastered on their faces.

"We have surprise guests, and they specifically asked for Ms. Kemper's class."

I'm suddenly regretting telling him my last name and where I worked during our disaster of a meal two days ago. I mean, I know he would've found out eventually, but I was not planning to see him so soon, and definitely not in my own classroom. I'm not mentally or emotionally prepared for this.

And then he pulls his hands from behind his back and presents me with a beautiful bouquet of flowers. "For you," he says, his voice soft and contrite. I can see the apology in his eyes.

"Awww," a bunch of my students coo, making me blush harder, and Ty grins wide at my reaction, his handsome face morphing with that same flirtatious smile that got me into his bed in the first place and started all of this.

"Thank you," I say.

He leans closer, his voice lowering. "I wasn't sure which flowers were your favorite, so I hope you don't mind these. I thought of you as soon as I saw them."

My heart melts a little as I drop my nose to smell the gorgeous pink peonies. "They're beautiful."

"Like I said, they reminded me of you."

I look at him, expecting him to still have a flirty smile on his face to go with that line, but when our gazes lock, all I see is sincerity and something that looks suspiciously like desire. I'm transported back to our night together—the way he looked at me while he thrust inside me and made sure I came before he shuddered with his own release. My breathing grows heavy until it feels like he and I are the only ones that exist in the room.

And then I realize the silence isn't just in my imagination. I break our stare-off to look over at my students and find twenty-eight sets of eyes watching us with utter fascination and glee.

My mouth parts to explain away what just happened, but before I even have a chance, one of the other guys that came with Ty—the one with short, cropped hair and piercing blue eyes—gets everyone's attention. "Who wants some LA Wolves gear?"

Chaos breaks out, and the intense moment between Ty and me is forgotten—for now. These are middle schoolers; they never forget anything except their homework. Thankfully, Mrs. O'Dell is deep in conversation with one of the other guys, who looks like a big terrifying beast but is giving her the kindest smile. The third guy—whose eyes seem to carry something heavy that looks a lot like the loss I see in my own eyes when I look in the mirror—catches my gaze, quickly glances at Mrs. O'Dell then back to me, and winks.

Relief floods my body. They kept her distracted, which means she didn't see my moment with Ty. Thank God, because I'm not prepared to answer the questions I'm sure she already has, let alone any she'd have if she caught on that Ty and I know each other in a more intimate nature.

I know I can't avoid the truth forever, but I'll put it off for as long as I can.

Ty wanders over to a group of my students while the other guys he came with do the same. I walk around the room, eavesdropping here and there on their conversations with the kids. That's how I learn that the big beastly man with the kind smile is Gabe Romero, the one with the piercing blue eyes and swagger is Dominic Smith, and the third man whose smile never quite reaches his eyes is Romel Watson. Apparently, the Fierce Four are the key to the defense of the LA Wolves football team —a team I've seen billboards for, but since I don't watch sports never paid attention to.

My students are buzzing with energy when the bell rings

for lunch, and for the first time ever, they are all reluctant to leave instead of rushing out the door. Once they're finally ushered out with hugs and waves to the guys, a sense of relief washes over me because this means Ty is leaving too. I can put my walls back up after he tore them down with the sweet way he interacted with my students. Gabe, Dom, and Romel head for the door, but Ty walks straight to me, a jersey in his hands.

"This one's for you."

I look down at the navy blue fabric in his hands. Then he flips it over, and I see RUSSELL written on the back and the number 31.

When I look up, he's already watching me. "I hope you'll wear it when you come to my game."

"You mean *if.*"

He leans closer, his gaze dropping to my lips briefly. "No, I mean *when*. I messed up, Lexi, but I'm not letting you go. You and this baby are mine. So, someday, hopefully soon, you'll be sitting in those stands cheering me on, and I want my jersey on your body so every man in there knows you're mine."

All the air whooshes from my lungs as I stare at this man who is making it really hard to keep my defenses up, especially when he sounds so sure. This man in front of me isn't the Ty who made me feel like a gold digger two days ago; this is the Ty who made me feel precious and cherished during our night together.

This is the Ty I could too easily fall for if I'm not careful.

He moves his hand up and brushes a lock of hair away from my face, his gaze still locked on mine. His mouth parts before he closes it again, and the corners of his eyes crinkle with slight strain. "I know you have every right to turn me down after how I reacted the other day, but I'm really hoping you won't, because I'm dying to spend more time with you," he rushes out before taking a measured breath. "We have an away game on Thursday, but will you go out with me when we get back in town?"

I have no good excuse to say no, and truthfully, my defenses are too weak after watching him with my students.

"Okay," I whisper.

The smile that breaks out across his ruggedly handsome face has my heart beating faster and my stomach tightening with need. He leans forward, placing his forehead against mine and closing his eyes. "Thank you, Lexi." He pulls away just enough to press his lips where his forehead just was, and emotion clogs my throat.

This man is so dangerous to my heart.

That weekend, we step into the restaurant, and Ty places his hand on my lower back as he holds the door open for me to go first. The second we're inside, my nerves flare to new heights.

This is a nice restaurant. Like, need-reservations-a-year-or-two-in-advance-and-everyone-here-drives-fancy-European-cars nice. I'm pretty sure it's been featured in magazines for its exclusivity, and I can immediately see why.

Every single patron is gorgeous—men and women alike wearing obvious designer dresses and suits. The women are covered in massive jewels, and the men wear watches I bet would cost as much as my yearly salary, if not more. The place settings look like something out of a high-end magazine for the elite, and the energy in the room screams power and wealth.

I am so in over my head here.

A stunning woman wearing a jaw-dropping off-the-shoulder gold dress walks by, and I try not to stare, especially when I realize she's an A-list celebrity, but I don't miss the way her cursory gaze drops down to my dress or the slight lift of her lip in a sneer that doesn't seem to fit the flawless beauty. My hands go to the skirt of my dress, rubbing my now sweaty palms on the suddenly cheap-feeling material I'd previously thought felt decadent against my skin. Can she tell this is a name brand knockoff I found on sale? My gaze darts around the other patrons, and even though I know they're not, it feels like everyone is looking at me—judging me.

I don't belong here.

What am I doing? I should be home on my cheap, comfy couch grading essays.

The heat of Ty's body next to mine is the only thing that pulls me out of my freak-out. He nods to the maître d', who greets him with a warm smile and guides us to our table. Meanwhile, I try to steady my breathing. I open my mouth half a dozen times to tell Ty this was a bad idea, but I can't make the words come out.

The truth is I want to see where this goes. I may feel like a fish out of water, but Ty doesn't seem to notice the stares. In fact, he's barely stopped touching me since he picked me up, so clearly he's not judging me for my dress. Why should I let other people's judgment impact my night with him?

I'm not on a date with *them*. Ty's opinion is the only one that matters.

I'm feeling slightly more confident when the maître d' seats us at a table near the back—tucked behind a wooden partition with a beautiful painting of the ocean at sunset—offering some privacy from the other patrons in the restaurant. He leaves our menus in front of each of us before walking away. A waiter quickly replaces him, taking our drink order and then giving us a few minutes with the menu.

"Do you know what you want to eat?"

"Um, I'm not sure yet." Honestly, there are some things on

this menu I've never heard of. I'm kind of terrified I'll be ordering bull's testicles or something. That's apparently a delicacy, right? I fight a grimace at the thought and focus on what sounds familiar.

He sets down his menu and leans forward. "I need to make a confession."

I set down my own menu, mirroring him. "Okay."

"I don't know what half this stuff is."

I can't stop the smile that breaks out on my face and the relief that courses through me. "Oh, thank God. I don't either."

"I was trying to impress you, but I think I might've been better off choosing a restaurant where I actually know what is on the menu."

My heart flutters. "You wanted to impress me?"

The lighting might be dim, but I don't miss the slight flush on his cheeks, and my own smile grows as all the stress and worry completely fade. "I don't know if I should be ashamed or not that you have to even ask. Of course, I want to impress you."

I pick up my menu, trying to hide the way I'm sure my own heated face is flushing. "I appreciate the effort."

He huffs out a laugh. "We'll see about that after you accidentally eat something that is supposed to be high-end cuisine, but is really something like bull's testicles or squid brains."

I drop my menu and stare at him with my mouth open. It's like he's in my damn head. This is what it felt like the night we were together too. Easy. Uncomplicated. Fun.

With everything that's happened since, I forgot how in sync we were that night, like two puzzle pieces fitting together perfectly.

The waiter comes over, and we each order a steak, and then while we wait, we talk. The conversation flows easily between us as he asks me more about my job and my students, especially the ones he talked to when he came earlier this week. I ask him about football, because truthfully, I don't know a single thing about the sport. I tried to watch his away game, but both Blaire and I were equally confused about what was happening as we watched.

The entire time we talk, Ty's gaze stays locked on me, as if no one else in the room exists. Our food is delivered, and we keep the conversation light as we tuck into our meal which thankfully turns out to be delicious. I'm only about three bites in when Ty puts down his fork and looks down at the table.

"I can't do this," he says.

My smile drops along with my fork, my appetite completely gone with those four words. How did I read him so wrong? I thought this date was going so well.

Then he looks back up at me, and his eyes burn with a heated intensity I've only seen on him once before. "I'm trying to be a gentleman, but I can't sit here and pretend I'm not dying to kiss you again. I can barely focus on what we're talking about because all I can think about is kissing your lipstick right off your face."

I gape at him in shock. That was not what I was expecting him to say. Then he shocks me further when he reaches around the side of the table and pulls my chair next to him instead of where I was seated across from him. He moves me like I weigh nothing, and then we're next to each other, and he drapes one arm behind my back, resting on the chair, while his other hand comes up to trace my cheek. His gaze eats up every inch of my face like he's memorizing each line and freckle and storing it away for all eternity.

I can hardly breathe.

His thumb grazes my cheek. "I'm going to kiss you now, so I can actually give you a proper date where I'm not distracted by that sinful mouth of yours...or at least less distracted, hopefully."

"Okay," I whisper, my voice raspy and filled with desire.

He watches me for another second and then his lips are brushing against mine in a kiss that's somehow both tender and passionate. My body melts against his as I let out the faintest moan and part my lips. His tongue swoops in, not needing any more invitation, and then nothing in the world exists but Ty. He groans deeply, but soft enough I'm sure only I can hear, before pulling away. He places one more kiss on my tender lips before he sits back, and I open my eyes to find his hooded and glazed with lust.

"Maybe that wasn't my best idea because now I just want to keep kissing you."

I cup his cheek, mirroring the way he held mine during our kiss, and he leans into it, his eyes closing like my touch is the best feeling in the world.

Only Ty.

He's the only man who's ever made me feel like this. Like I'm special to him, precious, worthy of being cherished and spoiled. I might be confused about a lot right now, but there's one thing I'm not at all confused about anymore. I want him. I want him to want me and love me the way I've always dreamed of being wanted and loved.

Doubt niggles in the back of my mind that he's only doing this because we're having a baby, but I push it aside for now. I want to live in the moment, and I need to remember that he made me feel this way before the baby even existed.

Maybe the baby is the thing that's brought us back together, but tonight, he's all mine. And I plan to enjoy every second.

"Fuck it," he murmurs before surging forward and taking another kiss that has me giggling. He pulls away, a radiant smile filling his face as he stares openly at my eyes and my mouth. "I love hearing you laugh like that."

I drop my gaze and nibble my lip, oddly embarrassed. This

man has seen me naked, and I'm carrying his child. But the idea of giggling like some innocent schoolgirl has my cheeks on fire.

He clears his throat and pretends to get serious. "Right, okay, so what were we talking about?" he asks as he picks back up his fork. His other hand rests on my thigh, keeping me close, and I don't hate it.

I don't hate it at all.

TWELVE

Ty

"I really thought once you found Lexi, you wouldn't be constantly glued to your phone anymore."

A smile tugs at my lips, but I don't look up until I finish texting Lexi. "Sorry not sorry."

Dom chuckles. "What are you? A teenage girl?"

"Oh, please, like you don't jump as soon as Alayna calls you."

He holds up his hands. "Guilty as charged." He takes a seat next to me in the locker room after our practice. "You seem happy. Things going good?"

I spin my phone in my hands. "Slower than I'd like, but that's my own fault."

"She's still keeping you at a distance since she told you she was pregnant?"

"Yes and no. We've been on a couple of dates since then, and she lets me kiss her, but she's still not as comfortable with me as she was before."

He shrugs. "Maybe the chemistry was just that night cause you guys had been drinking."

I shake my head. "We didn't have that much to drink that night."

I know the problem. She let me in and I treated her like shit. My reaction to her pregnancy announcement haunts me, and even though she lets me kiss her, I know I haven't fully earned her forgiveness just yet.

But I will. I'm not giving up on her—on us. No matter what hoops she makes me jump through to prove it. And maybe that's why I've brushed off Tanner's continued suggestions that I get a paternity test done. I'm not willing to risk the progress I've made with her even if I can't deny his doubts are valid.

"Honestly, I can't tell if it's her holding back because of how I reacted to her pregnancy announcement or me holding back because I'm afraid she's exactly who my brother thinks she is." I'd told the guys about Tanner's plea that I get a paternity test. They were much more supportive about it being my choice, although they didn't argue that a paternity test is the smart move to make given how little we know each other. I'm still torn about how to approach it because smart or not, I know without a doubt it'll derail any progress we've made, and I don't want that either.

My phone pings in my hand and I look down, frowning when I read her text in response to me asking her if we were still on for tonight.

LEXI

Can't tonight. Today was rough and I don't feel good. Maybe after you get back from Atlanta.

I leave tomorrow afternoon for our next away game. Tonight was my only chance to see her because of some teacher training classes she had earlier this week after work. It's been five days since I've gotten to touch her, and I've been looking forward to tonight all day.

"I gotta go," I say to Dom and then throw all my stuff in my bag and head out.

I make a pit stop at the store on the way to her place, which takes me longer than expected when I have to field some autographs for fans. The benefit of living in a place like LA is that they're pretty used to celebs here. Most of the time I don't get bothered when I'm out and about. So of course, I'd run into a tourist group filled with football fans on the one night I'm in a rush to get to my girl.

By the time I knock on her door, it's been two hours since she texted me. Movement inside can be heard from where I stand outside her door, looking around at the apartment doors in this hallway. It's not the worst neighborhood—in fact it's relatively safe, considering—but I hate that she lives here.

When she opens her door, her ocean-blue eyes hit me like a punch to the gut. Fuck, even tired and looking a little green, she's fucking gorgeous. She parts her lips, her brows furrowed in confusion, and I hold up the bag in my hands. "You said you didn't feel good."

I took Romel's advice and learned on our last date what her food triggers were and what snacks were working for her. One of those was eliminated the other day when she ate it right before someone walked into the lunchroom with a hot dog and she had to race to the bathroom to throw up. Now she can't have wheat crackers or even look at the box without thinking about that hot dog smell.

A soft smile lifts the edges of her lips and she moves aside, allowing me to enter. I drop a kiss to her forehead as I pass her, unable not to touch her when I'm this close and it's been so long already. Placing the bag on her kitchen counter, I start pulling out the items I got for her—Fruit Punch Gatorade, Tim's Cascade Original potato chips, Cheez-Its, pomegranate juice, ginger ale, and a frozen cheese pizza.

She leans against the doorframe leading to the kitchen, her head resting against the wall and her eyes tracing over each item. Her body seems to relax with every breath she takes, and her eyes soften when she looks at me. Her look tugs at something deep in my chest—something so much deeper than just wanting to bury myself inside her.

"Thank you," she says, her voice low but filled with gratitude.

This woman has no idea what I'd do for her—the lengths I'm willing to go.

Unwilling to stay away from her any longer, I move toward her and wrap my arms around her waist. Without hesitation, she leans against me, her arms wrapping around my neck. Her lips meet mine, and all at once, everything is right in my world. This right here is all I need.

"Is it your morning sickness?"

She tucks her head against my chest, and warmth moves swiftly through my entire body that she's seeking comfort from me.

"You mean all-day sickness?" she murmurs. "I swear it's gotten worse this week. I think I've just done too much the past few days, and I'm paying for it."

"How can I help?" My lips brush against her black hair.

She lets out a contented little sigh. "This is kinda nice."

I tighten my arms around her. "I'm happy to provide this whenever you need."

"Mmm."

I pull back enough to see her eyes closed as she rests against me. This close, it's impossible to miss the bags under her eyes. Has she not been sleeping well?

Bending down, I sweep my arm under her knees and lift her up. She gives a little mumble of protest, but her eyes remain closed, and her arms tighten around my neck. I don't bother stopping in the living room but head straight to her room, placing her gently on her bed and then covering her up with a soft fleece blanket from a small chair in the corner of the room.

When I move to go grab some of the snacks I brought to put on her nightstand, she grabs my hand, stopping me. Her tired blue eyes blink up at me, and there's a faint hint of vulnerability in her gaze. "Will you stay with me?"

"Yeah," I croak, unfamiliar emotion and need hitting me from all sides. God, I'd stay with her every night if I thought she'd let me. The fact she's asking me to now, and I have to leave her tomorrow, is already killing me.

I kick off my shoes, then climb into bed with her. She instantly curls into my side, her head resting on that spot between my shoulder and chest, her arm draped over my waist. She tucks her nose against my shirt and inhales. I wince, imagining that I probably smell like sweat since I didn't bother to shower before heading over here. Luckily we were only doing light drills today or else I would stink.

A deep sound escapes her throat, and her whole body seems to melt against me. "You smell so good."

I close my eyes and drop a kiss to the top of her head. "Glad you think so."

Her breath evens out quickly, sleep pulling her under, and I don't know how long I watch her, my heart aching with how badly I want her to want me like this all the time. How much I want her to let herself rely on me. How much I want to let all my own doubts go so I can really enjoy the feelings this woman evokes in me. Eventually, my eyes start to grow heavy as sleep drags me under, all my tight muscles loosening the longer her lavender scent hits my nose.

It's the best night of sleep I've ever had.

THIRTEEN

Lexi

"I am so sick of people telling me how to do my job," Blaire says as she bursts into my classroom during our planning period.

"Well, hello to you too."

She sits on top of one of the student desks in front of mine. "Seriously. Everyone and their mother thinks they can tell us how to do our damn job. Oh, I'm sorry, did you go to four years of college to learn how to individualize instruction for twenty-five plus different learners in one room? No? Then maybe you should sit down and shut up."

She growls, literally growls, and I sit back in my chair laughing, which only seems to make her ire rise. "How are you not pissed off by these new 'standards' they've thrown at us that are basically the old standards repackaged and with a bunch of fancy words that don't actually mean anything but come with a truck-ton of extra paperwork for us?"

I shrug. "Because I know what's best for my students, and the test scores for my kids prove it. Every year, they show growth, and since those numbers back me up, no one bothers to ask me how I'm doing it."

"How are you doing it?"

"I teach them the basics and then we go from there. They're meeting those standards whether I package it that way or not. I also adapt the lessons for my kiddos in a way that can also be helpful for all my students."

"That's why you only take Friday nights off. Damn, that's a ton of work. I didn't realize you were doing so much extra."

"I'm going to need to find a better way to do it once the baby is here. I can't sacrifice my own child for other people's, no matter how much I love my students."

Her gaze falls to the floor. "I don't know if I can do this profession forever," she whispers like she's confessing a sin. "I got into teaching because I wanted to make a difference, and if it were just the students, I would teach forever. But it's the damn adults. All the politics and administration bullshit that we have to deal with. It's crushing."

I don't admit it, but I've had the same thought. As teachers, we give and give and give, and then when we have nothing left to give, we're expected to give more. It doesn't make sense. And what's the most disheartening about it all is that the kids are the ones who suffer the most because of it.

But at some point, we're going to have to put our oxygen masks on first or else we won't be able to help anyone else.

"I'm thinking of starting a nonprofit," Blaire announces out of nowhere.

"For what?"

"For kids. I don't know the specifics, but if things keep on like they are, I'm going to rip all my hair out, and I love my hair."

I chuckle and shake my head.

"You'd join me, right? We could fill the gaps or start our own school or something."

I arch a brow. "I don't think it's that easy."

She tips her head, and her eyebrows reach her bangs. "*Anything* is easier than being a teacher."

"But we get summers off!" I tease sarcastically.

Her eye roll couldn't be any bigger if she tried. "God, I hate people sometimes. If getting summers off means going to trainings that are sometimes paid for and sometimes aren't—but expected for us to go to—or planning for the following year, or picking up a seasonal job since my salary barely covers the cost of living, then sure, we get summers off."

I cross my arms over my chest. "That nonprofit's looking extra good right now, isn't it?"

She drops her head back, staring at the ceiling. "I know this is probably just the October lull that comes every year, but seriously, this is not what I expected when I decided to become a teacher. I feel lied to."

"But you won't quit."

She lets out a heavy sigh. "No, I won't quit. Because I love my students, the little fuckers."

"Blaire!"

"Well, it's true. They're complete stinkers half the time and then they have that light bulb moment, and it's the best feeling in the world."

"Sounds about right."

She shakes her head. "Okay, talk to me about something else, anything else, since we only have"—she glances at the digital clock next to my door—"twenty minutes left of our planning period, and I need to get out of this funk before my next class."

"I haven't puked today," I say with a shrug, although I'm desperately hoping it's not a one-off but a sign that my morning sickness might be abating.

"*That* is what you have to distract me? That's terrible, but also, congratulations."

We stare at each other for a beat before we both break out in smiles.

"What are you calling it?" she asks.

"What do you mean?"

"The baby. Do you have a nickname? Like bug, or bean, or something equally weird and cute."

I unfold my arms and rub my flat belly. It's still weird to think I'm pregnant. If I didn't feel so awful all the time, I wouldn't believe it. "I've been calling him or her Peanut in my head."

Her face goes soft. "Peanut. It's perfect." We're both silent for a minute before she breaks it. "You're going to be an incredible mom; you know that, right?"

"You think so?" I have my doubts. I didn't exactly have any positive female role models in my life, and I remember so little of my own mom. Can I be a good mom if I don't even know what that looks like outside of movies or TV shows?

She pierces me with her fierce and serious gaze. "Lexi, you're the strongest person I've ever met with the biggest heart. Your kid is so stinking lucky that it gets to have *you* as a mom. I have zero doubts you'll be the absolute best."

Tears flood my eyes, and I don't bother getting frustrated with my overly sensitive hormones. I'm too filled with gratitude for this woman who has never given up on me, even when I was arguably quite prickly when we first became friends.

"You'll be a great aunt," I say, my voice choked and hoarse.

She smiles wide, her own eyes glistening with a sheen of tears. "You're damn right, I will."

We both laugh, and it cuts through the emotional weight that had fallen on the room. And for the first time since I found out about my baby, my fear recedes, and I finally start to believe that things are going to work out exactly the way they should.

FOURTEEN

Ty

As I pull up to Lexi's place to pick her up for our date, my eyes scan the neighborhood like I do every time I come here. I can't ignore the knot in my gut about her safety, and I don't like her living here where I can't protect her or our baby. With one more glance around, I get out of the car and jog up to her apartment. I've barely knocked before she's swinging the door open, and I have to remind myself to breathe.

Goddamn, she's beautiful. Her dark hair falls softly around her shoulders, over her deep-green sweater. She's wearing dark wash skinny jeans that hug her hips, and when she turns around to grab her purse, I have to bite back a groan at the sight of her luscious ass in those pants.

It's been a long time since I've had sex, and this woman turns me on more than any other woman I've ever met.

She spins around, not at all aware of the effect she has on me, and closes the door. I stand behind her while she locks up and then we walk side by side to my car. My fingers twitch with the desire to grab her hand, and I hold my breath as I reach out and twine my fingers with hers. She glances up at me, a soft smile on her face, and my breath escapes as I relax.

We're having a kid together, but sometimes I feel like a confused fifteen-year-old boy taking a girl out on a date for the first time with not a single clue how to act around her.

I thought I left those days behind me a long time ago, but apparently all it takes is this woman to bring it out in me. You'd think after the last several weeks, I would feel surer of myself with her, but that thin sliver of doubt I've held on to about her—thanks in part to my brother's continued texts and calls about a paternity test—has kept me from feeling stable in this growing relationship with her.

And I hate it because I don't want to doubt her anymore. I don't want to second-guess myself before I reach out to touch her. Especially when my body knows with one hundred percent certainty that it wants her and no one else.

When we get to my car, I step forward and open the door for her. A subtle blush streaks across her cheeks, and her eyes connect with mine for a second before she ducks her head and slides in with a quiet thanks.

I walk behind the car and slow my steps, taking a deep breath as I try to get my body under control. That split second of eye contact should not have me hard as a goddamn rock, but it does. There's something about the way Lexi looks at me that makes me feel seen in a way I never have been—even if only for a second. It was the same during our night together. Every look felt like she was seeing my soul, and it was impossible to hide from her.

It hits me then that even though she knows the truth of who I am now, she doesn't look at me any different. She doesn't look at me with dollar signs or like I can do something for me. She looks at me like she sees *me*.

I take a deep breath before I open my door and slide in, the doubts that have niggled at me since our first disastrous lunch when she told me she was pregnant finally starting to dissipate. I glance over at her to find her already watching me. There's uncertainty in her deep blue gaze.

"Everything okay?"

I rotate my body to face her, not even bothering to start the car yet as I stare at her. "Yeah," I say, my voice a little hoarse. Giving in to what I really want, I slide my hand around the side of her neck and lean forward, pulling her toward me until her lips meet mine in a kiss I've been dying for all day.

Her eyes remain closed when I pull back before slowly blinking open. "What was that for?"

"Because I wanted to."

Those soft lips that are a little wet from our kiss tilt up in the slightest smile, and her eyes go soft. "Oh."

My own smile lifts my cheeks. "Yeah, oh." And because I can't help myself, I kiss her one more time, not nearly as deep as I want to, but it's enough to tide me over.

I get us on the road and then slide my hand over her thigh, needing to keep touching her.

She clears her throat, and I catch her trying to stifle her smile. "So where are you taking me for our date?"

I squeeze her thigh. "You mentioned a craving for ice cream, so I thought we'd go to one of my favorite places on the board-walk. Then we can walk along the beach for a while. I figured low-key."

She'd also mentioned loving the beach but never getting enough time to spend there, so I wanted to make sure she got a beach night before the weather gets too cold.

I feel the weight of her gaze on me, so I glance over. Her eyes are bright and her smile soft. She's the embodiment of content, even if she still looks a little shy, but any tension in her body has completely faded at hearing my plans. "That sounds perfect. I've also been craving tacos if you feel like getting some of those later."

"I will never turn down tacos."

The rest of the drive goes by in silence, the low hum of the radio playing in the background as we make our way to one of my favorite spots. It's not as busy as I expected for a Friday night, and I'm grateful for that. But as we're in line for ice cream, a little boy, probably nine or ten if I had to guess, looks behind him and his eyes widen in a way that tells me he knows exactly who I am. He tugs on his mom's arm, and she glances down at him then back at me to see what she's looking at.

"It's Tyler Russell," the kid says in a voice like he's trying to whisper but forgot to turn down the volume.

I offer him a smile and then glance at Lexi to see how she's handling this. Past girlfriends used to either preen like peacocks that they were with me or get pissy about having to share me with fans—even if that fan was a kid. But it shouldn't surprise me that Lexi's not paying me any attention. She's smiling down at the kid like she thinks it's cute the way he's in awe of me standing right behind him.

Focusing back on the kid, I squat down so I'm more on his level. I've never liked towering over the kids when they come to meet and greets. "How's it goin'?"

His face lights up and he stumbles over his words. "Oh my gosh, I can't believe I'm really meeting you. My brother's gonna be so jealous."

"What's your name?"

"Preston. Can you sign my hat?"

"Sure thing." I look up at the counter and ask the employee if she's got a pen or Sharpie. She hands me one of each, and I use the Sharpie to sign my name and jersey number on his hat.

He stares at it in awe and then Lexi's voice speaks from beside me. "Do you want a picture together?"

I glance up at her, and she's looking at the kid's mom. "I can take one if you want to be in it too."

I'm not sure what the mom does or says because I can't stop staring at Lexi. She's effortless and unfazed. And there's no way I'm going to survive if this woman leaves me. I don't care if she ends up being a gold digger—although the evidence that she could be is completely nonexistent. In this moment, I let go of any remaining doubts as I soak her in and relish finally having a real partner who doesn't see my public-facing job as a burden or a stepping stone for something better.

Lexi grabs the mom's phone, and I stand up between the two of them for the picture, all of us smiling, and I know my smile in this picture will be bigger than any other fan photo I've ever taken because I'm smiling at the woman taking it.

FIFTEEN

Lexi

Ty slides his fingers between mine, entwining our free hands while we eat ice cream cones with our others. He's been throwing me soft smiles ever since we met that cute kid and his mom. It's the first time I've seen Ty interact with a fan in public, and I have to admit it was pretty cute to watch him.

We walk down the boardwalk a bit before he pulls us out onto the sand, and we move closer to the gentle waves lapping at the shore. The sun hangs low in the sky, but we've still got another hour or so before it'll get dark.

He pulls me to a stop and wraps his arm around me, pulling me in so my chest is against his as he finishes off his ice cream cone. I don't know how he's done with it already.

He stares down at me and then his gaze drops to my mouth. "What?" I ask, self-conscious that I have chocolate ice cream on my face.

My worst fears are confirmed when he goes, "You've got a little something right here." The last word is whispered against my lips before he closes the distance and slides his firm lips against mine. My body melts against his as I stay aware enough to keep my ice cream cone from tipping over.

He pulls back and hums. "Mmm, chocolate."

I bury my face against his chest as giggles escape. Freaking giggles. Only this man has ever been able to get me to giggle like some innocent schoolgirl. It's a novel thing to feel as light and carefree as this man makes me.

He rubs his thumb softly against my cheek, staring into my eyes, and my heart starts racing the longer he looks at me without saying a word. What does he see that has him looking at me like he's staring at the moon and stars in my eyes?

And how can I keep him looking at me like this always? No one has ever looked at me like this, and I know well enough that it won't last, so I choose to soak it up as long as I can.

"I want to know everything about you," he says, his voice low.

He wouldn't say that if he knew everything. If he knew how I grew up, the realities of an unhappy and endlessly lonely childhood. Not even Blaire knows everything.

He takes my hand again, and we keep walking along the beach. "I'm serious, you know. I want to really know you, Lexi. Are you close with your folks?"

I hate that one of the first get-to-know-you questions is inevitably about family. I suppose I should be grateful that he's waited this long to ask. "My parents died when I was young."

His face falls. "Oh Lex, I'm so sorry."

I shrug. "I was so young; I don't really remember them much anymore." That's the biggest tragedy of losing them when I was too little to have a lasting memory. The bits and pieces I do remember get harder to recall the older I get, and I worry about the day when I won't remember them at all. It'll be like losing them all over again.

"So did your grandparents raise you then?"

His voice is soft like he understands the delicate nature of our conversation, but it doesn't make it any easier. I really don't want to talk about this, especially not when I was having such a good time.

"No. I was in foster care until I turned eighteen. What got you into football?"

He glances at me and thankfully doesn't push anymore about my family. "I started playing youth football when I was eight. I was super active—all of us boys were—so my parents got us into sports pretty early. I played everything, but I fell in love with football and was more of a natural with it, so that's what I stuck with."

"Have you always played with the Wolves?"

"No. My rookie season I was on the East Coast, then played a couple of seasons in Atlanta before I got traded to the Wolves. I like being on the West Coast because it's the same time zone at least as my parents, and I like the weather here in California. Have you always lived here?"

"Pretty much. I had dreams of traveling to Europe, but never really had the time or money. I've always had to work to pay the bills."

"Maybe we can take a trip sometime." He says it as if our future together is so clear, and I wish I could see it like he does. I wish I could have that kind of faith in another person.

But I've never been that lucky, and even though we seem to be finding our footing, I'm still hesitant to completely let my guard down around him. But I also can't completely shut him down either because the truth is I *want* that future—no matter how implausible it might be for me.

"Yeah, maybe."

He stops walking, and it isn't until my arm pulls back from where we're still holding hands that I realize it. I spin around to face him, my breath stuttering in my chest at how handsome he is in the low light of the sun with the backdrop of the beach. This guy is so far out of my league, it's not even funny.

He pulls my hand, and I move the two small steps until we're toe to toe and I'm looking up into his brown eyes. As if he can read all my insecurities, he drops his head until our foreheads are touching, and it seems like all the air I'm breathing is coming straight from him.

"I want a life with you. I know the baby brought you back to me, but I was looking for you, Lexi, and I would've kept looking even with my friends telling me to stop. There's something about you—about us together—that I can't lose. I won't. I'll prove to you I'm in this for good, and I hope someday you'll trust me enough to tell me all about your hopes and fears and your childhood." He gives me a slightly pointed look that tells me I wasn't at all subtle when I changed the conversation earlier. "Okay?"

I want all those things too. It's exhausting always holding back and never really letting anyone in. It's especially exhausting when it's the father of your baby and the first man who's ever made you feel truly special.

"Okay," I whisper before his lips take mine in a soft kiss that feels like it sears him into my soul. It's not the kind of kiss I've read about—filled with passion and heat. Instead, it's the soft kiss of tenderness and security—two things I've never felt from another person before.

And it honestly scares the shit out of me.

SIXTEEN

Ty

When I woke up this morning, knowing about this appointment, I didn't quite picture it like this. If you'd told me three months ago I'd be sitting in a stark doctor's office surrounded by pregnant women, I would've laughed. But that's exactly where I am.

Lexi sits beside me, her hands in her lap and the fingernail of her right thumb rubbing over the top of her left thumbnail. It's something I've noticed she does a lot when she's nervous. It's so subtle, I wonder if she's even aware of it. I reach over and wrap my hand around hers. She looks up at me, and visibly relaxes as she turns her palm over, entwining our fingers together.

My chest expands with a sense of pride that I have the power to calm her—to ease some of her stress.

The high of victory on the field doesn't even come close to the way I feel when I get these small moments with Lexi.

My knee bounces as I look around the waiting room of the doctor's office until she sets her hand on my thigh, stopping the movement. I glance down at her, and there's a lightness in her eyes that's been growing with every day we spend together.

"Nervous?" she whispers.

"Maybe a little," I confess, wrapping her hand with mine and holding it tight. I can't remember a time when a woman's hand fit so perfectly in mine. "I don't really know what to expect."

I won't tell her the other fears I have. I've only ever spent a significant amount of time around Romel's daughter—who is weirdly wise for her age—and the kids at the pediatric cancer hospital I try to visit once a month, and those kids are just trying to survive. Neither of my brothers have any kids and aren't even close to settling down. I don't really hang out with any of the other players on the team apart from Gabe, Dom, and Romel, so I've never been around their babies.

I honestly hadn't seriously thought about the prospect of having kids before Lexi told me she was pregnant. I've been focused on football for the last several years, and before that I was focused on getting into the pros, so kids never had time to cross my mind. I might've thought about the idea of kids in that weird hypothetical way as something that would happen some-day, but there was never anyone I wanted to have them with.

Not until now. Now I can't imagine having a kid with anyone besides Lexi.

So, yeah, I have no fucking clue what to expect. But now that it's happening, I'm realizing I need to figure it out quick. And there's nothing that drives that point home more than being surrounded by a bunch of women in various stages of pregnancy.

Lexi licks her lips, and it reminds me of the present I bought her. I pull it out of my pocket and hand it to her. "For afterward."

She looks down at my hand then up at me with wide eyes and her mouth slightly parted in surprise. I don't know why she's shocked. She should realize by now that I'm always paying attention, especially when it comes to her. And it didn't take me long to figure out that the caramel apple pops were her craving right now. I bought several boxes and have them stashed in my condo, my car, and another in my other pocket in case one isn't enough. I know she can't suck on it now, but I figure she'll enjoy it afterward.

"How did you know?" she asks, a little awe in her soft voice.

"You had a couple of wrappers on your counter when I came over the other day, and you were sucking on one when I FaceTimed you during our last away trip."

She stares at me and then her lips quirk up into a small smile, but the way her eyes light up tells me I did a good job. My chest swells with something stronger than affection, stronger than anything I've ever felt before. I love making her light up the way she is now, knowing I contributed to her happiness, and I'll do just about anything to keep that look on her face.

A nurse walks out, a clipboard in hand. "Lexi?"

Both of us stand, and I follow Lexi as the nurse leads us down the hall to an empty exam room. A gray machine that looks like some space computer stands off to the side with a bunch of knobs and buttons. A long, thin, white handle sticks up next to a short, gray, fat handle. The rest of the room looks like your standard doctor's office. Some of my unease starts to settle.

Then I sit down in the chair beside the exam table, and directly across from me is a huge diagram that takes up a third of the wall and shows the size of a baby through each month of pregnancy. Lexi sits on the exam table and chats with the nurse, but I can't focus on anything they're saying because I'm staring at the image on the wall, and reality starts to sink in.

We made a baby.

A cluster of cells is growing into an actual person. A human being. That is fucking wild.

The nurse pulls out a black cuff and puts it on Lexi's arm, taking her blood pressure, and my gaze focuses on her face. From the outside, she appears relatively calm, but she has little tells I've discovered over the past couple of weeks we've been together. There's tension at the corners of her eyes that make the laugh lines there more pronounced, and while her face is a relative mask, her hands give away her nerves. The right thumb-nail scrapes over her left thumbnail again, slightly faster than it was out in the waiting room.

I want to stand beside her and offer her some support, but this room is small, and I don't want to get in the way of the nurse. When she's done taking her blood pressure, she asks Lexi how she's been feeling, takes some notes, and then tells us the doctor will be in shortly. The second she leaves and the door closes, I'm crossing the short distance to Lexi. From where she's sitting, her head lines up with my chin. Her legs open enough for me to position myself between them, and I immediately wrap my arms around her and hug her close. She's stiff for a minute before her arms wrap around my waist and she sags against me.

Something about this woman letting me give her strength makes me feel ten feet tall. Maybe because I suspect it's not something she does with just anyone.

"It's all going to be okay," I murmur in her hair.

"How do you know?" There's a shakiness in her voice which makes it seem like she's desperate to believe me, but doesn't.

"Because no matter what happens, I'm not going anywhere."

She pulls back, her eyes slightly watery. She's blamed her tears more often than not on her changing hormones, but a part of me wonders if it's because I'm starting to break through those thick walls she's built around herself.

She opens her mouth to say something, but then snaps it

shut. Her deep-blue eyes hold me hostage, emotion twisting her pretty face before a knock interrupts whatever she was about to say.

I spin around right as the doctor opens the door.

"Hi Lexi." The middle-aged doctor with thin, black-framed glasses glances at me and then does a double take. "You must be Dad. Has anyone ever told you that you look a lot like the football player Tyler Russell?"

I give her my fan smile. "I *am* Tyler Russell."

She lets out an awkward laugh and then puts her hand to her chest. "Oh my...I'm a huge fan. I'm Dr. Taylor. It's so nice to meet you."

"It's always nice to meet a fan."

She smiles wider and then thankfully focuses on Lexi. "How've you been feeling?"

"Tired," Lexi says, her body sagging. "All the time."

Dr. Taylor smiles kindly at her. "Totally normal at this stage. How's your nausea? Any other symptoms?"

"My nausea usually starts after lunch through dinner time. There are days it's not so bad and other days where it's still awful."

The doctor makes a note on the laptop she brought in with her and nods. "Again, normal. It should subside here soon since based on your last menstrual cycle you should be nearing the end of your first trimester. Most women see a drop in morning sickness once you pass that twelve to thirteen week mark. Very rarely does it linger into the second trimester, but it is possible. Any other symptoms or concerns?"

Lexi shakes her head.

"Okay, great. Let's have you lie down and we'll do an ultrasound to get some measurements." She moves toward the machine in the room. "Since you're far enough along, we should be able to do an external ultrasound, but if we can't get a good view then we'll do one transvaginally," she explains, pointing to the white wand I noticed earlier.

I stare at the long, thin, white wand and can't help but rub my hand over my mouth to hide my smirk. I'm way larger than that. My girl will have no problem with that thing if she has to use it.

Lexi lies back on the exam table, and Dr. Taylor has her push her pants down to the top of her pelvis. Lexi stares up at the ceiling while the doctor preps the wand with some gel and clicks a few keys on the ultrasound machine, her hands gripping the side of the table and her bottom lip trapped between her teeth. I stand, ignoring Dr. Taylor's glance my way, and focus on my girl. Lexi looks over at my movement, and the silent plea in her eyes nearly has me dropping to my knees wanting to promise her the whole world. I place my hand over hers, and she releases her grip on the table, flipping over her hand so we're palm to palm, her dark blue eyes locked on mine. My other hand brushes her hair away from her forehead.

I bend over, resting my head against hers, my mouth next to her ear because my words are only for her. "It's all going to be okay, Lexi. I'm right here, and I'm not going anywhere. Okay?"

I pull back to look in her eyes—to allow her to look into mine and see the sincerity in my gaze. She nods just as the doctor clears her throat.

"Ready?"

Lexi looks at Dr. Taylor. "We're ready."

I don't watch whatever Dr. Taylor is doing. Instead I watch Lexi's face, each expression giving me a small glimpse at what she's feeling, but I know it's just the tip of the iceberg. Lexi is guarded, more than most people I've met—men and women alike. But I want her to be able to trust me with her every thought and emotion.

I squeeze her hand, giving her any strength I can, and then a whooshing sound fills the room, and my gaze focuses on the screen of the machine the doctor is using. Dr. Taylor clicks a couple of keys, taking images of what looks like the old gray-and-white static I used to see on my grandpa's ancient television back in the day. But in the middle of that static is a small, round blob and a quick flicker that matches the rapid heartbeat now filling the room.

My vision blurs, and it takes me a second to realize the burning behind my eyes is tears. I can barely look away from the screen—from *my kid*—but I pull my gaze to look at Lexi. My heart nearly bursts out of my chest at the longing and pure love in her watery eyes as she stares unblinking at the screen.

"Is it okay?" she asks the doctor, her voice shaky.

Dr. Taylor nods. "Everything's looking great so far. Strong, steady heartbeat right where it should be. Baby is measuring right on track." She turns away from the computer and offers us both a caring smile. "Congrats, Mom and Dad."

And that's when the tears that have been building in Lexi's eyes start to fall. She doesn't make a sound, but the tears fall in a steady stream down her face. The doctor hits a few more buttons and then a small machine flares to life, spitting out several images of our little blob. She hands them to Lexi with a look of kind understanding before she starts to clean up. When she's done, she pats the table and tells Lexi to take as much time as she needs before she leaves us alone in the room. I can't stand to see Lexi crying, so I pull her up and wrap her in my arms. She burrows her head into my chest, her arms going around my waist, holding me tight to her. It's nothing like the tentative way she hugged me back earlier.

We stay like that for several minutes, but I don't complain. As much as I hate her tears, I relish in the chance to hold her close.

Lexi's the one who pulls away first, and I reluctantly let her.

She brushes her fingers under her eyes, wiping away any remnants of her tears. "Sorry about that," she mumbles.

I lift her chin with my finger, nearly forgetting what I want to say once those dark ocean-blue eyes meet mine. "You never have to apologize for crying, Precious."

She almost looks startled as the term of endearment leaves my lips. I've never really called any woman anything other than their name or baby, but neither of those seem enough in this moment—or seem right for Lexi. But Precious does because Lexi is the most precious person in my world.

Even if there was no baby, I would've chosen her. I *did* choose her. She was the one who left, and I'm bound and determined to make sure she never leaves me again.

I drop a kiss to her forehead, my own emotions swirling recklessly inside me. Today has been more than I ever expected. More than I ever dreamed.

"I'll step out and let you finish up, okay? I'll meet you outside."

"Okay," she says, her eyes still holding a vulnerability which makes me want to hold her tight and never let go. I drop one more kiss to her forehead because I can't help myself and then make my way out of the doctor's office. Once I get on the sidewalk, I pull my phone out and dial the one person who I know has been dying to hear how this doctor's appointment went.

It only rings twice before she picks up. "Hey, how'd it go?"

"Mom—" My voice cracks as pride and joy and a million other emotions fight to burst out of me. "The heartbeat was so fast."

She laughs on the other end of the line. Unlike my brother, she was happy for me when I shared the news. She didn't immediately jump to paternity tests and questioning if Lexi was just trying to trap me.

"That's normal."

"Yeah, that's what the doctor said. God, Mom, it was wild. I mean, it just looks like this little blob, but I could see the flicker of its heart going so quick. The doctor said everything looked great, so it's all good so far."

"Oh Ty, that's wonderful." There's a pause, but I don't fill it because I know my mom. She's careful with her words, only saying what she truly means, and I've learned it's best to never rush her. "You sound really happy, Sweetie."

I inhale a deep breath of the crisp fall air and look up at the still blue Southern California sky. "I am, Mom. I really am."

SEVENTEEN

Lexi

My pregnancy hormones are conspiring against me. For weeks, all I could do was eat, sleep, or throw up. My energy was at an all-time low, and I would've happily slept most of the day away. As it was, I was wiped every night after work.

But last week, my nausea completely subsided. And then a new symptom popped up. One that has me rubbing my thighs together trying to ease the ache. I give up trying to fight it, desperately needing to release some of this tension before I explode. I grab my favorite vibrator that never fails to get the job done and get comfortable on my bed, turning it on. I don't mess around. I've learned over the last few days that one orgasm barely does anything to sate me. Hell, three sometimes rarely does the job.

And that's why I'm convinced my hormones are conspiring against me because I suspect I would be more than sated if I gave in and let Ty fuck me senseless instead of keeping all this pent-up need to myself and trying to release the tension solo.

But we're going slow—apparently snail-paced slow. I refuse to let my stupid, horny hormones ruin what we've built over the past six weeks.

I turn on my vibe and then position it on my clit, going for gold. My back arches as pleasure instantly shoots up my spine, and my thighs start to shake with my impending release. The first one never takes long, and I'm already right on the edge when the damn doorbell rings.

I let out a groan of frustration, turn off my vibe, pull my yoga pants back up, and hustle to the door, wondering if it's a delivery again. When Ty was out of town last week, he had food delivered every day for me. It was different having someone take care of me instead of me feeling like I always had to take care of myself. Nice, but definitely something I wasn't expecting.

But when I open the door, it's not delivery. It's Ty. And like the devil himself is in charge of my body, my nipples bead in my bra, and my clit throbs between my legs at just the sight of this man who is too damn handsome for his—or my—own good.

"Hey. I thought you didn't get back until late tonight." I try to sound breezy, but I'm pretty sure I sound as frazzled as I feel. I'm teetering on the damn edge.

He tilts his head, his lips pulling up into a small smile. "Nope, we landed an hour ago, same time we were supposed to. I came straight here. That okay?"

I wave my hand and step back so he can come inside. "Yeah, sorry. I must've forgotten."

More than likely it's just my damn hormone brain that hasn't been able to stop thinking about sex for days, so of course the details about his flight home didn't register properly. But there's no way I'm confessing that to him as he walks in and places his bag down.

"You didn't want to go home and get settled?"

He spins around to face me. "Nope. I'm right where I want to be." He steps forward, that sexy smile playing on his face—and making a damn mess of my panties—and my gaze slides over his wide, bulky shoulders, down his gray T-shirt that hides the abs I licked during our night together, which was far too long ago. My mouth waters, and my clit pulses between my legs, as if I could forget it's there.

Then my gaze slides lower to the bulge in his jeans, and I swallow thickly, wondering if he tastes the same.

God, I'm so fucking horny.

"Precious, as much as I love these sex eyes you're giving me, if you don't stop, I might get the wrong idea."

"Huh?" I say, reluctantly pulling my gaze from his body to focus back on his face. His mouth is tilted up while humor and heat fill his eyes. His cheeks are a little flushed, and that only makes my heart beat faster and my need increase.

He steps closer, his tongue darting out to lick his lower lip. His breathing picks up as his hand rises and he grazes my cheek with the back of his fingers. I close my eyes at the feel of his skin against mine, even if it's not a sexual touch. Then my cheeks heat in embarrassment when a moan escapes.

Stupid hormones.

Ty makes a low sound in the back of his throat—a cross between a groan and a growl—and then steps even closer so his front is plastered to mine, his chest brushing against my achy nipples in such a way that has my knees going weak. His other hand wraps around me, holding me tight against his body where I can feel his thick, hard length between us. Raw, needy desire pulses through me like a live wire, and when I look up, his eyes shine with the same longing I feel.

"I'm so horny," I cry, tears of frustration burning my eyes after too many days of denying myself what I really need. "Please, make it better."

"Fuck, Precious. Why didn't you say so?"

He doesn't give me any time to answer before his lips are crashing on mine, and all thoughts disappear as I wrap my arms around his neck, holding his head to mine as his tongue plunges inside my mouth, sliding salaciously against mine. We both let out a moan, and then he's sweeping me up in his arms and carrying me to my room, all the while his lips never leaving mine.

Not until he sets me on my bed and then pulls back. His chest heaves as his hungry eyes stare down at me.

"Take 'em off," he says, his voice ragged and deep.

It takes a minute for my foggy brain to understand his words, but once they register, I can't get naked fast enough. He lets out a chuckle, but I'm too far gone to be embarrassed anymore. Once I've discarded all my clothes, I lie back on the bed, my thighs rubbing together, trying to ease some of the ache. One of my hands goes to my nipple, pinching it lightly since they're still tender, but the bite also adds to my release so I've learned to go with it. My other hand slips between my legs before I can even think to stop it, rubbing my clit in slow circles—anything to try to ease the tension building inside me.

His smile falls as his eyes darken and flare, his gaze sliding down every exposed inch until he stops at my glistening sex. I can feel how soaked I am.

"Goddamn," he murmurs. Then he drops to his knees, spreads my legs wide, and gives one long, languid lick from my seam to my clit.

My hands shoot to his hair, holding his head there. "Oh God, yes. That feels so good."

He hums against my plump bundle of nerves and then he stops fucking around. His mouth suctions around my clit, while his tongue flicks at it. Simultaneously, he slides one, then two fingers inside my pussy, curling them up to hit that tender spot inside.

Stars shoot across my vision as my first orgasm explodes inside me. It's so powerful, I can't even make a sound as my back arches off the bed and my toes curl. The pleasure is so overwhelming, I nearly black out. But Ty's right there, easing me through it with that glorious mouth of his. When the last tremors fade, I sag against my bed, my chest heaving and my horniness sated more than it's been in days. My thighs shake around his shoulders.

"Fuck, I needed that," I mutter, my words slightly slurred from how blissed-out I feel.

Ty places a kiss on my clit and then stands, slowly removing his clothes while his eyes seem to memorize every inch of my body. Just witnessing the way his heated gaze peruses every inch has my desire humming again in my veins.

"You ready for round two?"

"God yes," I say on a sigh.

His smile lights up his whole face and sucks the breath straight out of my lungs. This man is so insanely attractive. Some days I still can't believe he really wants me. He could easily have his pick of any woman out there, yet it's me he keeps coming back to.

I won't argue with it. I'll keep him for as long as he wants me, especially when the way he makes me feel—precious and cherished—is too addicting to give up.

Once he's naked, he rests his hands on either side of my body and holds his bulky frame just barely away from me, teasing me with the idea of skin on skin without giving me what I really want. He kisses my stomach, lingering a moment, his gaze snapping up to mine while his lips press tender kisses where our baby is growing. My heart nearly stops in my chest at the sight.

This man is going to break my heart someday, and I think I'm going to let him, simply because this memory would be worth it.

He kisses up my body, spending time giving attention to

each breast until I'm a writhing mess underneath him, when he finally reaches my mouth.

"Do I need a condom?" he asks against my lips. "I haven't been with anyone since you."

I stare into his brown eyes, not wanting a single thing between us. I want every inch of this man for as long as I can have him. "No," I say, my voice quiet but sure.

He nods once and then kisses me hard as he slides his thick cock deep inside me. We both let out groans as he stretches me wide.

"Fuck, fuck, fuck. Never felt this good," he murmurs against my lips, kissing away any response I can give. Despite the fact we haven't had sex together in almost three months, our bodies move together as if we've been having sex every day and know every move that will bring the other person the most pleasure.

Ty slides a hand underneath my ass, tilting my pelvis to hit a different angle inside me, causing fireworks to go off behind my eyes. This time, I scream as my release hits me, my orgasm causing me to contract against him so tightly, he has no choice but to follow me over the cliff.

We both shudder as little tremors go through us, but for the first time in days, I feel completely sated. I have no idea how long it'll last, but I'm thankful for the slight reprieve—and for finally feeling like I have my sanity back.

These pregnancy hormones are no joke.

Ty holds my body tight to his, dropping little kisses along my neck as we readjust so my back is to his front, his arms around me.

I close my eyes as sleep threatens at the edges, a calm washing over me along with something else—something scary and yet something I want more than anything—a sense of being wanted and belonging to this amazing man who I don't deserve.

EIGHTEEN

Ty

My gaze darts to the sidelines where one of the trainers stands near a bench. He meets my stare and shakes his head, causing my stomach to tighten as worst-case scenarios grow in number in my head. Lexi was supposed to come to the game, but she wasn't here by the time it started, and there's still no sign of her.

I've always been able to separate my personal life from what's happening on the field—until Lexi. All my usual tricks to get my head in the game aren't doing a goddamn thing.

What if she got into an accident on the way to the stadium? What if she's in the hospital hurt? What if something happened to the baby?

All the what-ifs nearly bring me to my knees. My phone is in the locker room, and she doesn't have any of my friends' or family's numbers if she needed another way to get ahold of me. Why didn't I think of that beforehand? She needs those numbers if there's an emergency.

Lexi is not a flaky person. If I've learned anything about her over the past couple of months it's that she's kind, caring, and conscientious. She'd never just not show up unless there was a good reason.

There's movement on the field, and my head snaps up to realize the play is in progress.

Fuck.

That hesitation is all the momentum they need. I chase after the player I'm covering, trying to fix my error, but it's clear he's going to catch the ball. The only thing I can do is hope it slows him down enough for me to tackle him. I push forward, channeling all my worry over Lexi and using it to move my body faster. The sooner we can end this, the sooner I can get back on the sidelines and beg that trainer to grab my phone and call Lexi.

I get closer and shove my body against his, but he twists at the last second, causing us to rotate on our way to the ground, and I hit the turf hard, followed by him landing on my right shoulder and head. Stars burst across my vision, and pain flares down my arm. He rolls off me quickly, but the damage is done. I don't think anything's torn, but my head throbs and my shoulder aches like I spent too many hours at the gym lifting weights that were fifty pounds too heavy.

Romel rushes over. "You okay?"

A groan escapes as I attempt to sit up, and he puts a hand on my shoulder. "Woah, hold on."

A team medic runs over and kneels next to me. "Where were you hit?"

I grit my teeth, knowing how I answer this will determine if I can play or not, but I'm not about to mess around with my health. "Shoulder and head."

"Headache?"

"No."

"Any nausea, ringing in your ears, or blurred vision?"

I grip my shoulder, trying to rub away some of the ache. "No."

The team doctor joins us on the field and crouches down. "You okay, Russell?"

"Shoulder hurts."

"He hit his head too," the medic shares.

The doc nods. "Can you walk?"

"Yeah." I shift, trying to get up, but three pairs of arms grip me and help me to my feet. Fans cheer as I slowly walk off the field with Romel at my back and the doc and medic on either side of me. The doc ushers me straight to the medical tent set up on the sidelines, and a part of me wishes we were doing this in the locker room so I could check my damn phone.

The game resumes play while he runs through a series of questions designed to help determine if someone has a concussion. I answer them all. My head might still throb, but I've had concussions before, and they didn't feel like this. I'm not confused, disoriented, or dizzy.

But I am distracted, and that's a stupid thing to be in my position.

The doc stands tall, shoulders back. "I can clear you for a concussion, but how's the shoulder?" He moves my arm, and at my wince, he frowns. He pushes on a couple of spots that are especially tender and doesn't miss the way my teeth clench or the hiss of pain when he tries to rotate my arm back.

"I'd like to check this shoulder out in the locker room where we can get these pads off and see what's really going on."

Focusing on the ground in front of me, I nod. "Understood."

When we exit the medical tent, the fans cheer wildly in the stands, and I plaster on my fake smile and wave to them, easing their concerns about my well-being. Guilt eats away at my gut when I see my replacement not moving as fluidly with the rest of the Fierce Four as I do.

I should be out there, and I'm pissed at myself for not being able to compartmentalize. Casting a glance, I find the trainer I talked to before the game who was supposed to keep an eye out for Lexi. I gesture for him to come over to me as the doc and I make our way to the locker room.

"She still isn't at her seat," he says without preamble.

My jaw clenches, but there's nothing I can do. No one else has her number, and I don't have it memorized—although I will after today—to have someone else call her. I'm going to need to make some changes so this doesn't happen again. I can't afford to be this distracted during my games, and apparently where Lexi's concerned, my brain can't just put her in a box and set her aside to focus on football.

The walk to the locker room feels like it takes an eternity, but the second we get in there, I ignore the team doctor who tells me to hop on the table that's been set up and go straight to my locker, grabbing my phone.

There's a text, and I can't get my fingers to move fast enough to open it, my heart already racing and images of all those worst-case scenarios flashing through my mind.

LEXI

> Hey Ty, I'm so sorry. I'm not going to make it tonight. I thought the morning sickness was over, but apparently not. I can barely keep anything down right now and feel like I've been hit by a truck. I hope you see this before the game starts. Score lots of points! (Or whatever you say for football...you'll have to teach it to me someday).

My whole body sags down onto the bench in front of our lockers, and I push my fingers through my hair, taking a long, deep breath of relief. She's okay. Nothing happened to her.

"Ty?"

I glance over at the doc and the medic who must've entered after us, both of them staring at me with arched brows. "Sorry.

My girl was supposed to be here today, and when she didn't show up, I was concerned."

The doctor frowns. "The only thing you should be concerned about right now is that shoulder. Come over here and let's get you checked out."

The doc examines my shoulder without all my football gear in the way and determines I tweaked it enough that he'd rather I sit out the rest of the game and let it rest. I stay in the locker room until halftime when the rest of the team comes in. Romel, Dom, and Gabe head straight for me.

"You good?" Romel asks.

"Sore shoulder. Doc wants me to sit out the rest of the game."

"Damn," Dom says, his brows furrowed in concern.

I point my chin the direction they came from. "How's it going out there?"

"We're ahead," Gabe says.

"And we'll stay that way. Their offense won't get past us," Dom adds, his tone brooking no argument.

I should be on the field with them. We've always had each other's backs, and I feel like I'm letting them down because I lost my focus and let a run go south.

Gabe claps me on my nonwrapped shoulder. "Don't worry. They won't score on us. We've got it covered, okay? You just rest up for the next game."

"What happened out there anyway?" Romel asks, fatherly concern in his gaze. I'm not sure he'd know how to shut it off even if he tried.

I grip the back of my neck and then tell them about Lexi and how I was late moving after the snap. These guys get it. Both Gabe and Dom would do anything for their women—including being distracted on the field if they thought something might be wrong—and Romel's biggest priority is his daughter. I don't have to explain myself, but I still feel guilty.

"Don't beat yourself up about it," Gabe says. "We all would've been the same way."

"When are we gonna get to officially meet your woman anyway?" Dom asks. "We didn't really get to talk to her that day we crashed her class."

"I was hoping you'd get to know her today, but now I don't know. I don't want to push her into anything until she's ready."

Romel watches me carefully. "You're falling for her, aren't you?"

I drop my gaze to the ground, not entirely sure how to answer. I've never been in love before, but I can't deny the way I feel about Lexi is more intense than I've ever felt for another woman. I look back up, locking my gaze with Romel's. "Yeah, I think I am."

Of course, I won't tell her that. Not yet. We might be having sex now—and thank fuck for that because her body calls to me in a way I've never experienced before—but that doesn't mean she's ready for me to confess all my feelings to her.

But someday soon, I hope she will be.

NINETEEN

Lexi

Carrying a bowl of popcorn and my apple juice, I head to the couch. It's not a weird craving, but it's one I've had for a few days.

Ty settles next to me, leaning forward to grab the remote before he turns to me. "Ready?"

I nod, my mouth already full of buttery popcorn. The corner of his lips quirks up in a boyish smile that has my stomach swooping. "What?" I mumble around a mouthful of popcorn.

He shakes his head. "Nothing. You're cute."

My cheeks heat like I'm a thirteen-year-old girl with my first crush all over again. But unlike that boy who seemed repulsed by my crush on him, Ty never makes me feel less than the most incredible woman he's met. He treats me like my time is a gift to him instead of the other way around. It's taken a lot of getting used to, but I think I'm finally starting to fully embrace all the happy feelings he makes me feel.

This is genuinely the happiest I've ever been in my life—and it's a type of happiness I wasn't sure I'd ever have.

He presses play on the movie we queued up earlier—a

romantic comedy I've really wanted to watch—and then spreads his arm along the back of the couch, allowing me to snuggle up next to him.

A deep calm washes over me as I lean against his warm body while his fingers play with the loose strands of my hair. Ty came over right after his team meetings today. He manages to spend all his free time with me and texts me every day that he's away, just checking in on me. It's been a completely new experience to have a man as attentive as he is.

If I'm honest with myself, it scares me a little bit. Nothing good in my life has ever lasted, and after the last several weeks with Ty, I'm worried that this time, having the rug ripped out from under me might truly break me beyond repair. I can feel my walls crumbling with every hour we spend together. The way he kisses me on the forehead, runs his fingers through my hair whenever we snuggle on the couch, always has my favorite snacks on hand should I ever want them, and looks at me like I'm his whole world. It's all eating away at any chance I had of keeping him at arm's length.

And then there's the sex, which is just as earth-shattering as it was that first night we spent together.

"How'd you get this scar?" he murmurs, and I glance away from the movie that I wasn't even paying attention to and find him staring at a spot on the back of my neck, the corners of his lips turned down in a slight frown.

I brush his hand away and move my hair back to cover it. "Oh, it was nothing," I say, forcing my gaze back to the movie, hoping he'll take the hint and not press it.

He doesn't.

"It looks..." he trails off and my curiosity gets the better of me. I turn my head to find him already staring at me. "My cousin tried to look like a badass one time and put a cigarette out on his pants, but they were thin and it burned through to his skin. He had a scar that looked kinda like this, but not as bad," he finishes, his voice trailing off as his gaze moves from mine to the spot now hidden by my hair. When he looks back into my eyes, there's something dark in his gaze that I've never seen from him before. His nostrils flare slightly as he growls out, low and rough, "Did someone put a cigarette out on your neck?"

I swallow thickly, my mouth dry and my heart racing. No one's ever asked me outright, and I typically wear my hair down so it's never noticeable. On the off chance I wear it up, I use makeup to hide it. Makeup can cover a multitude of sins.

He cups my face, and tears burn behind my eyes at his gentle touch when it looks like an inferno is raging in his eyes. "Who? Who fucking hurt you like that?"

My nose burns as I fight back the tears with everything I'm worth, but it's no use as they escape silently down my face, giving away the pain I try so hard to keep buried.

His anger fades as he shakes his head. "Precious," he whispers, and then he's pulling me into his lap, holding me tight to him, grounding me with his strength and comfort.

We sit there like that for a long time before I get my tears under control and find my voice. "Tell me about your family," I say, my voice low but pleading.

"Will you tell me about yours?"

My heart clenches as that old familiar pain flares. "I don't have a family."

His arms around me tighten. "Yes, you do. You have me. I'm your family now."

I close my eyes, wanting that to be true more than I've wanted anything in years. "Please, Ty. Tell me about your family, your friends, your childhood. Don't make me talk about mine. Not yet."

"I hate that someone hurt you," he whispers against my hair and then lets out a heavy sigh. "Well, I told you I have two brothers, Tanner and Taron. My mom really loved the idea of us all having *T* names. My dad's name is Tim and her name is Tina. We've always been close and played a lot of sports growing up in Vancouver. Tanner got interested in football, so like a typical little brother, I followed along. He plays for another team down south." He says it with a smile in his voice that has a small one gracing my lips. "Taron, however, fell in love with hockey, and he plays for a pro team out east."

"Wow, three boys and you all went into professional sports. Your parents must be so proud."

"Oh yeah. But my mom won't hesitate to put us in our place if she feels our egos are getting too big." He chuckles and the sound fills me with warmth, chasing away the darkness that surrounded me when he mentioned my scar. "My dad is a big softie."

"Kinda like you?" I ask.

He pulls away from me so he can look at my face and arches his brow. "You know there ain't nothing soft about me. Feel these abs."

My smile grows and then so does his, his eyes softening around the edges with that look of affection I'm quickly getting addicted to. "You're so beautiful," he murmurs. He leans forward, putting his forehead against mine. "I hope you'll trust me enough one day to tell me your story—all the parts, good, bad, and ugly. I want to know *you*, all of you."

"Some of those parts might be too ugly," I whisper. *You might never be able to love me when you learn no one else ever has.*

He shakes his head, his face more serious than I've ever seen it. "There's no way, Lex. The ugliest part of your history doesn't change how beautiful and incredible you are. You've survived the ugly and still shine."

My breathing turns shallow as I stare at this handsome man

who grew up in a home with happy siblings and two loving parents who would do anything for him. I never want to see the pity in his eyes when he learns how truly horrible and utterly lonely my life was. Our childhoods couldn't be any more different.

But it's the certainty shining in his eyes that has my heart racing for a completely different reason. I don't know what miracle brought this man into my life, but I don't want to regret a single second with him. Leaning forward, I place my lips against his. His hands tighten on my waist, shifting my body over his erection, and even with the material of my clothes in between us, my clit throbs. A moan escapes from deep in my throat, and that's all it takes for him to let out a groan and slide his fingers into my hair, holding my mouth against his as he takes over the kiss.

My fingers grasp at the hem of his T-shirt, pulling it up and revealing those hard abs he joked about earlier. I slide my nails down them, causing him to groan again, and then he's flipping us over so I'm under him on the couch. He kisses my jaw and then my neck, sucking slightly and making my back arch as shivers of desire spread through my body.

"Goddamn, I love watching you get worked up. You're so sexy," he says, his voice deep and ragged. He pulls my shirt up my body and over my head and then tosses it to the side. Before I fully lie back down, his hand is at my back, unhooking my bra until I'm topless beneath him. His hungry gaze eats up my exposed body before he dips his head and takes one of my overly sensitive nipples into his mouth. He doesn't bite or nibble because he knows they're tender, but he does suck them gently. All the while, his darkened gaze is locked on mine, watching my every reaction—the way my breath hitches, my eyes dilate, and my nipples pebble until they're hard nubs. He moves to the other breast, giving it the same treatment. While his mouth is busy at my breast, his hands pull down my yoga pants and underwear until I'm completely naked and bared for him.

He sits back on his heels, staring at my no-doubt soaked core.

"Ty," I plead. "Please."

His hungry eyes meet mine. "Lexi, I'll give you anything you want. Literally anything," he says, his voice hoarse with desire but filled with sincerity.

You. I want you to never leave me.

My greatest wish fills my heart, but never leaves my lips. Instead, I say, "I need you to ease my ache."

He stares at me for a moment longer, like he's trying to determine if that's really all. "Precious, I'm going to make you ache for me until you feel like you'll explode if you don't come before I ease it."

My jaw drops at his words, my clit throbbing from the desire in his eyes as he lowers his mouth to where I need him most. He swirls that wicked tongue of his over my clit, teasing me relentlessly before sliding one finger at an unbearably slow pace inside me.

"Ty," I moan, gripping his hair in my hands.

"That's it, Mama. Say my name like that while I worship your body the way it deserves."

God, this man.

I can barely think with him teasing me with soft swirls of his tongue while that one finger slides in and out so slowly it makes me want to scream. He knows what I need. We've been having sex regularly since my horny hormone brain took over. I tighten my grip on his hair and attempt to rock my hips to get his mouth to move faster, but all that does is cause him to remove his finger from inside me and hold my thighs apart with both hands while he licks me.

"Fuck, you taste delicious." He inhales like he's savoring

every aspect of eating me out, his eyes closing as a look of bliss spreads across his face. He opens his eyes, and the burning desire in them tightens my chest. His mouth descends back over my clit, and he sucks and flicks it with renewed vigor, never breaking eye contact. When my orgasm hits me like a tidal wave, it's not from the ministrations on my clit but the look in his eyes. The look I want to memorize and hold on to forever.

The look that says I'm *his*. He's claiming me. And God, how badly I want that to be true.

TWENTY

Ty

It's mid-November when I'm finally able to introduce Lexi to the guys. I hold her hand as we walk up to Romel's house, my thumb rubbing soothing circles on her hand. She's been nervous about this get-together—it's one of the reasons I suspect she still hasn't attended a home game—but I'm determined to make it as stress free as possible for her.

These guys are my family as much as my brothers are. Now that she's become an important part of my life—arguably the most important part—I'm desperate for her to get to know the group and see how great they are. I don't know what I'll do if they don't get along. It's not something I've planned for, and I hope it's not something I need to worry about, but I guess we'll find out soon enough.

I knock on the door, and a minute later it's pulled open by a cute little toddler with the biggest mischievous grin on her face, a flustered Romel right on her heels. "Kay, what have I told you about answering the door?"

Her smile falls as guilt fills her light-brown eyes which look identical to Sydney's. I wonder how hard it is for Romel to look at his daughter when she looks so much like her mother. "Sorry, Daddy," she says softly.

He smiles gently as he crouches down in front of her. "I just want you to be safe, Princess. I know it's Uncle Ty, but you still shouldn't answer the door, okay?"

She nods, but her eyes still hold a shimmer of tears from his reproach. Romel lets out a heavy sigh and then lifts her into his arms, holding her tight. He offers me a small smile that doesn't come anywhere near his eyes and then opens the door wider and gestures with his free hand for us to come inside. Once we're in, he closes the door and extends his hand to Lexi, his smile growing. "It's nice to finally get to meet you for real. This guy doesn't shut up about you."

"Wow, thanks, man. What happened to bro code?"

His brows lift in surprise. "I thought bro code was just about not poaching each other's women, which has never been our thing anyway."

"Thank God for that. But you're also supposed to keep my secrets."

His smile grows like the Cheshire cat, and I brace myself for the embarrassment I'm sure he's about to serve me. "Sorry, man, but she deserves to know you're obsessed with her." He looks at Lexi. "I've never seen a man more smitten, and that's saying something considering how Gabe and Dom are with their ladies. But you've got yourself a keeper here." He slaps me on the back. "He'll go to the ends of the earth for the people he loves."

I rub my free hand down my face. That wasn't as bad as it could've been, but I've been trying not to pressure Lexi too much. She doesn't need to know I talk about her all the time to anyone who will listen. When I glance down at her to see how she's taking it, I find her already looking up at me, a thoughtful expression filling her eyes while the corners of her pink mouth tilt up in a sweet smile. My heart stutters because I know without a doubt I've fallen in love with her, and I have no idea if she feels the same way.

She looks back at Romel. "Thanks for the heads-up."

Kay pulls her head from where she's had it buried against his neck. "You're pretty," she says, her lilting voice soft.

Lexi's cheeks flush, but her eyes brighten as she gives a friendly smile to Kay. It's the same one she had when we were in her classroom—her teacher smile I called it at the time, designed to put the kids at ease and make them feel seen.

"You're pretty too. I love your curls."

Kay sits up in her dad's arms, her smile wide, and it has the infectious effect of making all the adults around her smile.

If possible, I fall even harder for Lexi for making Kay light up like a firefly. I can't wait to see her love on our kid when he or she arrives in May.

Romel starts walking toward the living room and we follow, Lexi's hand still firmly in mine. Everyone stops talking when we enter the room, and four sets of eyes stare at us.

I clear my throat. "Everyone, this is Lexi," I announce. "Lexi, this is Gabe and his wife, Danae. And that's Dom and his wife, Alayna."

"If you hear Dom say Laney, he's talking about me," Alayna adds with a smile at her husband.

"And that's only my name to use," Dom says before dropping a quick kiss to her lips.

Lexi waves at everyone, but whatever ease she found with Kaylee in the hallway has completely vanished. Her palm is now clammy in mine, and she can barely hold eye contact with anyone but the floor.

Everyone seems to snap out of whatever stupor they were in when we walked in and comes bustling over. Gabe and Dom start telling embarrassing stories about me from the locker room while Danae and Alayna roll their eyes at them. But I'm not sure Lexi hears a word. She's got this slightly vacant look in her gaze I've never seen before, and her pulse flutters like crazy in her neck.

"Should we eat?" Romel asks. Everyone starts talking about the next home game as we walk to the dining room where Romel has a whole spread laid out.

"Lexi, you should come with us," Alayna says, turning back to Lexi.

Lexi's steps falter. "To the game?"

"Yeah." Alayna's brow quirks like that should've been obvious.

"Uh." Lexi looks at me, and I can't quite read her expression, but I can definitely pick up on her unease.

"That game is on Thursday. Lexi has work the next day."

Alayna's smile slowly fades from her face as she moves her quizzical expression my way. "We all do."

"I'm not sure, but I'll let you know," Lexi says. Her voice carries an air of calm, but the tight-lipped smile she gives Alayna doesn't come anywhere near her eyes.

Does she not want to see me play? I thought she'd really put it off because she hadn't been feeling well, but what if she just doesn't want to come?

The idea curdles the hope in my stomach. I don't expect her to come to every game, but I'd love for her to try to watch at least one. I want her there in the stadium with my jersey on her body.

In my family, we all supported each other and showed up. Even now, my parents fly out as often as they can to attend my games—and my brothers'. I don't know much about Lexi's childhood, but I know it wasn't filled with the kind of familial support mine was if her scars are anything to go by—and those are only the ones I've seen on the outside. The longer I'm with her, the more it becomes obvious she's got scars on the inside she's never let anyone see.

Alayna watches us more carefully as she sits down next to Dom and starts dishing up her plate. When my gaze slides around the table, everyone is darting glances between the food and Lexi and me. My jaw tics as my back teeth grind. This night is not going how I expected or hoped.

When conversation picks up, I lean over and whisper in Lexi's ear. "You okay?"

"Mm-hmm."

Frustration and unease builds, sliding up my back and making my body tense. "You aren't eating, and you've hardly said a word." Her eyes meet mine, and once again I wish I could read her better. I lower my voice even more, not wanting anyone to overhear. "These are good people. You don't have to freeze them out."

I know the minute the words leave my mouth they're the wrong ones, which is only confirmed when her whole body stiffens.

"Um, if you'll excuse me, I need to use the bathroom." She doesn't even look at me as she pushes her chair back and looks to Romel. "Where's your restroom?"

His brow furrows slightly, but it's gone in a blink. "Third door down the hall on the right."

"Thanks," she mutters, spinning on her heels and making a dash to the bathroom without a backward glance. I watch her until she turns the corner and is gone from my sight.

"She okay?" Danae asks.

I rub the back of my neck, not sure what to do here. Should I follow her? Give her some space? "I'm not really sure," I reply, feeling helpless. This night already wasn't going great, and I'm pretty sure I just made it worse.

"This crew can be pretty intimidating to a newcomer,"

Danae says with sympathy in her eyes. She would know, since she was thrown into our group without much warning.

"What should I do?"

She cocks her head to the side and then to the other, thinking. "It depends on her personality. Does she do better if you give her space?"

That helpless feeling grows. "I'm not sure, to be honest. We haven't exactly been in this situation before."

"Haven't you taken her out on dates?" Gabe asks. "That can get pretty intimidating too, especially if the press finds out where you are."

I shake my head before he's even done talking. "Not really. She's wanted to keep things low-key so she doesn't have to answer questions from her students and the staff at her school if our picture is taken. We've only been out in public together a couple of times."

Everyone nods in understanding. They get wanting to keep a low profile, especially Dom and Alayna, who've remained out of the limelight as much as possible since their PR-stunt-turned-real relationship started.

"Is the pretty lady okay?" Kay asks, her mouth half full of her bread roll.

Romel leans over. "I'm sure she'll be fine, Princess." He looks at me and nods with his head toward the direction Lexi disappeared to.

That's the only push I need to go check on my girl. I can still salvage this night, but I can't do anything if I don't know what's wrong.

And there's only one person who can tell me.

TWENTY-ONE

Lexi

I stare at my vacant reflection in the mirror, my hands gripping the sides of the countertop as I try to ground myself.

Romel has a gorgeous house, and it's a far cry from any of the ones I grew up in. So far, in fact, I feel like an imposter for even being here. What am I doing with a guy like Ty? Or maybe the better question is what is a guy like Ty doing with *me*?

My nose burns as the threat of tears builds behind my eyes. Gah, fucking hormones. I'm so sick of being an emotional basket case. I've met pregnant women before, and while I was never friends with any, I don't remember any of them talking about the emotional land mines everywhere. Or maybe it's just my hormones further conspiring against me.

My gaze drops from my eyes in the mirror to the reflection of my stomach. It's still mostly flat, not much sign that there's a little life growing in there, except for a small bit of pudge that I could brush off as bloat.

I have to remember the real reason Ty's with me is because we're having a baby. I can wish for more, but wishing's never gotten me anything in life. I know better than most that reality is a cruel bitch just waiting for the next chance to tear me down. I rest my hand over my belly and close my eyes.

"It's going to be okay," I whisper, but I'm not sure if I'm telling myself or the baby.

I turn on the faucet and splash a little cold water on my face. Meeting new people has always been hard for me. I'm better with kids. Adults, in my experience, always had ulterior motives. Their words carried double meanings I was often too young or naive to fully comprehend, which put me on edge. They couldn't be trusted. The kids had simpler motivations for saying or doing what they did, and it was always easier to let my guard down around them. It's one of the reasons I considered teaching elementary school, but it was a middle school teacher who saved me when I was younger—when I was so close to giving up completely. I wanted to be that person for someone else, to pay it forward.

I'm pretty sure I'd be a hermit if it weren't for Blaire, and who the hell knows what she saw in me that kept her coming back and chiseling away at my icy exterior. It's not something I do on purpose—more like a self-defense mechanism. All of Ty's friends are boisterous and friendly, but are they really being that way just because Ty's here, or is this genuinely how they are around new people? What must that be like to be so carefree when meeting someone new?

Will Ty think less of me now that he's seen this side of me?

Probably.

And I can't even blame him. Hell, he wouldn't even be the first to do it.

I hate that I'm this way. I hate that I can't laugh and make small talk with his friends easily. I hate that I second-guess the meanings behind every sentence they speak. I hate that my brain immediately starts worrying about what they're thinking of me, but instead of trying to fit in, I shut down.

A knock on the door pulls me out of my thoughts. "Just a second," I call out.

"It's me," Ty's voice comes through the door. "Can I come in?"

My eyes close briefly as I take a centering breath and then open the door. His handsome features are etched with concern, and as soon as the door is open, he doesn't hesitate to push his big body through, crowding me against the sink. His warm hands cup my face, and he drops his lips to mine in a featherlight kiss. Warmth from the small sign of affection infuses my bones and eases some of my tense muscles, but doubts still niggle in my gut.

He pulls away just enough to look at me, his brown eyes filled with care instead of the scorn or judgment I expected. "I'm sorry for what I said out there. It came out wrong."

I shake my head, my gaze dropping to the floor. "No. I'm the one who should be sorry. I'm...I'm not good with new people. I should've told you before we came."

"You didn't seem to have a problem when we met."

Butterflies flutter in my stomach as I remember the first time I saw him. The way speech completely escaped me and I had to remind myself to breathe. "That was different," I whisper.

"How so?"

"Well, for starters, I'd had quite a bit of alcohol at that point or else I would've probably frozen up or stumbled all over my words."

His mouth quirks up on the right in a small grin. "And why is that?"

I roll my eyes. "You know exactly why. You're too hot for your own good. It's not fair."

He chuckles, leaning his forehead against mine. "I spent that whole night thinking you were too good for me. Too sweet. Too beautiful."

There's no way that's true. This man could be surrounded by supermodels and I wouldn't be the least surprised. I'm nowhere near as beautiful as what I'm sure he's used to.

He brushes away a tear from my cheek that I didn't even realize had fallen. "You made me feel things I'd never felt before, and I'm not just talking about the earth-shattering sex. Lexi, I was devastated when I woke up and you were gone."

"You were?" God, I want to believe him. I want to believe in *us*, but I'm so fucking scared.

He brushes his fingers through my hair, and it feels so good, my lids grow heavy. "Walk me through what's going on in that brain of yours. How can I make this night better for you?"

I shake my head. "I don't know. I've always been like this."

"What makes you feel comfortable?"

I stare up at him. "Being at home in my pajamas."

He smiles again, his eyes softening as he looks at me with such tenderness, it makes another tear escape. "Please don't cry, Precious. Tell me how to make this better."

I shake my head again because I feel completely helpless and don't know to explain it to him. "I don't *know* how," I whisper. If he thinks I enjoy being this way, he's an idiot.

There's another knock on the door, and when Ty opens it, Danae is standing there. "Hey, sorry to interrupt." Her kind eyes look past Ty to me. "Mind if we chat for a minute?"

"Uh, sure," I say, hating the uncertainty in my voice that gives away how I feel, putting me at the disadvantage. And there I go again. God, why can't I just assume the best in people?

Ty looks back at me to make sure I'm really okay with this, and then steps out in the hall. "I'll just be right out here."

Danae closes the door and then moves to sit on the edge of the bathtub. She looks around the room that's bigger than my bathroom and walk-in closet combined and offers me a smile. "I still can't get over the fancy bathrooms these guys have. It's a far cry from what I grew up with."

I let out an uncomfortable laugh. "Same here."

She nibbles her lip for a second. "Feel free to tell me to mind my own business, but I feel like we might be kindred spirits."

"How so?"

She closes her eyes and takes a deep inhale. When she opens them again, there's a haunted expression in them I know all too well. "Do you ever feel like sometimes you see a person and just *know* they've been through some tough times?"

I nod, but can't speak over the lump in my throat. I rarely see it in other adults, at least not the adults I've been around. But I've had a handful of students in the foster care system—or ones that ultimately ended up in the system due to being removed from their homes by CPS—during my time as a teacher and recognized it, whether in how they looked or how they behaved. Behavior was often a better indicator that things had gone bad for them.

She continues. "I'm not saying we've been through exactly the same thing because even if you go through the same event, everyone experiences trauma differently. But trauma recognizes trauma."

"And you have trauma?"

She hesitates, and man, do I understand that hesitation better than any other part of this conversation so far. "I was in an abusive relationship," she says, and I can't imagine the amount of therapy she's probably had to be able to say it as if it doesn't haunt her every move.

"Foster care," I whisper, but my shoulders feel lighter as I voice the truth.

She nods, and I appreciate that it's not sympathy in her eyes, but solidarity. She's not judging me; she's recognizing a survivor. And that takes even more of the weight of this night off my shoulders.

"These people are some of the best I've ever met. I know you don't really know me, but I'm hoping you'll give them all a chance. They aren't the type of people to judge you for where you came from, but to lift you up as much as they're able. You're safe here. You can be as open or as closed as you want, and we'll accept you. The truth is, you make Ty happy and that speaks volumes. You don't have to do anything else to prove your worth to us, okay?"

"Okay." Because what else do I say to that?

She stands up and walks toward the door, but stops before turning the handle, looking back and giving me a sincere smile. "I'm really glad you're here tonight. See you out there."

With that, she walks out, and Ty is immediately standing in the doorway, looking at me and then glancing at Danae's back as she walks away.

"Everything okay?" he asks, the corners of his eyes etched with concern and his jaw tight.

I nod, meaning it this time, and feeling much lighter than I did before she came in here. I may not be ready to spill my whole life story, but for the first time tonight, I'm not terrified about sitting at the table and attempting conversation.

"I'm okay. Let's go back out."

"Are you sure? We can leave if you'd be more comfortable."

The fact he even offers makes my feelings for him grow so much stronger. He's not shaming me or making me feel bad for how I feel.

I step up to him, slide my hand around his neck, and kiss him softly. His arms instantly wrap around me as he falls into the kiss, moaning in objection when I pull back. He keeps my body pressed to his and his forehead on mine.

"What was that for?" he asks.

"For worrying about me, wanting to take care of me."

He kisses my forehead, and my heart feels like it grows two sizes from the tender affection. "I'll always take care of you, Lexi. I'm yours," he murmurs.

"I'm yours too," I whisper back. I'm his more than he could ever know, more than I've ever belonged to anyone.

"Come on." He steps back, taking my hand in his. "You'll tell me if it's too much? I have no problem leaving whenever you want."

And that's why I need to stay. He's willing to go to the ends of the earth to make me comfortable. The least I can do is try to get to know his friends.

"I'll tell you, but I'd really like to stay."

He nods, and together we head back out to the dining room where everyone is still chatting and eating. None of them stare at us as we take our seats, but they do bring us right into the conversation. Dom focuses on Ty. "Dude, remember that one time..."

And that's how the rest of the night goes. There's rarely a lull in the conversation—which is kept blessedly light—and by the end of the night, I've gotten to know Alayna and Danae some more and agreed to go with them to a home game sometime.

When we head to Ty's place for the night, my stomach is full, my heart is light, and for the first time in a long time, I feel hopeful that I might actually be able to keep this paradise Ty has brought into my life.

That is, until later that night when we're snuggled in Ty's bed, and he opens his mouth to say what I assume is goodnight, only to completely shock me.

"Will you come home with me for Thanksgiving and meet my family?"

TWENTY-TWO

Ty

We arrive at my parents' house in Vancouver, British Columbia, the day before US Thanksgiving. It'll be a short trip since we have to fly back on Friday, but it's worth it to finally get to introduce Lexi to my parents and my older brother, Tanner. He's been less than supportive over the phone, so I'm hoping once he meets her in person, he'll chill the fuck out.

I know he's coming from a place of caution, and while I can't deny it's wise given our profession, he also doesn't know Lexi. And at this point, his continued prodding about me getting a paternity test is only starting to piss me off instead of feeling like a big brother looking out for his little brother. Hopefully, this weekend he'll understand why I've been hesitant to bring it up to Lexi and push something that I don't doubt.

My dad picked us up from the airport and has been chatting with Lexi the whole way to my childhood home. Both my brothers and I tried to convince our parents to let us buy them something nicer, but they refused our offers. They said no other house would carry the memories this one does, and I can't deny there is something soothing about returning home and remembering all the love and laughter that filled our house during my youth.

I glance at Lexi, reminding myself she didn't have that kind of childhood. Maybe over the next couple of days, I can give her a taste of the kind of life I'd like to build with her. One where we're always surrounded by family, good food, laughter, and so much love it feels a little suffocating.

Dad pulls into the two-car garage, and we all pile out of his SUV. The door to the kitchen opens, and my mom is there, her hands up in the air and a huge smile on her face.

"My sweet boy. Come here!"

I rush over and lift her up in a hug. She squeezes me tight, and when I set her back on her feet, she's still smiling, her brown eyes bright and shimmering with happy tears. "It's so good to have you home, Sweetie. Isn't it great, honey?" she asks, looking behind me at my dad. Before he can answer, her mouth parts and she pushes me aside. "Oh my gosh. You must be Lexi!" She moves past me, quicker than I can blink, and wraps a surprised Lexi in a huge hug. "We are so excited to finally meet you. Tyler talks about you all the time."

Lexi looks at me over my mom's shoulder, her arms loosely returning my mom's hug and her eyes wide with shock and uncertainty. "He does?"

Mom finally releases her. "Of course he does. Every single call." I may not be able to see my mom's expression, but I can see Lexi's. My stomach tightens at the slight surprise she tries to hide. As if she's shocked I talk about her with my family—which she shouldn't be since the guys razzed me good when she met my friends last week. Clearly I haven't done a good enough job showing her what she means to me if she's still surprised I talk about her with the people closest to me.

"Well, come on inside. I bet you're exhausted after a full day of travel. You'll never guess who showed up this morning."

"Who?" I ask, my brow furrowing. I knew Tanner would be here since that was the whole reason we planned this Thanksgiving get-together, even though my parents usually celebrate Canadian Thanksgiving in October. This was really the only time both of us could get off during the season. Neither Tanner's team nor the Wolves play on Thanksgiving, and Tanner's game isn't until Monday while mine's on Sunday, so we were both free to come for a quick visit.

"Taron!" she shouts, practically vibrating from pure joy, and it's no wonder. I can't remember the last time my mom got all three of her boys under the same roof. Taron plays pro hockey and his schedule is insane.

"How the hell is he here? Doesn't he have a game today?"

"Achilles injury," a voice says from behind me, and I spin around to find my little brother, who's built just like you'd imagine a hockey player to be built. "I'm out for the next three to five games depending on how quickly I can recover, but I was able to get clearance to come here for a couple of days as long as I keep up with my exercises."

I wrap one arm around his back, pulling him into a tight hug. "Damn, man, it's good to see you."

He slaps me on the back. "You too. I hear you went and decided to pull a middle-child move for attention."

I look at him like he's just grown a second head.

"You know, knocking up your girlfriend." His gaze slides past me to Lexi, and his smile turns seductive. "Although I definitely would've found a way to keep a woman who looks like that."

I step in front of him, blocking his view of her, and give him a death glare. "Might want to move your eyes to something else before I punch you," I growl low, but apparently not low enough to keep Mom from hearing.

"Now, now, boys. That's enough. Let's head inside."

Taron throws me a typical grin, knowing he accomplished his mission of riling me up, and I spin around to find Lexi smiling at me. My breath stalls in my lungs at the lightness in her eyes, so different from the usual weight that I wish she'd share with me.

She grabs my hand, squeezing it once. "Not gonna lie; that whole caveman thing was kind of hot."

I pull her body flush against mine, wrapping my arms around her and dropping my forehead to hers. "Yeah?"

"Yeah," she says, her voice soft and breathy.

I brush her hair away from her face. "No one gets to look at you like that except me."

"Because I'm yours," she says with a subtle air of disbelief.

"Because you're mine," I say, my words strong and sure, never wanting her to doubt how much I want her.

How much I *love* her, even if I've been too scared of spooking her to say the words.

"Come on inside, you two. I've got food already prepared since I figured you'd be hungry," Mom calls from inside the house.

I keep Lexi's hand in mine as we walk through the door into the kitchen, and I nearly burst out laughing when I see the spread filling every inch of counter space.

"Is this just for us, or are you also planning to invite the whole neighborhood?"

Taron chuckles, even as he snacks on a baby carrot.

"Don't be silly. You boys practically ate us out of house and home when you lived under this roof. I wasn't about to run out of food during your visit."

"We're only here for two days, Mom."

She purses her lips and hits me with her mom glare. "Two days with professional athletes who eat six high-protein meals a day. Plus, Lexi's eating for two." Her attention moves to Lexi. "I hope you don't mind, but I asked Tyler what you were craving lately so I could have it on hand. It's been a few decades since I was pregnant, but I still remember how strong those cravings could be."

Lexi smiles at her, and from this angle, it looks like her eyes shimmer a little, but she blinks and they clear. "Thank you so much, Mrs. Russell."

Mom throws the dish towel she's holding over her shoulder and walks over to us, grabbing Lexi's upper arms softly. "Sweetie, you can call me Tina. You're family now, so no need to be so formal. I'm just so happy you and Tyler found each other." Mom's eyes get misty as her gaze drops down to Lexi's stomach and back to her face. "I'm so excited to be a grandma. I hope you two won't be strangers during the offseason. And we'll find time to come down and visit so we can help you out any way we can."

Mom's voice hitches, and I know she's getting emotional. She worries about us, and she's made it clear more than once she wants to see us happy and settled with families. This is a dream come true for her. Lexi is the daughter she's never had and always wanted, and I've never been more thankful for my mom being as loving as she is. Lexi deserves to have this in her life.

"So where's Tanner?" I ask, looking toward the living room.

An awkward look passes between my parents and my stomach drops. "He, uh, decided he couldn't get away for the holiday," Dad says.

My jaw clenches. That's total bullshit. I brought it up to him just last week, and he never said anything about bailing. I'm glad I didn't tell Lexi about his doubts, or else she'd think this is her fault, and the last thing I want is for her to have guilt over my brother being a fucking child.

"I'm sorry I won't be able to meet him. Ty's talked about him a lot," Lexi says. She looks up at me, a smile on her face and the usual creases next to her eyes missing. "All of you, actually. I think I've asked him to tell me a million stories at this point." Her cheeks get a subtle flush, and my heart pinches in my chest.

Fuck, I'm so gone for her.

"Well, then it seems only fitting we tell you some stories about your man here," Taron says as he walks over to her other side and wraps his arm around her shoulder, pulling her away from me as he leads her to the living room. "Did he tell you about that one time with the frogs?"

He's out of the room when I catch the tail end of his sentence, and I'm about to storm in there to stop him from telling one of the most embarrassing stories of my childhood when Lexi's laughter rings through the room and my steps stop.

Fine, he can tell her, but only as long as she keeps laughing like that.

"I'm sorry we didn't tell you about Tanner earlier. We only found out last night," Mom tells me.

"Kind of a coward move. I expected more from him."

It's clear she knows the real reason he didn't come when she doesn't look surprised or outraged by my comment.

"I know you're upset he's not here to meet her, but maybe try to cut him a little slack." A furrow forms between her brows. "I think he deals with a lot more than he ever tells us about because he's been more guarded in the last year."

"He doesn't need to take it out on me or Lexi though." Honestly, I'm fucking pissed he's not here. I thought for sure after he met her this weekend, we could finally put all this shit behind us, but now he's just going to continue to drag it out. "I'll be right back," I say before I duck back outside.

I pull my phone out of my pocket and click on his contact. It rings longer than normal, and part of me thinks the coward is going to let me go to voicemail when he finally picks up.

"I should've known you'd call."

"You're damn right you should've," I say. "What the fuck, Tan? You really bailed on spending time with our family because of Lexi?"

He lets out a heavy sigh like he's tired of this conversation already, and the condescension that rolls through the line only pisses me off more.

"I love her, Tanner."

"You can't be serious," he scoffs. "You barely know her!"

"We've been together for a couple of months now."

"That's no time at all to con you."

"That's enough," my voice goes hard as steel. "You don't get to make judgments about her or me when you can't even be adult enough to meet her. You don't know her, and frankly, I'm questioning if you know me at all anymore. Because if you did, you wouldn't be questioning my judgment like this. She's not conning me. And the more you push that assumption, the more you drive me away. So think carefully about what the endgame is here, brother, because if you make me choose between you and her, I will choose her. Always."

"You'd really choose a woman you barely know over your own blood?"

"You mean, my own blood who's being a pompous asshole and won't even meet her before deciding she's some gold digger? That blood? Because frankly, that's not the kind of blood I want in my family."

He's silent, but his silence speaks volumes. He's got nothing to say because he knows I'm right.

But maybe my mom's right too, because a year ago he wouldn't have reacted this way. I thought we were close and told each other all the important things, but I'm wondering if this is more personal for him. If something—or someone—made him this way. Before I have a chance to ask about my hunch, his cold voice rings through the line.

"Have a good Thanksgiving, Ty."

And then he hangs up.

TWENTY-THREE

Lexi

I was so nervous on our way to Ty's parents' house for Thanksgiving, but I'm realizing after spending a day and a half with them how unnecessary that was. I've never experienced so much love in one place. Last night after we first got here, I was overwhelmed by the love that was obvious between everyone. Ty's family welcomed me with open arms, and I couldn't get enough of their stories about their childhood or about Ty and his antics when he was little.

Apparently he was a bit of a daredevil as a child. I'm really hoping our kid doesn't take after him on that front. I don't think my heart could handle it.

His mom showed me pictures of him growing up, their family dog they had until a few years ago, and their sons' early years playing sports. All night long, I felt like I was being wrapped in a warm blanket made from unconditional love and acceptance.

Today was more of the same. Ty's mom made a huge feast for all of us, but it was the moment when dessert was pulled out when I nearly cried. His mom had made a pecan pie just for me. It's one of the few things I remember from my childhood before my parents died, and something I told Ty one night. I didn't realize he'd held on to that little tidbit of information so tightly— not until his mom presented it and told me Ty had requested it for me. It was hard to keep my emotions at bay at that point. I'd been teetering on the edge of tears since we arrived, but that moment made my heart feel like it had cracked into a million tiny pieces and been carefully and painstakingly glued back together. The tears fell unbidden, and his poor mom's face fell, until I shook my head and smiled at her through my tears. I couldn't tell her why I was so emotional about a damn pie, but she didn't ask either. She just set the pie down, walked over to me, and hugged me tight.

We spent the rest of the night playing board games until I could barely keep my eyes open and Ty took me to bed. I fell asleep with his strong arms wrapped around me and my heart feeling fuller than I could ever remember it.

But twenty minutes ago, my bladder woke me up—something that's been happening more and more frequently as my pregnancy progresses—and now I'm wide awake. So, once I finish using the bathroom, I head downstairs to get a small snack, hoping that might help like it usually does.

I'm surprised when I round the corner and find the light on in the kitchen and Ty's mom sitting at the table. She looks up from her book, her dark-green glasses sitting on the edge of her nose and her eyes wide.

"I swore I was only going to read one more chapter." She glances at the clock and then back at me, a guilty grin on her face. "That was about two hours ago, and now I can't put the dang thing down."

I laugh and walk into the kitchen. "I was hoping to sneak a snack."

"A snack sounds delicious. I think I'll have one with you."

She moves to get up, but I hold my hand out. "No, please, let me get it. You worked so hard on all the food today. You deserve to sit and relax."

She sits back in her chair, her smile still on her face, and nods in acquiescence as I move around the kitchen and put a couple of snack options together. I can't think of a single time since I got here when she hasn't smiled at me. It's been nice.

I've never met a boyfriend's parents before. I dated a few guys in my late teens and early twenties, but they were all older and, well, not exactly close to their parents. They weren't close to anyone, me included. So this experience with Ty's family has been more than I ever dreamed was possible.

I take the two plates of snacks over to the table and sit next to her. "What are you reading?"

Her smile turns a little mischievous. "A romance I saw recommended online." She lifts up the book, showing me the cover, and excitement thrums through me.

I look at what page she's on. "What did you think of her finding his ex in his bed?"

Tina's eyes widen. "You've read this?"

"Romance novels are my guilty pleasure."

Tina throws her head back and laughs. "Oh, sweetheart, there is absolutely nothing to feel guilty about. You don't think people who read murder mysteries or thrillers feel guilty for liking murder stories, do you? So why should women feel guilty for reading love stories?"

I smile at her logic. "I guess you're right."

"Of course I am." She shakes her head. "Pearl-clutchers trying to shame other women for enjoying a realistic love story. Sex is real life. To pretend otherwise is ridiculous. So don't feel guilty for a single second."

Acceptance hums in my bones. "I won't." How could I when this woman whose opinion I've come to desire and respect in such a short time is so adamant?

We nibble on the snacks and talk about our favorite books for a while before her expression turns more thoughtful. "Can I ask you something?"

"Sure."

"Tyler was vague when I asked him about your family. Were they okay not getting time with you during the holiday?"

My stomach tightens. Of course Ty was vague, since I've barely told him anything substantial about my family except that my parents died when I was young. He deserves to know the full truth of my upbringing. I've put it off for so long, and he's been patient with me, but I know I won't be able to keep the truth from him forever.

I look down at my hands, scraping my thumbnail with the nail of my other thumb. "I don't have any family."

A moment of silence passes. "Your parents?" she asks softly.

Emotion clogs my throat. "They passed away in a car accident when I was five."

Her hand reaches out, resting on my arm. When I look up at her, tears fill her eyes. "I'm so sorry. Who raised you?"

My eyes burn. "I did." It's the truth. My foster homes were not filled with love or happiness, or care for that matter. I was a mouth to feed and a regular check from the government. I taught myself how to behave, how to survive.

Without saying another word, she gets out of her chair and wraps her strong arms around me. For such a small woman, I'm shocked by how tight she squeezes me, but it's the hug of a mom comforting her child, and that breaks the dam. I wrap my arms around her, returning the hug as my tears cascade down my face. She holds me for several minutes, never loosening her hold until my tears finally subside. When she pulls away, she places her hands on my cheeks, making sure I'm looking right at her.

"I hate that you didn't have the love you deserved growing up, but I can promise you that's not the case moving forward.

I'm so grateful to have you in our family, and to see my son so incredibly happy with a strong, beautiful woman. It doesn't matter where you came from. You're ours now, understand?"

I nod, my heart feeling so full it almost hurts. She can't know how many nights as a child I dreamed of a moment just like this. She drops a kiss to my forehead and then sits back in her chair. We visit for a little longer before she starts to yawn, and we both head back to bed.

When I get back to Ty's childhood room, I crawl into bed and snuggle up next to him. His arm instantly wraps around me, pulling me tight against his body.

"Everything okay?" he asks.

"Yeah. It's better than okay," I mumble, my head resting on his shoulder and my lips brushing against his warm skin. I place a soft kiss on his pec, and he hums deep in his throat. "I love your family," I whisper, glancing at him. Now that my eyes have adjusted to the dark, I can see his profile clearly, his eyes still closed and a small smile lifting his lips.

"Yeah, they're pretty great. I got really lucky."

My heart races as I open my mouth, needing to say the words that have wanted to burst out for several days. "I love you too, Ty."

He turns his head, his eyes now wide open and staring at me like he's trying to see into my soul. Emotion burns in his deep-brown eyes as he rolls to his side, cupping my face and still keeping my body plastered against his.

A puff of air escapes his mouth as if in relief as he drops his forehead to mine. "Thank fuck, because I love the hell out of you, Lexi."

"You do?"

"So damn much." His lips brush against mine, just a tease, but I can feel the way his body tenses like he's holding himself back, especially when I feel the stiffness of his erection against my stomach. "You're it for me, Precious."

I close the space between us, kissing him with every emotion that's been building inside me. I kiss him with all the years I spent thinking I'd never have this. I kiss him with all the hopes and dreams of a real love I'd given up on until he showed up in my life. I kiss him with gratitude and so much love, I didn't even think it was possible for me to feel this much.

His hand wraps around my thigh, draping my leg over his hip as he rocks forward, rubbing his thick cock against where I want him most. He groans low in his throat as I rub against him, eager to feel him deep inside me.

"Fuck, Lex, I need to be inside you."

"Yes," I plead, my voice sounding breathy.

He pushes off his briefs while I pull off my T-shirt and slide down my pajama shorts and underwear. His mouth finds my breasts as he sucks and teases my overly sensitive nipples with his teeth. A whimper escapes my mouth, and he lets out a soft groan.

"As much as I love to hear your noises, we need to be quiet. My brother is right on the other side of us, and these walls are paper-thin."

I couldn't care less about his brother, but I definitely don't want his parents to hear us. Despite Ty's words, he doesn't make it easy on me as he continues to tease my breasts with his mouth while his finger rubs delicious circles against my clit. My back arches and my chest heaves as I try to hold back the moans begging to escape.

"Fuck, you're so goddamn wet."

"Ty," I whisper, my voice shaking.

He rotates us so I'm on my back and then kisses down my stomach, pausing just below my belly button to place a tender kiss while his gaze locks on mine. "I love you, Lexi."

"I love you," I say, my whole body feeling warm and not because of what he's about to do with that mouth, but solely by how his words make me feel. There's no doubt in them, no "I love you, but I wish you did this" or "I love you but I wish you were this way instead."

Just I love you.

It's there in his eyes that I'm enough for him. That I'm exactly what he wants. He may not know my full history yet, but he loves me anyway. And I'm no longer afraid that telling him will drive him away. I know he'll keep it safe, just like he's been keeping my heart safe this whole time.

He dips down, kissing just above my clit, then moves to my inner thigh, then the other. He places his face right over where I'm drenched for him and inhales, releasing a deep groan that I'm sure is way too loud, but neither of us seem to find the will to care.

His tongue darts out, sliding through my pussy and then circling my clit like it's the most decadent ice cream cone he's ever eaten. His eyes close as bliss streaks across his face, and when they open again, they burn with desire. That's the only warning I get before he licks and sucks me into oblivion. I come once from his mouth alone, and then a second time when he pushes two fingers into me while his mouth sucks my clit.

My whole body shakes, but I still want more. I need to feel him. I grab at his shoulders, then cup his face, pulling him up to my lips and kissing him hard. He hums against my mouth, my flavor still on his tongue, as he presses his thick cock against my core and pushes inside. We both shudder from the feeling of fullness and even deeper connection.

"God, I love you," he murmurs, rocking his hips back and then thrusting deep and pulling a whimper from me. "I love you so fucking much, Lexi."

"Ty," I start...to say what, I'm not sure because his pace

ramps up and obliterates all thoughts as he fucks me with abandon. Our bodies are sweaty, our hands clasped together over my head as his pelvis hits my clit again and again until I detonate like a bomb going off. With one more rough thrust, he follows with a groan, his head dropping to rest in the crook of my neck as his body shudders with his release.

We're both panting, trying to catch our breath when he collapses beside me, pulling my back to his front and holding me close. He presses kisses to my neck and shoulder, and I let out a soft hum of contentment.

Exhaustion seeps through the pleasure until I can barely keep my eyes open, and as unconsciousness pulls at the edges, I let those three little words free one more time, wishing there was something even stronger than words to convey how much he means to me.

The same three words I've never said to anyone else.

"I love you."

TWENTY-FOUR

Ty

It's later than expected by the time I get home from New York. Our team flight was delayed due to a winter storm, and by the time we landed in LA, it was already midnight. Lexi's spent every night with me since we got back from our trip to Vancouver, yet there's a confusing mix of joy and disappointment when I walk into my room and find her asleep in my bed. I love that she's here—coming home has a new thrill to it since she's been staying here—but I'm sad I don't get to talk to her and kiss her because she's asleep.

God, I've really become whipped.

I place my bag in my closet and then head to the bathroom to shower.

My clothes fall to the floor as the water gets hot. The second the warm spray of the water hits my sore muscles, the tension I've been carrying drains away. This last game was our worst of the season. I'm not sure what's going on, but our offense has been getting shut down more often and our defense is struggling to hold our line. The Fierce Four might be famous, but the truth is a defense can't be successful with only four strong.

I dip my head under the hot water, my arm stretched out to

hold the wall while I let the water pound down on my tired muscles. A hand slides up my back, and for a second I think I'm imagining it, but when I glance back, Lexi is standing behind me. She presses her naked body against mine, her lips brushing over my shoulder blade and her eyes heated.

Her hand wraps around my waist, sliding across my stomach and down until she grasps my quickly hardening cock in her hand. My eyes close in bliss when she squeezes and tugs.

"Fuck," I curse, my muscles tightening with a different kind of tension.

She rotates her grip, her wet hands sliding up and down in a salacious tease, but it's not the wet heat I want.

I grab her hand, stopping her movements, and spin around, my burning gaze piercing hers when I open my eyes again. "Are you horny, Precious?"

"Yes," she says, her deep, throaty voice making my cock even harder. I love it when she's needy for me like this.

I grip the back of her neck and haul her mouth to mine, plunging my tongue inside when her lips part on a gasp. Her hands slide down my sides to my back until they grip my ass, her nails digging in and making me growl. My cock pulses between us, aching to be inside her. But apparently she has other plans because she pulls back, her eyes darker than I've ever seen them and the hungry look in them making my heart race.

She drops to her knees and I swallow thickly, giving her free rein to do whatever the fuck she wants to me. She grips my cock in her delicate fingers, her hot gaze staring up at me like she's daring me to tell her what I want her to do.

It's a dare I accept. "Put my cock in that pretty mouth."

Her eyes flare with heat and then she licks up my shaft before wrapping her plush lips around the head and sucking lightly—too lightly. My fingers slide into her hair as my eyes burn into hers. "Someone's feeling like a little cocktease tonight."

The corner of her mouth tilts in the smallest of smiles before she goes back to those delicate little sucks that have my spine tingling, but are too soft for what I really need from her. I tighten my grip on her hair, and her eyes close in bliss. She hums around me, and I have to close my eyes against the pleasure racing up my spine.

"Suck it like the dirty girl we both know you are," I say, my voice ragged.

Her eyes flash and then she takes my cock deep until I hit the back of her throat. A guttural groan rips from me, and I toss my head back when she swallows, the tightness of her throat dragging me to the goddamn edge.

I pull her head off my cock and slip my hands under her arms, hauling her to her feet. My lips crash on hers, kissing her with all I'm worth.

"I'm not coming down your throat. The only place I want to come is in your tight pussy."

I spin her around, bending her over, and slide my hands appreciatively along the round curves of her ass. God, she's fucking perfect.

I keep one hand on her back while the other grips my cock as I notch it against her slick folds. Sliding into her is how I imagine heaven to be. A feeling of pure bliss spreads from my cock, through my blood stream, firing off every nerve ending from my toes to the tips of my fingers. Her pussy flutters around me, and I have to grip her hips to keep from thrusting vigorously inside her right off the bat.

"Ty," she moans against the wall, her head tilted so she can look back at me. The wanton desire in her blue eyes sets my pulse pounding. "I need it hard and rough."

There's nothing hotter than hearing her tell me what she needs, and I'm all too happy to oblige.

I grip her hips hard, a moan escaping her immediately, as I begin to pummel into her, hitting deep inside her and pulling out almost completely before I do it again.

She feels too fucking good, too fucking tight, too fucking perfect. My body becomes mindless as pleasure builds until I'm nearing the tipping point. I need to get her over the edge before I come. It's the one thing I've always prided myself on—making a woman come first—and that's never been more important than it is with *my* woman.

Moving one hand from her hip, I slide it around her belly where a slight bump now presents itself, and slip it to that needy nub between her legs. I circle her clit as I pound inside her, increasing my pace, knowing what she needs.

Leaning over her back, I put my lips right by her ear. "Come for me, dirty girl."

Her pussy convulses around me as her eyes squeeze shut, and a deep moan rips from her throat. With her pussy gripping me tight, I follow her, coming hard inside her.

Lexi has completely ruined condoms for me. Before her, I'd never had sex without them, so I never knew what I was missing, but holy fuck, the feel of her bare around me is a new kind of bliss I couldn't have imagined if I'd tried.

I'll never get enough of her.

I place delicate kisses along her upper back, both of us needing a minute to catch our breath before I pull out. I instantly miss the heat of being inside her.

I rotate us so she's under the spray of the water and wash her hair for her. Her eyes close, while the corners of her lips tilt up in a smile. Her cheeks are still flushed, and she has a glow that I know is more than just pregnancy hormones—it's happiness. A sense of pride greater than anything I've ever known fills me—I'm the one who makes her happy.

When her eyes open, they're sated and sleepy. I clean us both and then shut off the water. I dry her off before drying myself and don't bother with pajamas for either of us, preferring to hold her naked while we sleep.

As sleep pulls us down, I know without a doubt that I'll do anything for this woman in my arms.

TWENTY-FIVE

Lexi

I squeeze Ty's hand as we walk behind the ultrasound tech heading into our anatomy scan. We get to find out the sex of the baby today, and I've never been so excited. My bump has gotten much more prominent over the last few weeks, and it really feels like I'm pregnant now, even though I'm still able to hide it at work with baggy shirts and dresses.

When we get into the room, I lie on the exam table, lower my pants, and raise my shirt, exposing my small bump. The ultrasound tech tucks some medical tissue paper in my pants, protecting them from the warm gel she squirts on my stomach. She asks a few questions, and I confirm I'm twenty-one weeks pregnant, my name, and birthdate.

There's a large screen on the wall in front of us so we can see what she sees on her computer as she gets started. It's my first ultrasound since the initial one where we heard the heartbeat. My eyes tear up to see how big my little Peanut has gotten. It actually looks like a tiny person with a distinct head, arms, legs, fingers, and toes. A cute little nose becomes visible as she moves the transducer over my stomach. She points out the heart, which beats quick but steady, then she points out the eyes and how the hands are tucked by baby's cheeks.

"Do you want to know the sex of the baby today?"

I look at Ty just to confirm, although we'd already talked about it before this appointment. He nods.

"Yeah, we want to know," I tell the tech. She smiles and focuses on the screen, moving around until she's looking between the legs. We hold our breaths in anticipation, and I know I'm not an expert, but it becomes obvious there's an appendage not present.

"It looks like you've got a little girl in there."

Tears fill my eyes as I stare at the screen, at the little face with tiny features.

Her face.

A baby girl.

I'm having a daughter.

I'm terrified of what kind of world she'll live in and what she'll have to face as a woman, but thrilled beyond belief. I didn't have a preference either way, but I find myself smiling impossibly wide at the thought of a daughter. When I turn to Ty, he's staring at the screen, stunned.

"You're gonna be a girl dad," I say, keeping my voice soft, although it does nothing to hide the emotion.

He turns his watery eyes to mine and leans forward, one hand holding mine while the other settles on top of my head. He kisses my forehead and then rests his forehead against mine. "There's no one else in the world I would want to be a girl dad with than you."

We both focus our attention back on the screen, watching and listening as the tech describes the different parts of our daughter's anatomy. The appointment drags on a little bit when our daughter rotates and makes it hard to get one of the measurements the tech needs, but after a cup of ice water—which supposedly helps to get babies moving when they're like this—she moves into a better position.

We leave with a handful of ultrasound pictures and both of us still in stunned awe. I can't stop looking at the pictures as Ty drives us back to his place.

I'm having a daughter.

"What are we going to name her?" Ty asks, breaking the silence.

I tear my gaze away from the pictures, and my mind instantly draws a blank. "I have no idea."

He looks away from the road briefly, his gaze connecting with mine, and I catch the slight uncertainty in his eyes.

"What?" I ask.

He nibbles his lip for a second, and he looks a little timid as he asks, "Do you want to name her after your mom?"

"Which one?" The words are out of my mouth before my brain processes what I just said, and my eyes widen as he does a double take.

"You have more than one?"

I swallow thickly. I was not prepared to have this conversation today, not when I'm already emotional after learning I'm having a daughter. But I've put it off long enough. He deserves to know; it doesn't mean I have to tell him everything.

"I was adopted. I never knew my birth mother."

"Did you ever try to find her?"

"No," I respond, staring at the window, but apparently Ty doesn't take the hint that I don't want to talk about it anymore.

"Why not?"

My jaw drops as I turn my head and stare him down. "Why not? Why would I? She clearly didn't want me, so why would I bother wasting my time to find someone who never wanted me to begin with?"

He stares out at the road, his lips thinned and his brows low, thinking hard. Silence fills the space, and for a minute I think he's going to let it drop.

"Maybe she did want you, but she couldn't take care of you. That kind of thing isn't unheard of."

"You don't get it," I mumble, unable to look at him anymore. His questions have dampened my mood, and I don't want to think about the person who gave me up.

"Explain it to me," he says.

Why can't he just read the room? Why does he have to keep pushing?

Anger sizzles, building abruptly. "Explain it? I can't explain it to someone like you."

"Someone like me?" he says slowly like he's trying to understand the words.

"Someone who grew up with two loving parents and a happy family. You can never understand what it feels like to be abandoned."

"Maybe not, but I can empathize. I don't have to experience something to know it was hard and it hurt you. But I also can't understand being angry at someone when you haven't taken the time to find out why she gave you up, which was why I wanted you to explain it to me so I can understand better. I'm not trying to piss you off or pick at old wounds. I'm really just trying to understand."

I stare out the window. I can't explain it to him because then it'll reveal my greatest fear—that I'm unlovable.

That's why I've never searched for her. I didn't want to find out all my deepest fears were true. I would never recover from that kind of confirmation.

And I'd never recover if learning my parents never loved me made Ty question why he does.

"I need you to drop it," I say, not looking away from the passing scenery.

He doesn't respond, but when I glance over, his jaw is clenched tight, and he's staring at the road like it's personally offended him.

My stomach sours. This isn't how I wanted today to go, but now I don't know how to fix it.

We end up back at his place and he makes us lunch, but neither of us talk—both of us lost in our own heads. And then I feel it, clear as day, and drop my fork to my plate, my hand instantly going to my bump.

"What is it?" Ty asks, his face awash with concern.

My smile could probably light up his whole kitchen. "She moved. I felt her kick!"

He rushes around the counter and places his hands on my belly. I move them to where I felt her, and we both wait with bated breath.

"I don't feel anything," he says, but just as he finishes his sentence, she kicks right against his hand, not super hard but enough that he felt the subtle pulse under my skin. He stares at my stomach in awe and then drops his forehead to it.

His voice is low as he talks to our daughter, and tears well in my eyes. "Hey sweet baby. Do you hear your daddy? How you doin' in there? Your mama and I can't wait to meet you."

Whatever frustration I felt earlier melts away at the sweet way he talks to my belly, the way he's so obviously smitten with her already.

I grip his cheeks and pull his lips up to mine, kissing him through my tears. "I'm sorry," I whisper.

"I'm sorry too. I didn't mean to push you or ruin today."

"I know."

He pulls away, his brown eyes darker than normal. "I love

you, Lexi, no matter what happened in your past. You believe me, right?"

I want to, and maybe that's enough. "Yes," I say, even if it's not the complete truth.

I have to believe that someday I'll believe his words. Because the alternative is unbearable.

TWENTY-SIX

Ty

The field explodes into chaos as the offense moves into position. I keep my eyes focused on the player on my side of the field that the quarterback seems to be favoring today.

Sure enough, the QB throws the ball straight to him, but he barely makes it two steps before I tackle him to the ground and bounce back up on my feet. The next three plays result in no forward progress, and it's time to let our offense on the field to try to score some points.

We run to the sidelines as Dom slaps me on the back, a shit-eating grin on his face. "You're crushing it out there today."

I shoot him an arrogant smile. "I know."

He puts a hand to his chest pads and throws his head back laughing. "An arrogant Ty. I never thought I'd see the day. You're going to ruin your nice Canadian rep."

"No way," Gabe interjects. "Everyone knows Ty's the nicest of us all. No one would ever buy that he's arrogant."

My grin turns more sincere, and I shake my head at these guys. Then my gaze moves up to the seat I had reserved for Lexi, next to Danae and Alayna. There she stands, with Alayna leaning in and whispering something as she points at the field—

likely explaining the game to Lexi. Alayna's been a die-hard fan of football ever since she became friends with Dom in high school. Lexi's gaze moves to the sidelines, searching, until it lands on me. My smile grows to match hers, and my heart beats double time as some weird caveman desire flares through me when she turns around and shows off the back of the jersey she's wearing. My name is stitched on the back, and a certainty I've only ever felt on the field pulses through me.

Someday that name is going to be hers.

I never really got why the guys cared so much about their girls wearing their jerseys.

I get it now. Oh fuck, do I get it now.

My thumb slides across my lower lip as images of her wearing *only* that jersey start infiltrating my mind.

"Get your head out of the gutter," Romel mutters, handing me a tablet.

I shoot Lexi a wink and then take a seat between Romel and Gabe on the sidelines. I look at the tablet, reviewing a couple of potential plays this team is known for but hasn't used tonight.

"How's it going with Lexi?" Romel asks.

"Great," I say.

"And Tanner? Any word from him since Thanksgiving?"

I filled the guys in on Tanner's incessant demands for me to get a paternity test early on, but even they were shocked he didn't attend Thanksgiving.

A heavy sigh escapes. "Nope. This is the longest I've gone without talking to him."

"Have you brought up the idea of a paternity test to Lexi, or at least filled her in on what's going on with him?"

I look over at him. "How would you start that conversation without sounding like a dick? We're finally in a good place. She's been opening up to me more. She told me she loved me," I admit, my chest expanding at how good it feels to say it out loud.

We might've had a little hiccup after the anatomy scan, but since then things have been better than ever.

His eyebrows shoot up. "Seriously?"

I nod. She tells me she loves me every day, and there's no way I want to do anything that will risk the strides we've made.

"I'm worried if I bring it up now, she'll go back to shutting me out." The idea guts me.

"Listen man, I get it. I know you don't want to rock the boat, but I also think if you two have gotten as close as you claim, then you can explain it to her in a way she'll understand. We all know this isn't coming from you, but you can't deny in our profession it's a good idea to have those test results on hand. When the press finds out—and they will, especially once she can't hide her bump—there will be questions. And you're lucky she's gone so long without showing much. Sydney was showing by eighteen weeks, and there's no way she could've hidden it this long. It'll be easier on you both if you have those results to dispel any rumors before they even start. Look at it as your insurance policy against getting hassled by the press. Because if you think Tanner is bad now, he's nothing compared to the press vultures."

"Fuck. You're right."

"I know."

I glare at him. "Does it ever get boring being right all the time?"

He smiles wide. "Nope. Just wait until you're a dad and can pull the 'I told you so' card. It feels darn good."

I chuckle to myself. It's always funny to me when Romel replaces a swear word with the child-friendly version. The rest of us talk like a bunch of sailors and then there's Romel who acts like he's auditioning for a role on *The Good Place*.

Another play and we're back on the field. I spend the rest of the game playing the best I've played all season, and I can only attribute it to my good luck charm in the stands—the woman with dark hair, blue eyes, my name on her jersey, and my baby growing in her belly.

When the game ends in another win for the Wolves, I'm eager to get through the postgame interviews and out to my girl.

I rush through my shower, get dressed, and then I'm out the doors with a backward wave to the guys, who just laugh at me as they quickly finish so they can get out to their women too. I push through the door to find Lexi standing there with Alayna and Danae, and my breath fills my chest. Goddamn, she's beautiful. I never want to take this feeling for granted.

She sees me, and her eyes brighten as I walk over to her with purpose in every step. I can't even rip my gaze away from her to acknowledge the other women before I reach her, wrap my hand behind her neck, and haul her mouth to mine.

She melts against my body as her tongue dances with mine, and I relax into the kiss. This is exactly what I needed.

"Hot," Alayna says, breaking through my daze.

I break the kiss, remembering we're in public and Lexi still wants to keep this under wraps until she tells her principal about us. She's on winter break right now, but when she goes back, she's planning to tell her, especially now with her bump becoming more noticeable every day.

"Sorry," I murmur against her lips, my forehead resting on hers.

"For what?" she whispers.

"For forgetting we're still in public."

"We're in public?" she asks, and I pull back, letting out a laugh. My whole body feels light knowing she's as affected by me as I am by her.

Her eyes brighten as her lips twitch with a small smile, and her hands rest on my chest. "You were amazing out there."

"I had some great motivation in the stands."

"He was trying to show off," Dom says behind me.

I glance back to see the other guys coming out, Gabe and Dom both making a beeline for their women, while Romel is already on his phone, probably texting his babysitter to check on Kay who's likely asleep by now.

"I was not," I argue, as Lexi slides her arm around my waist. I glance down at her and nuzzle her ear, whispering so only she can hear, "I thought you didn't want to be too close in public yet."

Her deep ocean-blue eyes meet mine, and I swear my heart skips.

"I love you, Ty. I don't want to pretend you don't mean the world to me. There's only another week left of winter break anyway, so things will be out in the open soon enough."

This woman. She's completely ruined me for anyone else. Thank fuck I don't want anyone but her. Without another thought, I wrap my arm around her, keeping her close to my body as we all start heading out to our cars.

On the drive home, my fingers are restless against the steering wheel as I debate how to approach this conversation with Lexi.

"You okay?" she asks.

I glance over at her before focusing back on the road. Maybe there's no time like the present. "Actually, I was hoping we could talk about something."

"Okay," she says, and I hate the caution in her voice. She's bracing herself for the worst, and I'm worried what I'm about to say will land under that definition.

"The press are going to get word of this soon, especially once we're not hiding our relationship anymore."

"Uh-huh," she says when I stop talking.

"They'll pick apart our relationship if they think it's juicy enough, and considering we haven't been together that long and you're pregnant, they'll jump to a lot of conclusions—maybe even say some nasty things."

"Like what?"

"Like questioning the paternity."

I swear her whole body freezes in the seat next to me.

My words rush out of my mouth like a torrent of water. "*I'm* not questioning it. I want that to be clear. I have zero doubts our baby girl is mine. Do you believe me, Lexi?"

I glance over to find her staring straight out the window. Her body is so stiff it doesn't even look like she's breathing.

"Lexi?"

"Y-yeah."

"You believe me?" There's no way she can miss the pure panic in my voice.

"You want me to get a paternity test." It's not a question.

My stomach tightens, but we've already come this far. "I'm thinking it wouldn't be a bad idea to get one if we can. To prove those rumors false before they can take off."

"I have nothing to hide from you, Ty. This baby is yours. If you want a paternity test, I'll give you one."

I pull up to my place and put the car in park, thankful I can give her my full attention. I grab her hand and hold it tight in mine. Her blue eyes don't reveal any of the emotion I've grown so used to seeing there, and my heart sinks to my stomach.

"Lexi, I don't doubt you." I place one hand on her stomach, and her eyes flare and start to shimmer. So she hasn't shut me out completely. "This baby *is mine*, no matter what, because *you* are mine. Test or no test, I still choose you and our baby. I *trust* you. But the press can be vultures, and they don't trust anything but receipts and irrefutable proof. I don't want your name dragged through the mud if they think this is a ploy to bag a pro athlete. I don't want that to ruin your reputation since there is no such thing as innocent until proven guilty when you're a public figure these days. You're tried in the court of public opinion, even if evidence comes out way later that shows all the accusations were false. I don't want to get to that point. I want to be prepared to put out any fires they try to start the second they light the match. Does that make sense?"

She stares at me, her gaze still more guarded than it's been in weeks.

"Please believe me," I beg. "I trust you. This is not for me."

"Okay," she says, her voice whisper soft. "I'll ask my doctor about it at my next appointment."

"I love you, Lexi."

A flicker of emotion fills her eyes, but then she looks away from me, down at my hand holding hers.

"I'm really tired. The game really took it out of me. Can we head in?"

"Sure," I say, not feeling sure about anything at all, except that I just set us back, especially since she didn't return those three words I've grown so used to hearing.

TWENTY-SEVEN

Lexi

The Monday after a long break is always bittersweet. I'm excited to see my students, but it's hard to get back into the groove after having two and a half weeks off, especially when I spent at least a week of that time catching up on grading. But there's always a little anxiety about how hard it will be to get back into school mode—for both me and my students.

Except today, most of my anxiety is about talking to my principal and finally telling her about my pregnancy. I've been getting looks all morning since there's no way this dress hides my bump well. I'm grateful I was able to keep it under wraps for so long so Ty and I would have some time together to figure things out, but I've put this off long enough. Truthfully, I don't want to hide it anymore, even if my bump wasn't noticeable. I'm proud of my relationship with Ty, and I'm so excited to meet our baby girl.

Mrs. O'Dell's office door opens and she steps out with a huge smile. "Hey Lexi, come on in."

She moves around her desk as I shut the door behind me. "How was your break?"

"It was good. Ended too soon," I say with a weak grin, my nerves getting the best of me as I take a seat across from her.

She laughs. "Doesn't it always. But it's nice to get back into the routine of things."

"Definitely."

"So, what's up?"

I scrape a fingernail over my thumbnail in my lap, trying to quell my nerves. "Well, I have an announcement."

Her face freezes. "You're not quitting, are you?"

"No! No, I'm not quitting, but I will need to take some leave time at the end of the year." She arches a brow, and I take a deep breath. "I'm pregnant. Due in May. I plan to work as long as I can until the baby comes, but then I'll be taking maternity leave for the remainder of the year."

Her face still seems frozen as she stares at me then down at my stomach. "You're pregnant?"

I can't help the smile that spreads as I say, "Yes." My hand rests on my belly where I've been feeling her kick for over a week now. It's surreal, but also incredible. Just touching my belly seems to calm my nerves.

"I didn't realize you were—" She cuts off the rest of her sentence, and my smile fades.

"I'm what?"

"Well, to be honest, I didn't expect this from you, Lexi. You're not married or engaged last I heard. Your students look to you as a role model, and what kind of message does it send when you get pregnant without being in a serious relationship?"

She delivers her words as if she's just a concerned friend instead of the thinly veiled insult it really is. My stomach knots as I stare at her desk, not even able to look at her as I process her words.

I knew I might get some looks, especially from a few of our

more judgmental teachers, but I didn't expect it from Mrs. O'Dell.

When I finally look up at her, she's staring at my stomach, her lip slightly curled in distaste. She catches me watching her and replaces it with a smile that never felt fake before, but now I see it for exactly what it is.

"Is the father in the picture at all?" Her tone once again takes on that caring inflection which now feels like total bullshit.

I have to swallow around the lump in my throat. "Y-yes." I don't want to tell her it's Ty, not because I'm embarrassed, but because now I'm questioning if she can be trusted with that kind of information or if she'd be the first person to run to the press.

She sits back in her chair, relief crossing her face. "Well, that's something at least."

I'm so stunned, I can't even speak.

As if she has no idea the way her condescending attitude has impacted me, she continues, "I'll need you to prepare a statement for me to approve before you tell your students. I want to ensure we don't get any angry parent phone calls."

"Angry parents?"

She looks at me like it should be obvious and she's disappointed it's not. "Well, obviously, many will be uncomfortable with their child's teacher having a child in this way."

I look around the room for a second just to make sure I didn't experience a time warp when I walked in here. Nope. It's definitely not 1950.

It hits me then that I don't have to sit here and take this. So, I don't. I stand from the chair and move to the door without a backward glance.

"Lexi," she calls behind me, "where are you going?"

I don't turn back as I respond, "Back to my classroom. I have work to do, and I'm not wasting my entire planning period being treated this way."

I walk out of the office and down the empty halls, but instead of going to my room, I head to Blaire's. We have the same planning period, so I know she'll be free.

She glances up when I open the door, and as soon as she sees my expression, her eyes darken and she stands from her desk. "What did she say to you?"

I shake my head and realize I'm trembling, like a low-level vibration going through my entire body.

Blaire comes over and moves me until I'm sitting in her chair while she perches on the edge of her desk. She hands me a spare water bottle she pulls out of the mini fridge on the floor against the wall.

"What happened?" she asks after I've taken a sip.

"She basically scolded me." I recount the whole interaction, and by the time I'm done, Blaire's rage-pacing back and forth in front of her desk.

"So, just to recap to make sure I'm understanding this correctly, she basically, in so many words, suggested you were a slut and your students and their parents would judge you."

"She didn't call me a slut."

She shoots me a look. "Please, that holier-than-thou attitude? The comment about whether or not the dad was in the picture? I bet she'd eat her words faster than she could blink if she knew the dad was Tyler Russell. She practically tripped all over herself when those guys were here."

"She wants me to prepare a statement."

Blaire's eyes bug out. "She what?" She seethes, and for a second I think she's going to stomp down to the office and raise hell, but instead she sits in one of her student desks and puts her head in her hands. When she looks up at me, her shoulders have sagged. "Lexi, this is completely unacceptable. This is the twenty-first century for fuck's sake."

"I know." I'm not shaking anymore, but a feeling of dread mixed with exhaustion pools in my stomach.

"What are you going to do?"

"Write the statement."

"You can't be serious."

"What can it hurt?"

She stands up as if she can't sit still because she's so enraged on my behalf. "Because it's none of her damn business! It's literally no one's business but yours and Ty's. They don't have a right to an explanation. All they need to know is you're pregnant and will be taking the rest of the year off once the baby comes. That's it."

I let out a heavy sigh. "Maybe if I'd gotten pregnant with any other guy that might be true. But Ty is a public figure. The press will be all over this, and nothing will be private after that."

Her face pales as if she hadn't processed that. "Shit," she mutters.

"Yep."

"You should talk to the union rep. There's no way what she said to you is appropriate. I can understand you wanting to write some kind of statement because of Ty's job, but I don't think she has the right to demand that of you. She wouldn't ask that of anyone else."

"I'm not going to get the union involved. At least not right now. I'll write the statement and be done with it."

Then she perks up, and her smile grows wicked. "You should have Ty hire a fancy PR person to write up the statement you'll use for the press and use that for O'Dell and your students. The kids will just be excited about Ty being involved. They're not going to care how it happened. If their parents want to be judgy assholes about someone else's life, that's for them and hopefully their therapist to work through. That's not your responsibility. And O'Dell can go fuck herself."

I laugh. "I'd pay money to watch you say that to her face."

She points a finger at me. "Don't tempt me. No one gets to make my best friend feel like shit and get away with it." Her expression softens. "I'm serious, Lexi. You did not deserve this treatment. You know that, right?"

I nibble my lip and then nod. I know I don't deserve it, but that doesn't mean I didn't expect some form of this treatment. Maybe it's because of my upbringing or because so many people have let me down, but it's often easier to expect the worst than to be blindsided. If anything, it's a testament to how much hope Ty's brought to my life that I wasn't prepared for O'Dell's response.

By the end of the school day, my mental exhaustion and physical exhaustion are competing to make me feel like I've been hit by a bus, but I can't leave until after our staff meeting. I grab a snack and meet Blaire outside my door so we can walk to the auditorium together. We're two of the last ones to get in and get settled in our seats. Blaire elbows me, and when I look at her, she nods her head to the front corner where O'Dell is talking to one of the assistant principals, Melanie Peters. Right as I look at them, they both look away, and that knot in my stomach that O'Dell put there earlier today tightens.

"They keep staring at you," Blaire whispers. "I don't have a good feeling about this."

I don't either, but O'Dell wouldn't do anything since I haven't had time to prepare the statement she wants. Or at least I hope that's the case.

But not ten minutes later, I'm reminded why hope has always let me down. O'Dell starts our staff meeting as usual with announcements. She shares that the head custodian is retiring at the end of the year and reminds us that the sub shortage is a problem and to always leave lesson plans on our desk and have emergency plans drafted just in case a fellow teacher has to cover us. And then she dashes all my hope when she says, "And one of our own is expecting. Lexi Kemper is pregnant and due in May. She'll be out the remainder of the year once she delivers, so we'll let you know once we have a long-term sub set up."

Everyone turns to face me, and the usual suspects shoot me dirty looks—the same ones I definitely expected that behavior from. I get several smiles from other teachers, some indifferent looks, and then some questioning.

"I hate her," Blaire mumbles, her glare pointed directly at O'Dell. "That was completely unnecessary and something she should've cleared with you first."

"Agreed, but there's nothing I can do about it now."

"I still think you should get the union rep involved."

Maybe she's right, but I'd rather not. I have nothing against our union rep, but I'm conflict-averse, and it feels like getting the union involved will only make this a bigger deal than it already is.

By the time the hour-long staff meeting is over, I'm beyond done with this day. Not even the idea of my date with Ty tonight can get me out of the poor mood I'm in now. And it doesn't get any better when no fewer than four people ask me when I'm getting married, about my relationship, or who the dad is.

I can't get my purse and work bag fast enough, but I hustle out as quickly as I can while Blaire plays interference. I shoot her a grateful smile and then book it to my car.

Once inside, I rest my head against the headrest and close my eyes, hoping the silence will give me one moment of peace, one moment to find the happy place I've lived in since Thanksgiving. But all I hear is O'Dell's condescending voice and the barrage of questions from other staff members. My eyes pop open, and I stare unseeingly out the windshield as reality hits me with its full force. Today was *nothing* compared to what will happen when the press finds out.

I'd felt sick and hurt when Ty first asked for a paternity test, but now I understand what he was talking about. No one's doubting it at my school, but then again no one knows that Ty is the dad. The press doesn't have the best history of giving the benefit of the doubt. A sliver of worry still remains over whether that test is really for the press or because he doesn't believe me, but I need to trust him.

With that thought, all I can think about is getting to him. Forget canceling our date tonight. I need his strong arms to wrap around me and remind me what we have. I need him to make me feel special in the way only he can, especially after being made to feel less than by so many people who I expected better from.

I turn the ignition and head straight to his place.

TWENTY-EIGHT

Ty

Lexi shows up at my door an hour before I was supposed to pick her up for our date, and I can tell right away something's not right. I cup her face and stare into her tired eyes swimming with frustration. "What's wrong?" I glance down, placing my hand protectively on her small baby bump. "Is it the baby?"

She shakes her head, stepping forward and wrapping her arms around my waist, then burying her head in my chest. "Today was really rough," she mumbles.

It hits me like a ton of bricks that she was planning to tell her principal today. I wrap my arms around her, holding her tight while she seeks comfort in my arms. As much as I hate whatever or whoever made her feel this way, I can't deny I love that she came running to me for strength and comfort.

"Come on, let's sit down and you can tell me all about it, okay?"

She nods her head, and I pull her inside, closing the door and guiding her to my couch. Already, my place feels better with her here. It feels like home more than it ever has.

On our way to the couch, she glances over at the kitchen island and her steps falter. "Is that a taco bar?"

"Yeah, you told me last night you were craving tacos with all the fixings, so I thought we'd have some tonight and watch some TV."

"But you were going to pick me up..."

I shrug. "Yeah, and bring you back here. I figured you'd be tired after a long day back at work and would just want to relax. I would've packed it up to bring to your place, but my couch is comfier."

"It is," she says absentmindedly, still staring at the taco fixings.

"Here, sit down, put your feet up, and I'll get you a plate."

I don't wait for her response, but instead, head to the island and fix her a couple of tacos with the toppings she said she was craving the most. When I turn around, she's already sitting on the couch with the soft blanket my mom sent her for Christmas covering her lower body. She's staring at her hands, and she looks so morose, my whole body hurts just watching her. Who put that look on her face?

I place her plate on the coffee table and sit next to her, pulling her into my lap. She doesn't hesitate to snuggle up to me, and warmth once again infuses my entire body knowing I'm her safe place.

I really thought I fucked things up after we talked about the paternity test, especially since she's been a little more guarded the past couple of days. But apparently it wasn't irreparable damage.

I brush my fingers through her long, silky, black hair. "What happened, Precious?"

"My conversation with my principal didn't go well," she starts, and then she tells me all about her day—the meeting with her principal, Blaire's outrage, then the disaster of a staff meeting. But more than just telling me the events with an air of detachment she usually has when she talks about something bad, this time she shares how she felt, the hurt their judgment caused her.

And my blood fucking boils.

How fucking dare they make her feel anything less than amazing. How fucking dare they suggest her students or their parents won't respect her.

How. Fucking. Dare. They.

My body is stiff as a board as she finishes telling me everything, and I desperately wish I had a game tonight so I could lay some poor fucker out on the field and take out all the anger coursing through me.

Lexi stiffens in my lap, and when she looks up at me, there's a hint of fear on her face. "Are you angry at me?"

I frown, some of my anger fading at her question. "Why the hell would I be mad at *you*?"

She shoves her hand in her hair and then rubs her forehead like this whole day has given her a headache. "I don't know. You seem angry."

"I am. I'm fucking pissed, but not at *you*. Lexi, you did nothing wrong." She looks up at me, doubt clear in her eyes. Why the fuck would she think she's at fault here?

Goddamn motherfuckers messing with my girl's head.

I rotate her so she's straddling me because I want to look into her face properly when I tell her this. "Lexi, you are incredible. Beyond incredible. You're awe-inspiring. The way you love your students, Blaire, *me*. I'm completely undeserving of *you*. And clearly so are those damn motherfuckers at your school for making you feel less than. No one gets to do that anymore. Not as long as I'm around. I'll help you write your statement, and I'll even do you one better and personally deliver it to your principal, if you want. We can see if she has the balls to say the shit she said to you to *me* because I can guarantee she won't get far before I shut that shit down. It doesn't matter whether this baby was conceived when we didn't know each other or if we'd been together and married for years. That night was the best damn night of my life because I spent it with the woman of my dreams. This baby,"—I place my hand on her belly—"she's a miracle. She brought you back to me. I love you, Lexi. Just the way you are. Don't let these idiots who clearly don't know a damn thing about you make you question your character. Your students know who you are, and they love you for always being there for them, pushing them, and encouraging them. If their parents feel differently, then fuck them. They don't deserve you either."

Tears pour down her face, and my heart aches with every one she sheds. My thumb rubs over her cheeks, wiping away the tears. She leans forward, resting her forehead on mine. "I don't know what I did to deserve you."

"Precious, you didn't have to *do* anything. You just need to be you, and you're more than enough. You deserve every good thing in this life. And if you don't believe me, then I'll spend the rest of my life proving it to you."

She stiffens, her blue gaze locking on mine. "The rest of your life?"

I cup her cheeks, wishing just by looking into my eyes she could see into my soul, see how she's changed my life in every possible way for the better. "As long as you'll have me, I'm yours."

Her face crumples as she wraps her arms around my neck and holds me tight, as if she's afraid I'll disappear if she's not holding on to me. And maybe that's exactly how she feels after losing her parents so young. I know that she was in foster care and has experienced abuse and an obvious lack of love—not the nitty-gritty details, but the basics of her experience. I know it probably wasn't as simple as she makes it out to have been. You don't carry the kind of guardedness she does without reason.

"I love you so much," she cries against my neck, and there's a hitch in her voice like it cost her something to admit the depth of her love for me, like she's out on a limb, scared shitless.

My arms wrap around her waist, holding her close. "I love you too." I'll say it as many times as she needs me to. I'll do whatever it takes to prove those aren't just words to me.

We sit like that for a long time, our arms never loosening their hold until she eventually pulls back, wipes her face with her hand, and then spins around to find the plate of food. Right on cue, her stomach grumbles, and I cover my smile with my hand.

"We should probably eat," she says.

"Yeah, we should, but there's one more thing I wanted to discuss with you first."

"What's that?" she asks, facing me. Her expression is open, and after the way she showed up at my door, I'll take that as a huge win.

Leaning forward, I grab her hand and pray she'll say yes. "Will you move in with me? I want to come home to you every day, no matter what time I get in from away games or if it's just practice. We can live here, or we can find a house with a back-yard, something where our daughter and any future kids we have can run around and play. Whatever you want to do, I'm down, as long as you're there. We're practically living together already—I just want to make it official."

She stares at me for a moment, her face the picture of shock with a gaping mouth and widened eyes. And then it morphs into pure, incandescent happiness. "You want to move in together? You want to buy a house with a backyard?"

"You forgot the part where I come home to you every day," I remind her, my own smile matching hers.

She throws her arms back around my neck, laughing—my

absolute favorite sound in the entire world. "Is that a yes?" I ask, laughing with her.

"Yes," she says, pulling back only enough to kiss me, and it takes no time at all for that kiss to turn into something more.

I slide my fingers through her hair, holding her head to me as my tongue slides across the seam of her lips until she parts them, granting me entry. My tongue dances with hers as her fingernails slide across the hair at the back of my neck, sending a shiver of need down my spine.

"You might have to eat after," I murmur against her mouth before kissing her again.

She lets out a soft moan as her hand slides down to my cock which now feels so hard it could cut glass. Yeah, we'll definitely have to eat after. Because right now, all I want to do is get lost in her body, hoping I can make her feel everything I feel.

TWENTY-NINE

Lexi

A month later, I'm emptying out the final box in our new house. I still don't know how he was able to close on it so quickly, but I went from agreeing to move in with him to house hunting over the next week and then finding this gem that was in a gated community and had a large backyard for our daughter and any future children, as he likes to remind me.

It's the house of my dreams, and even with my things here, it still feels surreal.

Thick, strong arms wrap around my waist, Ty's big hands cradling my bump as I lean back against his hard body. My eyes close in bliss as happiness warms every inch of me. If Ty never gives me anything else, this feeling of home, security, and contentment will be enough.

I try to ignore that saboteur in my brain telling me not to get too comfortable. Ty's been nothing but steady the whole time we've been together, so there's no reason to believe it, but my constantly fluctuating hormones don't always make it easy to ignore the negative voice in my head. I'm choosing to trust—and remind myself daily—that he'll keep my heart safe. He won't let me fall, and I don't want to ruin this happiness we've found.

Unfortunately, telling myself that doesn't necessarily stop the negative-thinking spiral, or the part of me that feels like I need to be on my best behavior in my own house. I have this irrational fear that if he gets annoyed by how I fold laundry or load the dishwasher or something else equally mundane, he'll stop loving me. It's ridiculous and there's not anything Ty's done to cause it, but it's there, nonetheless.

I must stiffen or do something that gives away the negative turn to my thoughts because Ty nuzzles against my neck.

"What's wrong?"

I shake my head. It feels so ridiculous, but Ty doesn't let me get away with not telling him. My shoulders fall as I confess, "I haven't lived with anyone since I was eighteen. It's an adjustment, and I don't want to do something that will end up being a deal-breaker for you."

He spins me around in his arms. "And here I was worried about how my bad habits might be a deal-breaker for *you*. I'll warn you right now, I hate doing dishes and more often than not they end up in a pile in the sink before I cave and put them in the dishwasher." He winces like this is a major flaw in him. It's annoying, but not a deal-breaker. He brushes my hair away from my face, and his expression turns serious. "Did your foster home kick you out? I may have done a little research and read that you can get extensions before you're expected to just be out on your own, especially if you were still in school."

I don't like talking about that time, but there's not the same panic clawing at my throat as when I usually think about those years. "No. It just wasn't a good place. I had my bags packed for weeks—not that I had much of my own. I'd been working since I was fifteen, so I'd saved up as much money as I could. On my birthday, I left and slept in my car for a couple of weeks before I got an apartment. I got a tuition waiver as a benefit of being in foster care, so college was paid for, and I worked to afford books and housing. It might've been easier—certainly cheaper—if I'd been willing to get a roommate, but after so many years of living with other people, I wanted my own space. I wanted to feel safe when I was home." It's more truth than I think I've ever revealed to anyone.

His eyes darken as his face gets stormy and protective. "Is that the placement where you got the burn?"

God, I love how this man immediately wants to fight all my demons. It's addicting having someone instantly come to your defense this way. I rub my hand over his hard pec. "No, I didn't get my burns with that family."

That doesn't mean I didn't experience abuse there. Physical scars aren't the worst things that can come from abuse. Truthfully, I look at those scars and barely remember the pain anymore. But I can still remember clear as day the insults and the way those people made me feel—worthless, unlovable. The emotional abuse left much longer-lasting, albeit invisible, scars. Those are the scars that have kept me from letting Ty in all the way, even if I know he deserves to hear all of it. It's hard to relive that pain to explain it all though, and at this point, that's the only thing really stopping me from sharing it all with him.

He leans forward and kisses my forehead. "You're safe here, Lex. You don't have to act or be on your best behavior. You just have to be you."

That's a lot easier said than done. There's something about simply having someone else in my space that makes that spot between my shoulder blades tighten. I'm always thinking about if I'm leaving dishes out or my laundry on the floor. I catch Ty staring at me as I spit out my toothpaste before we go to bed that night and instantly wonder if he saw something that's put him off. But all he does is smile at me, pat my butt, and then start brushing his own teeth. I rinse my mouth with water and then on my way out, pat his butt in return, meeting his grin in the mirror before I scamper to the bed, my heart beating rapidly. A weird giddiness takes over me. This isn't the first time we've slept together, but it's the first time we're sleeping together in *our house*.

I slide into bed and lean back against the pillows, my hand resting over my bump. She was active earlier after dinner, but she must be sleeping now because she's not moving much. Knowing her, she'll wake up right as I finally fall asleep. Some nights I can sleep through her flipping around in my stomach, but most nights she wakes me up. After unpacking a million boxes today, I'm hopeful I'll be too tired to be woken up by her nocturnal acrobatics.

Ty flips off the light to the bathroom and then makes his way to the bed. I struggle not to stare at the hard lines of his toned body and the tattoos over his arms and torso as he gets into bed wearing only his black boxer briefs that hug every bitable curve of his ass. Seriously, this man is too attractive for his own good.

When my gaze slides up to his face, it's to find him already smiling at me, one dark eyebrow arched and his lips quirked in the corners like he's fighting back a grin.

My cheeks flush. "Oh, come on. You can't blame me. I mean, look at you!" I gesture to his perfect physique.

"You won't ever hear me complaining about you ogling me. Don't worry, I was doing the same thing. Your tits in that top are fucking tempting."

I glance down, and sure enough, my stomach has pushed my breasts up until they're almost obscene, practically falling out of my tank top. They've gotten so big in the last few months, and I know Ty enjoys them.

I glance back at him with my own smile and arched brow. "Oops."

He tips his head back and lets out a full belly laugh that has me laughing with him, and suddenly all my stress about the day and having to be on my best behavior around him disappears. It's hard to be self-conscious when you're laughing this hard. Happy tears are sliding down my face when his hand reaches out and brushes them away.

"I love your laugh. It's one of my favorite sounds," he says.

"One of them? You have others?" As soon as the words leave my mouth, I know what he's going to say.

"Oh yeah. Let me show you another one."

And then he slides down to his stomach, pulls off my sleep shorts, and spreads my thighs apart before burying his head between my legs, his tongue doing magical things to my clit that has my whole body tensing as a moan—his second favorite sound—rips from my throat.

THIRTY

Ty

Lexi snores.

After how stressed she was about doing something embarrassing or something that could be a deal-breaker for me—which isn't possible because I'm so far sunk for this woman it's not even funny—I don't have the heart to tell her.

I also don't think it's something she normally does, but the pregnancy has changed her body, just like Romel suggested it might. I love this woman, but the sounds that come out of her in the middle of the night are downright terrifying. The first time I heard it, I thought a lion had broken into my penthouse.

I watch her sleep for a little longer, loving how peaceful she looks when she's asleep, especially in *our* bed in *our* house, then get up and head down to make her breakfast. She's been on a waffle kick for the last couple of weeks, so I decide to make some batter. I've got music playing low in the background as I drink my coffee and make us waffles and bacon. I also whip up some egg whites for myself since I try to eat relatively clean, even in the offseason.

When the waffles are done, I turn around to put them on

the plate on the counter only to find Lexi standing at the edge of the kitchen, her eyes wide as she looks around. I follow her gaze and wince a little at the mess I made.

I wasn't kidding about the dishes, but I guess I haven't cooked enough for her to realize I'm kind of a messy cook. I clean it up when I'm done, but the during often looks like something out of a disaster movie.

I look back at her. "I'm going to clean all this up. Promise."

She stares at me for a second, her bottom lip trapped between her lips, and I start to panic that maybe this is a deal-breaker for *her*. But that panic doesn't have much time to grow because she walks up to me, wraps her arms around my waist, and nuzzles against my chest. Her body starts to shake, and I almost think she's crying which makes me feel like the biggest asshole in the world, until she makes the most unladylike snort and I realize she's laughing.

She's laughing at me.

She tilts her head up, her face flushed as she tries to compose herself, and I can't help smiling down at her. God, I fucking love this woman, even when she's laughing at my expense.

She shakes her head and looks back around the kitchen before smiling up at me. "You weren't kidding."

"No, I wasn't."

"Is it weird that this mess actually makes me feel better?"

My shoulders relax as I hold her closer to me. "Not at all. I already told you; you can't do anything that will make me run away from you. I'm in this, Precious. All in."

She pushes up to her tiptoes, bringing her lips to mine, and I get lost in the kiss until I smell something burning and realize the bacon is well past crispy.

She smacks my butt as she moves over to the cabinet to grab

more plates, and we move around the kitchen together getting breakfast dished up. It's the first time it really sinks in that this is my life—the woman of my dreams making breakfast with me and carrying our baby. It feels like a dream come true, and if it weren't for the continued distance between me and my brother, my life would be downright perfect.

THIRTY-ONE

Lexi

"Danae's here to take you to girls' night," he says, placing a kiss on my neck.

"Mmm," I hum, pleasure coursing through me. The best thing about living with Ty is unfettered access to his body that I can't seem to get enough of—at least right now since my hormones are raging. I've never been hornier in my entire life than I have been during this pregnancy. We're having sex every day, sometimes multiple times a day because I can't stop. He doesn't seem to mind. If anything, his hunger has been rising to match mine. He's always finding small ways to touch me, kiss me, caress me. It's enough to drive me crazy with need, especially now when I have to leave, and I can already feel my clit throbbing for him again.

"Ty," I whine, causing him to chuckle.

"Sorry not sorry. I'm addicted."

"But I have to go and now I'm horny."

"Well, we can't have that, can we?" He spins me around, lifting me up until my ass is sitting on the edge of our bathroom counter. He's down on his knees before I can even question him, his hands lifting up my skirt and pulling my underwear off.

His gaze locks on mine as he licks up the seam of my soaked pussy lips to my achy, needy clit. The second his lips wrap around that pulsing nub, my hands are in his hair, holding his head to me. "Oh God," I moan, rocking against his mouth. God, I wish we had more time so he could make this last forever, but I know Danae is waiting downstairs.

"Ty..." The word is barely out of my mouth when he thrusts two fingers inside me, curling them to hit that spot that always makes me see stars. He thrusts once, twice, then sucks on my clit hard as he thrusts a third time and I shatter, my orgasm ripping through me as if I haven't had one in weeks instead of this morning in the shower.

He eases away as the last of my orgasm washes through me. "Damn, I love this. I might have to get you pregnant a lot if this is how it's going to be, because I can't get enough of your needy little moans."

I choke out a laugh, and then he's helping me put my clothes back to rights. He holds my hand as we walk downstairs and find Danae relaxing on the couch with her phone in hand. My cheeks flush for making her wait so long, but she just looks up at us with a knowing grin and asks, "Ready to go?"

"Yeah." I kiss Ty, not acknowledging his wolfish grin when my eyes flare at my taste still on his tongue, and then walk out the door.

"Bye, Ty," Danae says, tossing back a wave and following me.

"Drive safe, Danae. You've got precious cargo in that car," he calls out, leaning against the doorframe looking all casual and relaxed in his faded jeans and T-shirt. The guys are meeting at Romel's house while the girls are hanging out at Dom and Alayna's. Once the guys got wind that Alayna wanted to have a girls' night with me and Danae, they were planning their own.

"Do you know what the guys are doing tonight?" I ask Danae as she drives us to Alayna's.

"Didn't Ty tell you?"

My cheeks heat. "He probably would've if I'd asked, but we were a little preoccupied."

She laughs, the sound light and airy. "Oh girl, I've been there. Most days I'm still there. It's a wonderful place to be," she says with wistfulness.

I can't help smiling. "Yeah, it is."

She shakes her head as if shaking away a memory probably similar to the one going around in my mind of what Ty and I were doing ten minutes ago. "The guys are probably going to play board games."

"Board games? Really? I would've imagined they'd have poker nights or something."

She arches a brow. "Have you not seen Ty's collection? He's got a whole closet full of board games. They rotate through some of their favorites, and sometimes he'll bring one that they've never heard of. They do this once a month typically."

I lean back in the chair. "Oh my God, I can't believe I never put it together before. The boxes that Ty put in one of the spare rooms. I thought it was sports memorabilia or something."

"I can't believe he hasn't told you about his collection. He's known for it."

I can't either. Especially when I think about how many boxes were in that room. I wonder why he's never pulled out a board game when we were having a date night in.

A prickle of worry filters through my happy bubble, wondering why he hasn't shared something that is such a part of him that all his friends know about it—that saboteur looking to remind me nothing good ever lasts in my life.

I close my eyes and take a deep breath, hold it for four seconds, then let it go. I'm not going to let those thoughts win.

Things are going just fine, better than fine. I'm sure there's a good reason he didn't tell me about his love of board games.

We pull up to Alayna's house, and she opens the door with a pitcher of lemonade in her hand. "I just kicked Dom out to go play with the boys. Come on in, ladies."

We walk in and follow her back to the patio, and my jaw drops because this has to be the nicest patio I've ever seen. It's like something out of a magazine. A huge deep-green lawn spreads out with a great view of Los Angeles. There's a pool on the right, while on the left is a covered patio with thick wooden beams and Edison string lights serving as a canopy under the wooden roof. A plush-looking, cream, L-shaped couch faces a large square firepit. There's a big-screen TV on the wall, and on the other side is a bar and grill.

"Holy shit," I whisper, although apparently not quietly enough because Danae laughs.

"That's what I said the first time I came over too. I'm still getting used to the luxury these guys live in."

"You didn't grow up like this?" I ask as we take a seat and Alayna serves us tall glasses of cold lemonade.

"Oh, God no! I was barely making ends meet before I met Gabe. In fact, I'd just been fired from my job when Gabe offered for me to work with him and live in his pool house."

"You mean the job he was partially responsible for getting you fired from," Alayna adds with a smile.

Danae shakes her head. "I've told him a million times that was not his fault. But it all worked out for the best regardless." She looks at Alayna. "Same for you and Dom. It's so good to see you two finally settled down together."

Alayna looks down at her wedding ring, a serene smile on her face. "Yeah. Kind of funny how just when you've given up hope, things start to fall in place exactly as they were supposed to."

Her words strike a chord in my heart, and before I even realize what I'm doing, the words are tumbling out of my mouth. "That's how I felt before I met Ty."

They both turn to me, their attention riveted. I don't normally open up so easily to other people, but after bonding with them over the past month or two, it almost feels easy to peel back my layers and let them see a little more. Blaire and Ty are the only other people who've made me this comfortable, but maybe it's time to let more people into my circle.

"I was pretty set in my routine and had convinced myself I was fine living a mostly solitary life, and then I met Ty when I was out with my friend Blaire, and..." I'm thrown back to the memory, the way he made me feel, my desperation to leave before he could ruin how perfect the night was. "It was the best night of my life."

Alayna nibbles her lip and then leans forward as if telling a secret. "You know, from what Dom told me, Ty was wrecked when you were gone the next morning. He said Ty spent every spare moment trying to search for you online. The guys were worried he was one desperate attempt away from hiring a private investigator."

My mouth drops open. "No way."

Both women nod. "Gabe told me the same thing," Danae confirms.

I take a sip of my lemonade, processing this information. It offers me some comfort and helps quiet the saboteur in my mind. And for the rest of the night, it serves as a reminder that he truly did want to find me. He's not just with me because of our daughter—another lie the saboteur has planted, despite repeated evidence he wanted me before he knew about the baby.

"How are things going at work?" Danae asks. They both know about the initial response my principal gave me and the statement I had to get preapproved before I told my students. Ty was insistent on coming in with me that day, but considering the press hasn't gotten involved in our situation yet, I didn't want to give my principal anymore fuel, so I made him stay home.

"They're actually going pretty well. I'm mostly ignoring the people who give me weird looks, and my students have all been so excited. A few parents even sent in baby gifts as a congratulations for me. It was super sweet."

"I love that," Alayna says. "I'm so glad they've been supportive. Proves your principal is an idiot."

I take a sip of my lemonade. "Yeah, I can't say our working relationship has improved since her reaction to my pregnancy. Blaire thinks we should find new jobs next year, but I'd hate to leave my students behind. They love coming back and saying hi —even after they've moved on to the high school—so it still feels like I'm severing all those ties, ya know?"

They both nod. "At the end of the day though, you have to do what's best for you," Danae says, placing her hand on my arm and giving it a quick squeeze like she understands it's a tough decision to make.

The conversation shifts, and I spend the rest of the night laughing and talking, getting to know these two incredible women more and hearing about their own love stories. But even better than that, I open up more. I let them in.

And it feels really good.

THIRTY-TWO

Ty

Romel lays down three train cards and claims his route while Gabe makes a sound in the back of his throat. He hates to lose, and Ticket to Ride is one of his favorite games.

My parents used to have family game night every weekend when I was a kid, usually on Sunday nights. As we got older, sometimes it would be every other week, but they made it so enjoyable that it was something we prioritized even as we got into high school. I'm sure that's where my collection started. As I look around at the serious expressions of my friends who have adopted this game night tradition, I can't be mad about it. I love that these guys are cool with sitting around a table playing board games and shooting the shit rather than partying all the time. Normally we try to do it once a month, but with everything going on this year we haven't had nearly as many game nights as usual.

"So how are things going with Lexi?" Romel asks.

A smile graces my lips. "Great."

It's an understatement. Things are better than I ever could've imagined. We can't get enough of each other, and I don't think it's just because of her raging pregnancy hormones. I think I'd still want her this desperately even if I wasn't incredibly turned on by seeing her body grow and change as she carries our daughter.

Who knew it was so hot to watch your woman go through pregnancy?

"How'd she do during the away game trips?" he asks.

"She did okay. Alayna, Danae, or Blaire hung out with her while we were away. I think that helped." It still burns that we didn't make it to the playoffs this year, but I'm also glad we're now in the offseason, and I can focus on getting ready for my daughter to grace us with her presence.

"Syd hated those when she was pregnant with Kay."

I wonder if he realizes he once again spoke about Syd without his voice hitching. I've noticed lately it seems to be easier for him to talk about her. I can't imagine how he feels having lost her. I'd never recover from losing Lexi, and I've only had her in my life a fraction of the time Romel and Sydney were together.

"Laney loves her," Dom chimes in, drawing a card.

"So does Danae. I think she's even trying to convince Lexi to hang out with her and my sisters," Gabe says with a fond smile on his face, and I know how much it means to him that his family and Danae are so close.

If only I could say the same about everyone in my family. My mom calls and texts Lexi regularly, and Dad and Taron ask about her whenever we talk on the phone. Tanner is the lone holdout as far as accepting Lexi with open arms.

As if he knows I'm thinking about him, my phone buzzes in my pocket, and when I pull it out, I see a text from Tanner that immediately grates on my nerves. He hasn't talked to me in months and this is what he leads with? What the fuck?

"What's up?" Gabe asks, and when I look up, everyone is already looking at me with arched brows.

I rest my elbows on the table and lean forward. "Remember how I told you Tanner was not on board with Lexi?"

They all nod.

"Well, we haven't talked since he bailed on Thanksgiving, but he just texted me."

Romel arches a brow. "Didn't you tell him you were getting the paternity test?"

"I was going to, but then decided against it since he won't return any other text I've sent him. If he's going to be an asshole, then he doesn't deserve that information."

They all nod. "That's fair," Gabe says.

My phone buzzes on the table, and I sit back in my chair as I open the text. My jaw clenches when I see his latest message.

TANNER

> I've seen too many good guys get taken down by manipulative women. I refuse to watch it happen to my brother.

"You should call him," Romel says. "Nothing gets solved over text messages. You can't hear each other's tone, and things tend to get misunderstood."

"Give me a minute," I say, pushing away from the table and heading out onto Romel's patio.

The phone rings once before my brother's deep bass rolls through the line. "Hey."

For a second, I'm surprised he picked up at all, and then I cut to the chase because I'm sick of this shit. "I need you to let this go."

"You need to stop thinking with your dick and think with your goddamn head for once."

"Fuck you," I seethe. "When did you turn into such an arrogant shithead who thinks he knows what's best for everyone around him? You don't know shit about Lexi—"

"And you do?" he cuts me off, his own voice rising. "You think you know her? What has she told you about her life? Have you done a background check? Hired a PI to look into her history?"

"She's a fucking schoolteacher, Tan. Not a goddamn hooker I picked up off the street."

"Doesn't mean she doesn't have skeletons in her closet. You're one of the most well-known defensive players in the league right now. You think she's above wanting to take advantage of your success and fame? In my experience, no one is above that."

I shake my head, my fingers digging in my hair. "Who the hell are you and what did you do with my brother?"

"I am your fucking brother, Ty. That's why I'm doing this—because someone needs to. I can't believe your friends haven't. I expected more from them."

"They're treating me better than you are," I spit out, my anger rising with every word out of his mouth.

"Have they looked into her?"

"Have *you*?"

Silence.

My stomach drops. "Tanner."

"You need to listen to me, Ty—"

"Fuck you," I seethe into the phone. "Fuck you, Tanner. How dare you look into her? Why can't you fucking trust me? Why can't you trust her?"

"What has she done to deserve our trust?" he shouts back.

"She's *mine*. That's enough. She doesn't have to *do* anything else. You need to respect that."

"Ty—"

"No. I'm done. Leave Lexi alone. And leave me alone too while we're at it." I end the call, and it takes every ounce of strength I have not to chuck my phone across Romel's pristine lawn.

What a piece of work. I cannot even *believe* him.

I pace the patio, trying to cool down, but I know I can't stay out here forever. When I'm convinced I won't break something, I head back inside. Three sets of eyes settle on me as I sag into my seat.

"Call went that well, huh?" Gabe asks.

"I've never fought with my brother about anything serious, but this time...this time he's crossed the line, and I don't think I can forgive him so easily." I rub my face. "I think he's looking into Lexi's history."

"Has she told you about it?" Romel asks.

"Some."

"Now might be the time to get her to tell you all of it, so you're not blindsided by whatever Tanner shows you."

I shake my head. "I'm not going to push her to share unless she's ready. I know it was bad. That's enough for now."

I don't tell them I suspect it hurts her when she talks about it. As much as I want to know every piece of her—good, bad, and ugly—I don't want her to have to relive a pain I can never understand just to fill in those gaps in information for me. She'll tell me when she's ready, and that's what matters.

Maybe he's right and I'm being naive, but I'm trusting my gut. She's been honest with me since the beginning, and I'm choosing to trust her. She's the mother of my child, and hopefully someday soon, she'll agree to be my wife.

I will protect her at all costs, even if it's from my own brother.

THIRTY-THREE

Lexi

Sunlight shines softly through the windows as I part my eyelids. On a sigh, I sink back into the warmth of Ty's arms wrapped around me, cocooning me.

I've never felt safer than I do in his arms. It's not a feeling I thought I'd ever get to experience, not after the way I grew up. But I'm growing more addicted to it by the day.

I'm so in love with him it scares me.

He hums against my neck, his arms tightening slightly before he slides his hand down to my stomach. "How are my girls this morning?"

Butterflies swarm in my stomach. "Good," I murmur. Good is an understatement. Blissful might be closer to the truth.

He nuzzles my neck, his stubble tickling me, and a giggle escapes. He chuckles and then his deep, husky voice whispers in my ear. "I love your laugh. I want to wake up to it every day."

"You already do."

He hums again in his throat and then rubs his face against that sensitive spot on my neck that's always so ticklish. I burst into a fit of giggles that has him laughing until both our phones ping with an alert. I reach over to the nightstand and pick mine up, seeing the notification for a new email.

I open it and lie back in Ty's arms, letting him see the paternity results that are likely sitting in his email as well. I knew what they'd say, but there's relief in knowing he now knows for sure. I still don't fully believe these results were just for the press. Now that I've been in his life for several months, I understand why he needed them. While I wish he would've trusted me blindly, he needs to be smart about this, and at least now we have irrefutable proof so no one can question him.

He kisses my head and snuggles me close. "Thanks for doing that, Lexi."

Before I can say anything back, his phone dings again, and then again. His brows furrow as he rolls over and grabs it off his nightstand. I can't see his screen from this angle, but it's clear when he shoots up to a sitting position with a curse that it's not good.

I sit up. "What is it?"

"Fuck," he mutters, his thumb scrolling through what looks like an article. He scrolls back to the top, and my heart freezes in my chest when I see my school picture next to a picture of Ty in his Wolves jersey.

He pulls up another article and then another. Each headline worse than the last. His phone rings, but he ignores the call.

I can't stand not knowing what they say, so I grab my phone and search my name. All the breath in my lungs whooshes out of my body instantly when I see the first headline and click on it. My awful childhood is plastered all over the page. The next article is more of the same. The third calls me a gold digger from the wrong side of the tracks.

For the first time in months, nausea rises up so rapidly, I'm sure I'm going to vomit, but I can't stop staring at the train wreck in front of me.

How did they get all this information?

And then the next thought hits me. *My students are going to see this.*

"Is this true?" Ty's voice cuts through my devastation at having my entire sordid history plastered all over some of the biggest news outlets in the world—things I barely want to remember, let alone have anyone else know.

I glance up at him but can't read his expression through my own emotional turmoil. Instead, I stare at his phone screen which he holds up to show me. I read the paragraph, nausea swirling until I can't hold it back. I throw off the covers and dash to the bathroom, barely making it to the toilet before bile climbs up my throat. There's nothing in my stomach to expel.

The demons of my past have finally caught up with me. No matter how much good I've tried to do with my life, secrets never stay buried. Or maybe they would have if I'd fallen in love with someone else. Someone without a public following. Someone without a fan base that will no doubt tear me to pieces, if they aren't already.

"Lexi."

I look up from my position on my knees bent over the toilet.

"You have a record?"

I shake my head. "It was supposed to be expunged when I turned eighteen."

A storm cloud brews in his eyes, and the saboteur in my head that's been whispering lies in my ears laughs at me. This moment right here is what I was afraid of. I can practically feel the pull of the carpet as it's ripped out from under me. Ty isn't looking at me like the woman he loves.

Maybe it's *loved* now. I know better than most how little that word can mean to some men. It's why I've never said it aloud until Ty.

And now I'm thinking that was a mistake. All of this was a mistake.

I push to my feet and brush past him.

"Lexi, we need to talk about this."

I spin around to face him. "Talk about what? My entire life being splashed all over the media for the entire world to see? Some of my worst mistakes are now out in the open. You think I'm proud that I got banned from a department store at sixteen and sent to juvie for stealing? I never broke a single law after that, but ask me why I broke that one." Anger fires through my blood because anger feels like a safer emotion than devastation and heartache. Anger is powerful instead of weak.

I need to take some of my power back and remember who I am. I'm not the girl that gets the fairy tale. I'm not the girl who's lovable. Maybe I got to be her for a minute, but it wasn't real.

This. This right now is real.

"Ask me," I demand through clenched teeth, fighting back the tears begging to be set free.

"Why?" he asks, his voice hoarse and some emotion in his eyes I can't comprehend.

I hold my head high. "Because my foster brother at the time threatened to strangle me to death if I didn't. Considering he'd already gotten away with burning me with cigarettes several times, it wasn't a meaningless threat. Want to know where he is now?" I don't give him time to answer. "In jail for murder. So, while I'm painfully embarrassed that I still can't step foot in that particular department store, I'd choose my life over that stupid store any day of the week. I did what I had to do to survive. No one was going to look out for me except *me*." I point to my chest, anger nearly suffocating me as my heart feels like it's being ripped to shreds inside me, piece by piece, while Ty just stands there staring at me.

"I survived," I say, my voice cracking, and I know I'm close to losing it, but I refuse to lose it here. I wouldn't be in this situation if it weren't for the man standing in front of me. I wouldn't be exposed like this, reliving every nightmare of my youth. I could've kept it in the box where it deserved to stay hidden.

"Lexi," he starts, but I cut him off by putting my hand up. He snaps his lips shut and watches me walk to the closet where I throw on some sweats and a maternity T-shirt. I throw some clothes into a duffle bag and walk out to find him sitting on the edge of our—*his*—bed, staring at his hands in his lap.

He looks up when he hears me, and his eyes instantly shoot down to the bag in my hand. He's on his feet in a heartbeat. "Where are you going?"

"Anywhere but here," I mumble, already heading for the door.

"Lexi, wait a minute. It's not safe out there. The press is probably swarming the place, and if they aren't yet, they will be soon."

The pieces of my heart that were still intact begin to crack. He's not objecting to me leaving, just my safety. Another thought—insecurity—slams into me. Is his worry about *me*, or about the baby? Was I right at the beginning thinking he was only in this because I was pregnant?

I close my eyes against the pain. My emotions are a mess, and I don't think I can blame it all on pregnancy hormones this time.

"I can't stay here." My voice is devoid of the emotion ripping my insides to shreds. I spent years learning how to never give anything away, and I hate how easily it comes back to me. "I can't even bear to look at you right now."

He sucks in a sharp breath, and I can almost hear the pain my words inflict, but I'm hurting too much to take on his hurt too.

"Lexi, I'll fix this."

Of what little he's said this morning, that one sentence might hurt most of all.

I turn around to face him, and I must not be hiding my true devastation as well as I thought because pain fills his eyes. "You can't. The damage is done, Ty. There is no fixing this."

My tears are so close to the surface, my nose is starting to run. I need to get out of here where I can fall apart in peace, and I know he won't let me go if he thinks the baby won't be safe—I refuse to believe any of his feelings for me anymore. "I'll go to Blaire's. I'll be safe there."

He takes a step closer, but halts when I throw a sharp look his way. "Lexi, please," he pleads. For a moment, I wish he *could* fix it. I wish we could have the happily ever after that he made me believe was possible.

I wish I was anyone else.

But I'm not. I can't change my past, but I know for sure I don't need to be with someone who's a public figure. I can go back to being a nobody and hiding—maybe once all the current media attention dies down.

"I'm leaving," I say, but the words come out choked as a tear escapes.

His hands ball into fists at his sides, and his jaw clenches as if it's taking all his strength to keep himself still and not come to me. "I wish you wouldn't. Please, Lexi. I *will* fix this."

Another tear falls. My time is up. The anger that made me feel strong is sweeping out of my body like it's being washed out to sea, and if I'm going to fall apart, it's not going to be here.

I don't say anything—I can't—as I spin around and walk out.

THIRTY-FOUR

Ty

It takes every ounce of strength in my body to keep my feet planted and not chase after her, but I know my words aren't enough right now.

How the fuck did this happen?

I shove my hands through my hair, then call Gabe. He hired a bodyguard for Danae when shit with her ex was getting dangerous, and that idea is looking pretty good right now. I have no idea how feral the press will be, but based on the initial onslaught of articles, I'm guessing it's only a matter of time before they try to find her.

He answers on the third ring. "Dude, it's like six a.m. Some of us like to sleep in during the offseason."

"I need the name of the bodyguard you hired for Danae."

His voice is much more awake when he speaks. "What happened?"

I pace back and forth in the living room as I recount what we woke up to. "She just left for Blaire's house, but I don't want her alone without protection in case they figure out where she is."

"No, I totally agree. Let me make a call and see if I can pull some strings for you."

My entire body sags with the faintest bit of relief. "Thanks, man. I really appreciate it."

"Don't sweat it. It's what family does for each other."

We hang up so he can call the security company while I restart my pacing, trying to sort through next steps when all I want to do is hold Lexi in my arms and tell her everything will be okay. But I can't do that because I don't know that it will be. This is bad.

I'm about to call my PR rep to get them to take everything down when Tanner calls me for the third time this morning—no doubt to gloat over what I didn't know.

I don't bother with pleasantries. "Not now, Tan. I'm dealing with a shitstorm over here."

"You left me no choice. You wouldn't listen to me."

My hackles rise as a cold sweat goes down my spine. "Wait. Are you telling me *you* did this? You found out this information and leaked it to the press?"

He hesitates, but when he answers, he still has that slightly arrogant tone like older brother always knows best. "I'm sorry. But I needed you to see it, and you were being a fool when it came to her. She's not who you think she is, and the last thing you need is another woman like your ex trying to take advantage of you."

Lexi is exactly who I think she is, and I didn't need her entire awful history to know that.

My tone is deathly cold. "Are you serious right now?"

"Ty, I understand you're upset, but you'll see I did you a favor."

"A favor?!" I shout, suddenly glad Lexi isn't here to see me because I feel more violent than I ever have in my entire life. "You think you did me a fucking favor by sharing personal details about Lexi that were *none of your goddamn business?* What the absolute fuck is wrong with you?"

"Are you even sure that baby is yours?" he cuts in, his own anger clear through the phone.

"As a matter of fact, I'll send you the paternity test results so you can go fuck yourself with them."

He's silent, which is great because I still have more to say. "Did your PI happen to dig up why she shoplifted? Probably not, since that would require talking to both parties. Not that you've done *anything* to deserve this information, but she was threatened by her foster brother. That record was supposed to be buried when she turned eighteen. She's got scars from the abuse she suffered." I hear him curse softly, and for once I feel vindicated that he might finally understand how epically he fucked up.

"You just opened her wounds up for the whole world to read about. You act all high and mighty like you're protecting me, but as a high-profile figure, you know better than most that there truly is such a thing as bad press. If you're not the least bit worried about Lexi, think about what this has done to me. You think I deserve this? If you'd just pulled your head out of your goddamn ass and gotten to know her, you would've seen the truth for yourself. But instead you decided you know best, when the truth is you don't know a fucking thing."

"Ty..." There's remorse in his voice, but it's far too late for that.

"Tanner, let me be clear because I'm only going to say this once. Don't ever fucking talk to me again. You're dead to me. You not only violated my trust, but do you realize you've put Lexi and our daughter in danger? You know what the press can be like. How the fuck could you do that to your own family? What you did is unforgivable."

He starts to speak but I hang up, and this time my anger gets the better of me and I chuck my phone across the room. It shatters against the wall, falling to pieces on the floor.

"FUCK!" I shout, bending over and screaming into the floor.

Lexi was right to run away from me. Whether she knows the full extent of it or not, I did this to her. It was my own fucking brother who betrayed her, who put her history out there for the whole world to see. I can barely stomach the truth as I slide down the nearest wall, dropping my head back and wondering how I'm ever going to fix this.

If I were Lexi, I wouldn't forgive me either.

As the anger seeps away, I glance over at my destroyed phone. If I'm going to fix this, I'm going to need a new phone. I push myself up and head to my bedroom to get dressed. The mussed-up sheets taunt me, and Lexi's soft lavender scent hits my nose as soon as I walk in. She said she switched shampoos and lotions because the lavender soothed her and often helped ease her nausea. Now I can't smell it without thinking of her and what I'm missing.

I quickly get dressed, processing everything, and then realize I can start the process by sending an email to my PR rep. I head into the office and turn on my laptop, typing up a quick rundown of the situation, how I need it handled, and letting him know I'll call once I have a new phone.

I pull up the messaging app on my computer that syncs to the account on my phone and send Taron a message letting him know Tanner is persona non grata. Next, I message Dom, Gabe, and Romel. They're all quick to respond—Gabe letting me know Wyatt's on another job, but the company is going to send a bodyguard to Lexi's location if I can give him the address. Dom asks what we need, but it's Romel's response that has me standing up and pacing.

ROMEL

> This is not good for Lexi's stress, especially at 31 weeks pregnant. What can we do to help mitigate this for her?

My fingers grip my hair, tugging on it tight as I try to run through all my options, but betrayal hangs thick in the air, and it's clouding my thought process.

I can't believe Tanner did this to her. To me.

My laptop dings, and I glance at my email to find a response from my PR rep. They're sending a messenger with a new phone because he needs to be able to talk to me. I guess there are perks to being rich and famous.

Within an hour, the doorbell rings, and the messenger is there with a brand-new phone in hand. It takes me less than ten minutes to get it set up, and then I've got my PR rep and his team on speaker. They're already drafting a response from me, but the damage is done. The comments on social media posts about the article are slamming Lexi. Someone claiming to know her from foster care has already sold a story about her to a tabloid for God knows how much. My stomach roils, and my jaw is clenched so tight it's starting to hurt, but I can't stop moving until I feel like this is under control.

Until I know Lexi is safe from the vitriol.

I've already texted her several times with only one response —that she arrived at Blaire's safely and no press were there—but that doesn't ease any of my worry.

When my phone rings, I immediately pick it up hoping it's Lexi, only to have my mom's face on the screen. I answer because I won't protect Tanner, not when he couldn't be bothered to protect Lexi—and by extension, me.

"Hey Sweetie, Dad and I saw the news. Is Lexi okay?"

"Tanner did this," I spit out, my anger flaring again.

"What are you talking about?"

"Tanner gave this information to the press under some misguided idea that he was protecting me."

"No," she says breathlessly. She murmurs, and it's clear she's telling my dad what I just told her. "I've got you on speaker now, Ty. Are you sure?" I can hear the hesitation in her voice—the disbelief that her son would do this.

"He told me himself."

I can practically feel her shock and concern through the phone. "Damn," Dad mutters, disappointment hanging heavy off that one word.

"Is Lexi there? I tried calling her, but she didn't answer," Mom asks.

"She left." I leave off the invisible *me* that I'm feeling in my soul. The absolute betrayal on her face, the way she shut down and closed me out. She was protecting herself *from me*, all because of my stupid brother.

I can't lose her. I won't.

I woke up this morning holding the most beautiful woman in the world, feeling a peace I'd never known possible while our daughter kicked in her belly, and with one alert, my whole world has gone to shit.

I want to go back to two hours ago when Lexi was here, safe, with me. When I was the person she trusted the most. She doesn't even know the extent of the betrayal since it was my brother who did this to her. She only knows it was because of my fame that she's of interest to the media at all.

Questions and what-ifs run through a loop in my mind while my parents babble on the phone, trying to understand why Tanner would do this, why Lexi would leave, why, why, why.

"Ty, what can we do to help?"

I drop to my couch, putting my head in my hands as the

stress of the last few hours weighs me down. I'm drowning under it all, and all I want is Lexi back.

"I don't know," I choke out, my voice breaking.

"Sweetie," Mom says, her voice watery like she's fighting back her own tears.

"She's gone, Mom. She left, and I don't know if she'll want to come back. At this point, I can't blame her if she doesn't."

"She will." Her voice wavers slightly. "She loves you," she says, and this time there's no doubt in her voice.

But what if love isn't enough?

I love Lexi with every fiber of my soul, with every breath in my body, with every beat of my heart. But what does any of that mean if I can't protect her from my own fucking brother? From the vitriol the media is spewing about her childhood that she *survived*.

What good is love if she's hurting and feels safer away from me than with me?

THIRTY-FIVE

Lexi

The ticking of a clock is the only sound for a long time. I don't know why Blaire has it, but it's starting to annoy the shit out of me.

When I showed up on her doorstep, my cheeks tearstained and a no-doubt vacant look in my eyes, her eyebrows practically hit her hairline, but all she did was open the door and let me in. Once I explained, she went on a rampage for an hour while I sat on her couch, shock hitting me hard as I realized all the ways my life would never be the same.

My students and their families may not have cared about my pregnancy, but I can't imagine there won't be a lot of conversations about the information circulating about me now. Blaire took my phone away when it kept dinging with notifications from people who I was friends with on social media posting on my accounts or tagging me. The comments were my worst-case scenario brought to life.

Is this really you? Are you allowed to teach with a criminal history?

Wow, this is insane. They let this woman be a teacher? I wouldn't want my kid in her class.

I went to high school with her. She was the weird, quiet girl. It's always the quiet ones you have to watch out for.

More of the same, but it was never-ending.

All my hard work trying to put the past behind me, and it's gone in the blink of an eye. A record that was never supposed to see the light of day, foster kids who were in homes with me coming out of the woodwork for their fifteen minutes of fame while they tell lies about me.

I can only imagine how much worse it's gotten since Blaire took my phone away.

"What am I going to do?" I whisper, a sob building in my throat as my eyes burn with tears. All my anger evaporated as soon as I left Ty, and now I'm just left with a desolate emptiness.

Blaire sits next to me and holds my hand. "I don't know, but you're not going to do it alone. I'm going to be right by your side at work tomorrow."

I squeeze her hand because if I try to talk, tears will be the only thing that come out. She tilts her head to try to make eye contact. "I bet Ty would be there too if you asked."

I nibble my lip because a part of me wants to—the part of me that grew comfortable with the way he took care of me, loved me. But the other part of me—the part who's known only struggle, betrayal, and pain—is louder and telling me I can't really rely on anyone but myself. Not even Blaire.

I shake my head and catch her frown in my peripheral vision, but she doesn't say anything.

"I'm gonna lie down. I'm tired."

She doesn't stop me as I make my way to her guest room. She checks up on me at dinner time, but I'm not hungry. I don't know when exactly I finally fall asleep, my tears soaking the pillow, but when I wake up, the sun is just starting to rise.

Time to get up and see the damage of my life.

It's worse than I imagined. When Blaire and I pull up at work, I'm suddenly grateful for the bodyguard I found in Blaire's living room this morning when I came out for breakfast. Ty sent him, and at first I thought it was overkill, but now that I'm seeing the front entrance of my school swarming with press, I'm glad he's here. My heart races as he parks the car he insisted on driving, and we all stare out at the chaos that's spread across the walkway and the front lawn of the school.

"Are you sure about this? Maybe you should call out sick," Blaire suggests, not for the first time.

"I don't have lesson plans set up," I say numbly.

"Fuck lesson plans, Lexi. This is insanity. You can't be expected to teach with this going on right out front."

She's probably right, but I can't just sit at her house all day, and I'm not ready to face Ty again.

Summoning all my strength, I rub my belly, feeling my sweet girl's strong kicks and grounding myself in the fact that I've survived my whole life. I can survive this too. I prepare to open the door and get out of the car when the locks engage. I look over at the bodyguard whose dark gaze is assessing the situation.

"Is there a different entrance you could use?"

Blaire pops her head between the driver's seat and the passenger seat, pointing to the far right side of the building. "There's one over by the portable classrooms. It's used by the cafeteria staff and custodians because it's close to their supply closet."

He nods once, and then backs out of the space and follows her directions to the back side of the school. Fortunately, this entrance doesn't seem to have anyone around, although I notice a few extra cars with people sitting in them. On closer inspection, they have long-lens cameras.

Fantastic.

But it's better than the mob out front.

"On a count of three, let's run inside." Blaire looks at me expectantly.

"I'm thirty-one weeks pregnant and rarely work out. I'm not running anywhere. But I will speed walk with you."

A smile graces Blaire's face for the first time since I arrived at her house yesterday. "Speed walking it is."

We get out of the car, and my bodyguard follows as we hurry toward the door. Car doors open and close, and a warm palm presses on my back. "Walk faster if you can; I'll stall them," my bodyguard murmurs, spinning around and telling them to stop. There's commotion behind us, but I don't dare turn around to see what it is as Blaire gets to the door and opens it with her school key. We rush inside, and my bodyguard follows us. "Only key access?" he asks us.

We both nod, and he seems to relax slightly. "Alright, lead the way to your classroom."

We walk down the halls, the three of us silent until we turn the corner and find a crowd outside my classroom door, but this time it's not the press. It's my principal and several of the other grade level teachers who have classrooms in this hall. They all look over at us at the same time, but Mrs. O'Dell is the first to step forward, her face in a stern frown.

"Ms. Kemper, my office, please. We have much to discuss."

I'm thrown back in time to when I was thirteen and the principal called me into her office, accusing me of stealing food. Shame coats my body now the same way it did then. I *had* stolen food, but only because it was the only food I had access to, and I was starving. Kids in the foster system had automatic free breakfast and lunches at school, but I wasn't getting dinner at home, and the school lunches weren't enough. I'd been hungry for days before I finally caved and stole the muffin. I felt so guilty, I cried myself to sleep for two weeks.

We walk in silence to her office, passing other teachers in the hallway whose conversations stop the second they spot me. One guess what they were talking about.

When we enter her immaculate office, she gestures to the chair across from hers before she takes her seat. She places her folded hands on the desktop and arches a brow. "To say I'm disappointed about what's come to light is an understatement. We pride ourselves on excellence here, Ms. Kemper, and I think it's safe to say that we need to investigate the claims that have been brought forth."

Saliva turns to sawdust in my mouth as I stare at her wordlessly.

She continues. "We've been getting calls all morning from concerned parents. The district representative and I met this morning, and we've agreed the best course of action is to put you on administrative leave for the time being."

"Administrative leave?" I whisper.

"Without pay," she adds, her chin lifted with an arrogance she doesn't deserve. I've worked for far better principals than she is, and I'm wishing I was sitting across from one of them right now. They would still treat me like a human being instead of the scum beneath her shoe.

"I—"

She holds up a hand. "You'll have a chance to state your case at a formal hearing in front of the board, but for now, I have to ask you to leave so there will no longer be any disruptions to the learning environment of our students."

"I can't even tell my students what's going on?"

"No."

Nothing else. Just no.

It always amazes me when higher-ups in education conveniently forget that we're working with kids—human beings who deserve to have things explained to them so they understand why their teacher is here one day and gone the next. Talk about disrupting the learning environment. They don't even know where I am in my lessons. I can only imagine the subs they'll get to cover my class, if they can even find subs since there's a shortage. Likely, it'll be a fellow teacher who doesn't even teach my subject and just gives the kids a study hall or worksheets. How is *that* not disruptive to the learning environment?

I get out of my seat since I know nothing I say now will change her mind and walk out into the main office. Flashes of light go off on the other side of the doors as students try to enter the building, and tears of frustration build behind my eyes as I'm faced with reality. Maybe she's right. My students—any student at this school for that matter—don't deserve to be hounded by press as they come to school.

I turn around and walk down the hall, back toward the side door, my bodyguard once again at my side although I didn't notice him join me at first.

"Is Blaire in her classroom?"

"Yes, ma'am," he replies, his eyes scanning the hallways as we move.

I'll text her when we're in the car. I don't want to stay in this building any longer than I have to. Another layer is added to my sadness knowing what was once a happy place for me now is not. It's just another place I've lost.

I brush away a stray tear and close my eyes for a second, hoping to push any other tears back. When I open them, I halt in my tracks. Ty is standing in front of me, his face as weary as mine looked in the mirror this morning. There are also deep bags under his eyes, and his hair is a crazy mess. His clothes are wrinkled, but it's his eyes that have my heart aching.

Love, concern, longing, and fear are all wrapped up together and shining through the eyes that just yesterday morning brought me so much comfort.

"I hope you don't mind I'm here," he says, his voice hoarse. "Blaire called me, and I rushed right over." He steps closer like he can't keep himself away from me any longer. "I'm so sorry, Lexi. I *will* fix this. Please come home with me."

His gaze drops to my stomach, and the relief that fills his eyes has my heart clenching painfully in my chest. Is he really worried about me or is it just the baby?

Does it matter anymore? I can't stay with Blaire because eventually the press will figure out where I am, and I won't bring this madness to her house.

"Okay," I say.

His eyes perk up. "Okay?"

I nod and then walk back toward the side door, which Blaire must've told him about since he's parked next to the car we came in this morning. I get inside and look out the window as we drive away from my school, feeling like I've just lost another piece of myself and not knowing if anything will be left of me when all's said and done.

THIRTY-SIX

Ty

When Blaire called me this morning, I was so grateful I'd given her my number in case there was ever an emergency when she was with Lexi. The bodyguard did his job, and I'm thankful for him too, but I need to get my girl home where I know she's safe from the madness.

I glance over at her sitting in the passenger seat, her hands cradling her baby bump, and her vacant eyes staring out the passenger-side window. The corners of her lips are pulled down in a frown, and as I watch her, a small tear streaks silently down her face. She doesn't brush it away. She doesn't move at all.

I grip the steering wheel tight in my hands. I slept like shit last night without her while also trying to figure out how to fix this. I have a few ideas, but I don't know if she'll be on board with any of them.

The easiest solution would be to pull out the ring that's been taunting me from my underwear drawer and get down on one knee. But I haven't been holding on to it for two months just for her to think I'm proposing as a solution to a problem instead of the real reason—that I can't fucking breathe without her.

"Are you cold at all?"

No response.

"Hungry?"

Nothing.

I switch on the radio to her favorite station, but that doesn't elicit the smile it usually does. Instead of pushing her, I drive silently all the way home as my brain goes a hundred miles per hour with things I need to do to make sure she's safe until we get this under control.

I haven't even had a chance to ask her what happened when she was at school. Blaire told me about the reception they received when they arrived, and I knew Lexi had been in a meeting with her principal, but I don't know what was said. Based on Lexi's vacant look, I'm guessing it didn't go well. She looks like all the fight has been zapped right out of her.

When I pull up to the house, I park and run around to her side, opening her door for her and coaxing her out of the car. My chest aches at the despondent look on her face and the bags under her eyes that match mine. Did she get any sleep last night? When was the last time she ate?

My gaze drops to where she protectively cradles her belly, and I know the only way I'm going to convince her to take care of herself is to remind her that she's taking care of our little girl too. She loves our baby so much. It might be the only way to get through to her.

She sits heavily on the closest chair to the door, and I squat down in front of her. When she continues to stare at her hands in her lap, I lift her chin, forcing her usually vibrant blue eyes that are now dull and tired to meet mine.

"Precious. You have to eat and then get some rest. If not for yourself, then for our baby. She needs her mama to stay strong right now." I place my hand on her bump, feeling our little girl give a strong kick. In the darkness of the last twenty-four hours, feeling her sweet kick brings a smile to my face.

I glance up at Lexi, knowing she felt it too, only for my stomach to sink as pain seems to streak across her face. "What's wrong? Is it the baby?"

She bites her bottom lip and breaks our gaze, shaking her head. I feel like I've been doused with cold water. Something just happened, but I'm not sure what.

"Lexi?"

She pushes herself to standing and I rise to help her, but she holds her hand up. "I've got it. You're right. I should rest."

But she doesn't head up the stairs for our room. She makes her way to the kitchen. Halfway there, I stop her with a hand on her arm, gripping her gently. She still won't look at me. "Lexi? If you're hungry, I'll make you some food. You can go upstairs and I'll bring it to you, okay?"

She nods and turns around, once again not saying anything. I watch her walk to the stairs until she disappears. When I get in the kitchen, I stop and place my hands on top of my head. That sick tightening in my gut has only gotten stronger since we got home.

I'm messing up.

I'm not sure how exactly, but the feeling that I just made things worse coats me like I'm covered in heavy molasses.

It might be time to call in reinforcements.

THIRTY-SEVEN

Lexi

My back hits the bedroom door as I close it and finally let the tears fall freely. A sob works its way up my throat, but I cover my mouth to hold it in. My heart—or what's left of it—hurts beyond reason. It's a pain I've felt once before, but as time dulled the memory, I forgot how truly painful it was. How I felt like my body was being ripped apart from the inside out by some invisible force that wanted to inflict maximum pain.

He's here for the baby.

That's good. That should be enough. She'll always have him; I know that beyond a shadow of a doubt. But a small part of me hoped when he arrived at my school that maybe he was there for me.

I've never felt more like a vessel for the truly precious cargo I carry as I did when he put his hand on my belly and lit up at our daughter's kick and then had the nerve to remind me to take care of myself for her.

I would *never* risk our daughter. It's why I made sure to force down a banana and my prenatal vitamins this morning even though I had zero appetite. It's why I tried meditation videos last night to bring down my stress because I know it's not good for Peanut.

I know how to put my daughter first. He doesn't need to remind me she's important. She's my whole fucking world now.

She's the only solid thing I have left.

A small part of my brain, which has been questioning everything on a loop, wonders if I'm too emotional to look at this situation objectively. Maybe he was just showing general concern.

But he wasn't. He was making sure I understood if I wasn't taking care of myself, I could be hurting our daughter.

Another sharp pang tugs at my heart, and a small sob rips free. I rush to the bathroom and lock the door. My face stares back at me in the mirror, my cheeks blotchy from my tears, my eyes red and dull, my mouth dry, and my nose a runny mess.

But none of that hits me quite as much as the despair in my gaze. Those dull eyes are lifeless; they're broken. All my pain, all my fears, all my doubts—a lifetime's worth—are reflected back at me.

Unlovable.

No one wants you.

No one will ever want you.

Ty was supposed to be different. He was supposed to be the one who would love me. He made me believe those whispers in my head were lies. That I was lovable. That I was wanted. By him.

But it's not me he wants, is it? Was it ever? Or has it always been about our daughter? By keeping me close, he wouldn't have to fight for access to her.

He grew up in a two-parent home, so naturally he would want that for his child.

I close my eyes, unable to look at myself for a single second longer. I was so stupid.

Sitting on the edge of the tub, I let myself feel it all, knowing when I exit this bathroom, I need to have my armor fully in place. I won't leave again. Ty's right; it's not safe for me outside this house. But more than that, I will give our daughter what I never had.

A family.

I can accept that Ty doesn't love me, that none of his actions have been about me. I can remind myself that I have survived all my worst hurts, and Ty will make an incredible father. Now that I know the truth, I can protect myself. I can accept—something I should've done years ago—that this is my life. That I may be unlovable, but that doesn't mean I can't give all my love to my child. She'll never feel the way I feel right now. She'll never know this kind of agony.

Turning the water on, I splash my face, pulling myself back together. It's harder to put my metaphorical armor back in place than I remember. My heart aches at all the ways Ty chipped away at my walls over the last several months—all the ways he made me feel safe when I should've listened to my gut that none of it was real.

I firm up my resolve, and like a lock clicking shut, the final piece of armor slips into place and a numbness coats my bones. The only warmth in my body comes from my stomach, where my daughter grows.

This time when I meet my reflection, all I see is acceptance, resolve, and strength. It's not the peaceful kind of strength I felt before—it's the strength that's born from necessity. My eyes are dry, my face less red and splotchy. My mouth is still turned down at the corners, but I don't have the energy to fake a smile.

I can do hard things. I will survive this like I have survived every day before this. Like I will survive tomorrow, and the day after. I have me and her, and that's enough.

Once I'm sure I won't crack, that my armor is secure, I exit the bathroom. Ty's sitting on the side of the bed, his head down, but at the sound of the door opening, his gaze finds mine as his body becomes alert. His hands rest between his legs as he sits there, clearly waiting for me, and he's so handsome, even with his brow furrowed in concern and those bags under his eyes. It's not fair. Hasn't life punished me enough? Now I have to raise a daughter with the sexiest man I've ever seen, knowing he can never love me.

My confidence wavers ever so slightly, but I take a breath and hold firm. Ty stands up and pulls back the covers. I crawl in, and when he rounds the bed and gets in on the other side, I turn away from him. I'm strong, but not strong enough to look him in the eyes without him seeing how completely broken I am.

His arm wraps around my waist, hauling me back into his body, and a traitorous tear escapes.

"Lexi," he breathes against my neck.

Exhaustion overwhelms me hard, the softness of the pillow, the warmth of the comforter, the strength and comfort of his arms all working to lull me into the sleep I didn't get last night, but I have to get this out first. He deserves to know that I understand.

"It's okay, Ty. I won't ever push you out of the baby's life," I mumble, my eyelids growing heavy. "I'm glad she'll always have you."

"So will you," he says, and I swear I can feel his heart racing through my back, but it could be my imagination as sleep pulls me further down.

"Because of the baby."

THIRTY-EIGHT

Ty

I don't like the way she's talking. She can't possibly think I'm only here because of the baby.

Can she?

My arm tightens around her waist, my heart racing in my chest. "No, because I love you."

She yawns, and her voice is whisper soft when she speaks, her eyes closed. "You don't need to lie anymore. I understand."

Her voice starts to fade, but panic claws at me. "Understand what?" I can barely ask, but I have to know what the fuck she's talking about.

"That I'm not lovable."

My heart stops as her breath evens out, and she falls into a much-needed sleep. But fear and hurt grip me so painfully tight I can barely breathe. She thinks she's unlovable?

I knew I messed up, but this is worse than I could've ever imagined.

How can she think that? It's not just that she doesn't believe *I* love her—which is bad enough. She doesn't believe she's worth loving at all.

I'm not lovable.

The sentence taunts me as she sleeps deeply next to me, and I hold her tight like if I let her go for a second, I might lose her forever.

That's not an option. And I'll do whatever I need to do to prove her wrong.

Proving her wrong is much easier said than done. Over the next few weeks, a change comes over her, and if I thought she had her guard up when we first got together, it's nothing compared to the woman who looks at me every day, her smiles never reaching her eyes and a slightly distant look in them whenever I catch her alone.

Her hand never leaves her belly though. She's always rubbing it in some way, murmuring softly to herself which I suspect is more for our daughter than her.

It gets worse when I realize she's buying her own groceries and not eating any of the ones I've bought. The more I watch her, the more aware I am that she's *only* using the things she's purchased with her own money. The only thing she accepts from me is the roof over her head and our bed to sleep in each night.

It chips away at my sanity, slowly but surely, because I'm losing her more with every day that passes even though she's standing right in front of me.

She won't even kiss me anymore.

Knowing what she thinks about herself—that she's unlovable—is both a gift and a curse. At least I know what I'm fighting against, but how do you fight a demon that lives inside your loved one's head? How do you fight something that doesn't take physical form but has been reinforced in small, painful ways over and over again her entire life?

Thinking you're unlovable doesn't come from one heartache. It comes from being shown repeatedly that you're not enough. That you're not worthy of love. That no one can love you.

It hadn't clicked how hard this battle was going to be until Danae explained it to me that way when I called in reinforcements. But not even reinforcements have helped; Lexi won't open up to Alayna or Danae either. I've heard her talk to Blaire on the phone, but their conversations sound surface level—the same shit she gives me.

I'm not proud of it, but eavesdropping on her conversations has been the only way to try to get insight into where her mind is.

It's not in a good place.

"How's she doing?" Mom asks me over the phone.

I release a heavy sigh, my chest pulling tight. "Not good," I choke out. "I don't know how to reach her, Mom. I can't get through. I love her, and she believes she's unlovable."

I filled my mom in when she called last week. I couldn't hold it back, and I needed advice from another woman, one who's never steered me wrong. She loves Lexi too, which just further proves that Lexi is nowhere close to unlovable.

I've never loved anyone more.

"How do I fix this?" I ask as my voice breaks.

"My sweet boy. Unfortunately, I don't know that *you* can. She has to believe it. Have you looked into the therapist like Danae suggested?"

I glance at the stairs, but I know Lexi won't come down, not while I'm here. She works hard to avoid the rooms I'm in. "I got her contact information. I haven't given it to Lexi yet. I don't know how she'll take it, and I don't want to make things worse."

"I know you don't. But she needs to talk to someone, a

neutral party. She might not like you for it, but she deserves to believe she's loved, Tyler."

Fuck. My worry is that bringing it up will push her further away from me, and I'm barely hanging on by a thread as it is. She's here, but I don't have her. She barely lets me hold her. I feel like I've been dropped in the middle of the desert and can see the water, but it's never within reach.

I need to hold her, to comfort her, to give her all the love inside me that's dying to burst free and surround her until she believes it's real.

I hate that my mom is probably right. None of it will matter until Lexi believes, and I can't battle the monster in her head—only she can.

"I've gotta go, Mom."

"Hang in there, Sweetie. Just keep loving her through this. We're ready to come down there as soon as you give us the go-ahead to help out any way we can, okay?"

"Thanks, Mom."

With a goodbye, I hang up the phone and then pull the business card I've been holding on to for the last few days out of my pants pocket. I twist it around in my fingers.

There's no reason to delay. I'm not leaving Lexi or giving up on her, even if she shuts me out further after I give this to her. I'll wait as long as it takes until she comes back to me, mind and body. My heart is hers, and only hers.

I climb the stairs, my feet moving heavy as dread curls in my gut. I may be doing what I know I need to do, but I'm not happy about the thought of losing her even more than I already have.

I'm about to walk into our room when her voice filters out of the nursery I set up across the hall. It was supposed to be a surprise before everything happened. I never got to do the big reveal I planned. I didn't realize she'd even looked in here. The door is slightly cracked, so I lean against the wall next to it peeking in to watch her and listening to her soft voice talk to our daughter.

She runs her hand over the crib rail and then grabs the little Wolves jersey I bought with my last name on it—the name I still hope will be Lexi's someday. She stares at it, holding it tightly in her hands as she moves to the large, cushioned rocking chair and sits down like the entire weight of the world is on her shoulders. The look of pure heartache on her face guts me. Worse than that, she looks lonely and lost, two things I never want her to feel again.

I can't stand the distance anymore. I walk into the room cautiously, and as if startled, she stands up quickly and then grimaces in pain.

"Are you okay?" I ask, closing the distance between us in a heartbeat.

She brushes me off. "I'm fine. I just stood up too fast. It's probably just round ligament pain. I should go lie down." She pushes past me and waddles out of the room. I shove my hands in my hair, my heart cracking and my jaw clenched tight. I hate everything about this. This wasn't how it was supposed to be.

A shout of pain breaks through the silence, and I don't think —I just move. Running across the hall into our room, I find Lexi in the bathroom bent over, tears streaming down her face and blood dripping on the floor. She looks up at me, stark fear permeating every inch of her face.

"Something's wrong."

THIRTY-NINE

Lexi

The drive to the hospital is a blur of fear and pain. My stomach cramps and my inner thighs are slick from the blood still coming out. Terror like I've never known fills me when Ty helps me out of the car, and I see the towel I was sitting on covered in dark red blood. A nurse wheels us into an exam room and rushes to get the doctor. Ty stays by my side the whole time, his hand holding mine tight like he's afraid to let go.

I move my other hand on my stomach, lower and then higher, searching. "She's not moving," I whisper, panic gripping my throat so tight it feels suffocating.

Ty's hand squeezes mine. "What?"

"She's not moving. She's normally so active this time of day and she's not moving." My voice rises in pitch, and my chest feels heavy as hysteria starts to slither under my skin.

Before he can respond, the doctor walks in. "Hey Lexi, I'm Dr. Price. Let's see what's going on, okay?"

The nurse wheels in an ultrasound machine, and Dr. Price squirts some warm gel on my belly and then focuses intently on the screen. The only sound in the room is the faint hum of the machine, until she puts the transducer down and faces me.

"Okay, Lexi, I want you to take a deep breath for me real quick because I can see you're panicked, and I need you to bring your stress down for the baby."

I nod my head like I'm some kind of bobblehead doll, but I'm hyperaware of what she hasn't said yet. "Is she okay?"

"Her heart has slowed and she's in distress. Did you have any kind of impact on your stomach at all?"

I shake my head profusely. She puts her hand on my arm. "I only ask because it appears you have a placental abruption which is usually caused by some form of trauma to the stomach, but not always. We're going to get you prepped for an emergency C-section and get baby girl out of there for her safety and yours."

"But it's too early. I'm only thirty-four weeks."

"I want you to take a breath for me, Lexi." She inhales, gesturing for me to mimic her, and I do, trying to slow my racing heart. As the panic lingers, I realize we're wasting precious time.

"Please save her," I plead. "Do whatever it takes."

"They're prepping an OR right now. Thirty-four weeks is a little early, but most of her development is done. Once she's out we'll assess her and see if she needs any steroids to help out her lungs, but right now the most important thing is getting her out and stopping the bleeding, okay?"

I nod, tears still streaming. I've lost a lot in my life, but nothing scares me more than the thought of losing my daughter before I've really had her. Before I get to see her smile or laugh or hold her in my arms.

It's a flurry of movement as nurses come into the room, prepping me. One tries to push Ty into the bathroom to change into some scrubs.

"I'm not leaving her for a second. I'll change right here if I have to, but I'm not letting go of her hand."

"It's okay, Ty. Go get changed. I know you want to be in there when she's out."

He bends over, resting his forehead on mine, his eyes searching mine like he's hunting for something. I'm confused and overwhelmed by the pleading and longing in his gaze.

"I'm going in there for you. *With* you. I'm not leaving *you*, Lexi. Not now, not ever."

Tears fill my eyes. This is not the time for this.

He grips my face, refusing to let me break our connection. "I love *you*," he says, his voice begging me to believe him.

My heart wants to—God, does it want to. "Now's not the time," I whisper.

"You're wrong about that, Precious. You're at risk here, too, not just our daughter, and like hell will I let you be wheeled in there thinking losing you won't rip me apart. I won't lose you. I wouldn't survive it."

"Mr. Russell," one of the nurses interjects, urgency filling her tone. "We really need you to get changed if you're going in there."

Without looking away from me, he tells the nurse, "Hold one side and help me put these on over my street clothes. I'm not letting go of her hand. I'm not letting her go," he repeats, but the second time I know it's for me, not the nurse.

I think all the women in the room swoon.

But they don't argue with him. They just work around him holding my hand. Once he's in scrubs, they wheel me to the operating room, and the whole time, Ty never lets go of my hand.

Throughout the entire procedure, he's there, always touching me in some way.

And then the most beautiful sound pierces the air. Our daughter's cries are loud and strong, and tears leak down the sides of my face as the doctors hold her up for us to see.

Ty kisses my forehead, his own eyes bright with tears. "God, she's perfect, Lexi. I love you so much. I'm so proud of you, and grateful for you."

I close my eyes, crying as his words find weak links in my armor. My hormones are all over the place, and I can't make heads or tails of anything except the way he makes me feel in this moment.

Like I'm the most precious gift he's ever been given.

In our hospital room, I hold my daughter—Lana Rose Russell—in my arms, unable to look away from her sweet face. Her almond-shaped eyes match Ty's, and her nose is a smaller version of mine.

It's so bizarre to see my features mirrored on someone else's face. I trace a finger over her soft cheek, mesmerized as she breathes in and out slowly, her eyes closed in sleep, her tiny little fingers curled into fists and nuzzled near her face.

She's perfect.

I know no one is perfect, but she is. I didn't know it was possible to feel this much love so instantaneously. I feel so full it's like I could burst. Tears fill my eyes and spill over every so often, but for the first time they aren't from sadness or heartache. They're from pure gratitude, pure joy that this shining little light is in my arms.

"My little Peanut," I whisper softly. "Mommy loves you so much."

I glance over to where Ty fell asleep on the couch that converts to a small bed they had in the room and find him awake, watching me. He's on his back with one arm under his head while the other rests on his stomach, his head turned in our direction, and something fierce and protective, yet soft in his gaze.

"Sorry, I didn't mean to wake you," I say softly, also not wanting to wake up Lana.

He shakes his head, his voice rough and low when he speaks. "You didn't."

"How long have you been up?"

The corner of his mouth tilts up. "A while."

Something heavy and charged passes between us. "You're the most amazing woman I've ever met," he says with such sincerity, it adds another crack to my armor.

I break our stare to look down at our daughter. "I'm sure that's not true. I've met your mom."

"She's got nothing on you." He doesn't even miss a beat.

My gaze shoots to his, my mouth slightly parted. His mom is incredible, loving, devoted. She's everything I always wished for growing up. She's how I remember my mom being—what few memories I have of her.

I'm not even close to her level, and yet looking in his eyes, there's such devotion and honesty there. He believes those words with everything inside him.

"Ty..."

He sits up, putting his elbows on his knees, but his gaze still determinedly locked on mine. "I know I fucked things up. I know I didn't protect you when I should've, but I'll do better, Lexi. Please don't shut me out. I'm in this 150%." He stands and walks over to me, and my breaths grow shallow, but I can't look away even if I wanted to.

"You are the only woman for me. The love of my life. The mother of my child and any future children I'll have. You're it. If you cut me out, I'll never love anyone the way I love you."

He sits on the edge of the bed, facing me, and cups my cheeks in his hands, his brown eyes pleading with me. "I will never stop fighting for you. Never stop protecting you. Never stop cherishing you for the precious gift you are. I didn't even know I was living in the dark until you brought your light into my life. I can't lose you. So please tell me what I can do to fix this. Because I'm dying, Lexi. I'm dying every day that you shut me out."

Tears well up in my eyes and cascade down. "I'm not enough for you."

He grips my face, but not so hard it hurts. "You're *more than* enough for me. If anyone's not good enough in this relationship, it's me. I didn't protect you when I should've."

I shake my head. "Ty—"

"You're lovable," he says, cutting off whatever words I was going to say. "You're the most important person in my world and the love of my life. You're so lovable, I never stood a chance of *not* loving you."

"But what if—"

He cuts me off again with his forehead against mine. "No ifs, Lex. Take the leap with me. Hold my hand and never let me go. Choose me. Choose to love me, to fight with me, to try with me, to have a life with me. That's what love is. It's choosing your person every day. Through good and bad. I choose you. Now. Tomorrow. Always. *Choose me.*"

I stare at this man, baring his heart and soul for me, and every ounce of my armor falls, disintegrating in thin air as tears —this time of relief—pour out of me. I nod my head. "I choose you," I choke out over my emotion.

He doesn't let me get another word out. His lips are on mine in a desperate kiss, both of us needing this connection after so long without it.

When we finally pull away for air, I look down at our still-sleeping daughter and then back up into his eyes, and for the first time in weeks I feel whole.

FORTY

Ty

There's a knock on the hospital room door, and when it opens, Blaire, Gabe, Danae, Dom, Alayna, Romel, and Kaylee come into the room.

Kay's eyes light up as she spots Lana, and she curls her little fists up to her cheeks and squeals. "Cuuute."

All the adults in the room smile and chuckle as she continues to coo at my daughter.

My daughter. God, that's weird to say. I'm officially a dad.

The women surround Lexi, and my heart feels like it's so full it's going to explode out of my chest, especially when they make Lexi smile.

Romel pats me on the back and gives me a knowing look. "How you holding up?"

I've never been so emotionally wrecked in my entire life. I'm on cloud nine that Lana is here, safe and overall healthy even if she came a little earlier than expected. And the fact that Lexi is choosing me—that I practically watched her drop her guard when she looked into my eyes and told me she loved me—makes me feel like I have everything I never knew I needed. But with that comes absolute terror of something happening to ruin this delicate happiness we've found.

But I keep it simple. "I'm really fucking happy, man."

"It'll be nice to have another father in the mix, someone else who will clean up his language, especially after that first slipup when your child starts following you around saying the swear word over and over." He gives me a wink, but I can't wait.

I mean, I can because Lana's still a baby, and I don't need her growing up too fast, but I'm also excited for all those moments that will come someday.

"We're happy for you, brother," Gabe says, pulling me into a quick hug and a slap on the back.

Dom is next. "Couldn't have happened to a better guy. You're going to be a great dad, Ty."

"Thanks, man."

I'm getting a little choked up, and unlike Lexi, I can't blame my emotions on hormones. Just pure and simple emotional exhaustion.

The door opens again and my parents walk in. Mom's eyes already shimmer with tears as she gives me a quick hug and then makes a beeline for Lexi and her first grandchild. The love that shines in her gaze as she looks at Lana and then Lexi tugs on something inside of me. Something that's aching to officially make Lexi a Russell.

My dad pulls me into a hug, and when he pulls away, his expression is serious. "How are you two doing?"

With all the chaos, I haven't had time to fill them in, but he must see the relief in my eyes. "We're good. We're really good."

He nods once. "Good. I was worried about you two."

"You and me both, but we're okay now."

He stares down at the laminate tile floors for a minute before his gaze turns fatherly. "We told Tanner about the baby."

I start to shake my head because if I never speak to my brother again, it'll be too soon. "Ty, hang on. He feels awful. We all know he made a mistake—"

"A mistake?" I seethe, low enough so no one other than the two of us can hear. "He nearly cost me the woman I love. That's not a simple mistake. He went too far."

Dad holds his hands up. "No one will deny that, Ty, least of all him. He's aware. I've never seen your brother look so awful. The guilt is eating away at him."

"Good," I spit out and then his sentence catches up to me. "Wait, you've *seen* him?"

"Well, yes." His gaze shoots to the door behind me just as it opens, and my stomach sinks with dread and betrayal.

I spin around, already bracing my body for seeing the traitor, but nothing can prepare me for the savage protectiveness I feel with Lexi and Lana only feet away.

"How dare you fucking show your face after what you did to her."

All conversation in the room ceases, and a gasp that sounds a lot like Lexi's pierces through the sudden ringing in my ears. But my eyes burn with rage as I face my brother. Dad wasn't lying—he looks like shit with bags under his eyes and remorse in his gaze. He holds a bouquet of flowers in one hand while his other is raised like he's trying to prove he's not a threat.

He didn't use his hands to threaten my girls before. Yet, he still caused damage that hasn't entirely been fixed. Lexi's job remains in limbo, and despite weeks passing, the press won't completely drop the story about Lexi's past.

"Get out."

"Ty—"

Before he can say anything else, I step up to him, but Mom is there in a heartbeat, her voice that stern mom voice that always made us kowtow as kids.

"Not here. I know you two have things to work out, but you

will not do it in this room where Lana and Lexi need to rest and not be stressed out. Take it outside, right now."

"I'm not leaving my girls," I say, my voice low and threatening while my gaze remains locked on Tanner.

"It wasn't a suggestion, Tyler," Mom says, and then lower, "If you want to do best by your girls, take this outside."

I finally rip my gaze away from Tanner to look at Mom, only for it to settle on Lexi instead, like two magnets snapping together. Her face is pale, her mouth parted, and tears fill her eyes.

Fuck. I never told her it was Tanner who leaked the story, and this sure as shit wasn't how I wanted her to find out. I try to give her an apology with my eyes, but I'm not sure how effective it is, especially considering we have quite the audience at the moment.

Turning back to Tanner, I mumble, "Fine," and gesture for him to go first. I'm sure as hell not leaving him in here with Lexi and Lana.

Once we're out in the hall, I notice Mom is following us. She arches a brow. "What? You thought I was going to let you boys work this out unsupervised? I don't think so. I know you both too well to think you can have a civil conversation right now without a mediator. I don't care how old you are."

I shake my head but don't argue. There's no point. She's right. Already my fingers are twitching with the desire to just knock Tan on his ass and let him have it for the hell he's put us through over the last few weeks.

We can't go outside the hospital because the press are still an issue, so I ask a nurse where we can go and not be disturbed. She points to an extra waiting room that's empty and has a door we can close. Once we step inside, I spin around and cross my arms over my chest, staring down the man I used to look up to and now can barely look at without wanting to punch him.

"Speak," I demand.

He sets down the bouquet he's still holding and drops his arms to his sides. "I really thought I was doing the right thing." I scoff before he's barely finished speaking. "Okay, maybe not with the press. That was uncalled for, and I'll own that mistake. But I had good intentions looking into her past."

"Intentions don't mean shit when they cause the kind of harm you did."

"You jumped in with both feet with this girl, Ty. You weren't thinking clearly. One night with her and then she shows up saying she's pregnant and you didn't even seem to question it. She could've been playing you for all you were worth, and you were acting like her little lapdog."

"She's not like that," I spit out, my body taut from holding myself back. I hate hearing him talk about Lexi like she's anything less than amazing. "You don't know her, so that meant I was an idiot for trusting her? Did it ever cross your mind to trust *me* to know enough about her?"

His jaw clenches, and remorse once again flashes in his eyes that are the same shade of brown as mine.

"Those paternity test results you were so on me about came in the morning the press broke the story. If you'd waited one fucking day... If you'd just *trusted me*." I have to look away because it's about more than what he did to Lexi, although that's the biggest part.

It's the slight against me. His actions showed how little faith he had in his own fucking brother.

"Ty," his voice comes out hoarse.

When I look at him, his shoulders are slouched, his eyes shining with the possible sheen of tears, and his mouth turned down in a frown. "I'm sorry," he chokes out. "I'll say it over and over again until you believe me. I fucked up. I'll own it. I'll come forward with the press and explain. I'll get them to stop talking about her."

I step forward, my jaw tight. "You think I haven't already tried? You set off a domino effect, Tan. There is nothing simple about 'fixing it' because if there were, I'd already have done it by now. You threw her entire life out there for the world to see. She's at risk of losing her fucking job! She loves being a teacher, and now she might not be able to because of how people are looking at her. You know the power of the press. How fucking dare you put her through that."

His hand grips the back of his neck, and I can practically feel the despair wafting off him, but it's not enough.

The damage is done, and I don't know if there's any way he can fix it.

"Are you done?" I ask, my voice flat and devoid of emotion.

He swallows thickly, staring at me like he hopes I'll magically forgive him.

I won't.

A quick glance at Mom tells me she already knows how I feel and how hard this is for her to have two of her sons fighting.

"I'm going back to my girls," I say and walk past him without another look.

FORTY-ONE

Lexi

A few days later, we're finally released from the hospital, and while I'm beyond happy to be home, I'm worried about Ty.

Ever since Tanner showed up at the hospital, there's been a tension in his shoulders, a stiff set to his jaw, and a harshness in his eyes when he doesn't think anyone's watching him. The only time it all truly seems to dissipate is when he's holding Lana.

It appears I'm not the only one completely wrapped around our young daughter's tiny little fingers.

Ty tucks me into bed for a rest since I have strict orders to take it easy while my incision heals. Lana is in my arms, sleeping soundly, while he makes multiple trips downstairs to make sure I have snacks, water, and anything else I could possibly need.

When he's about to move away from my bedside to go grab something else I probably won't need, I grab his wrist, stopping him in his tracks. He looks down at me, that slightly harsh and haunted look in his face. Except on closer inspection, it's not haunted—it's hurt. My heart aches for him because I know how close he is to his brothers, and it's breaking my heart knowing I'm the reason they're fighting.

I'm still reeling from the discovery that it was Tanner who

dug up my life history and handed it to the press. I never would've expected him to do that in a million years. I didn't realize I was the reason he skipped Thanksgiving until Ty and I talked about it after he left the hospital. This whole time I had no idea he hated me. Because you have to hate someone to destroy their reputation the way he's destroyed mine.

Focusing on Ty, I slide my hand from his wrist to interlock with his fingers. He squeezes once and sits on the edge of the bed. "Why don't you take a shower and then relax with me?" I suggest.

He shakes his head like he has so much to do, but he doesn't. His mom is staying in the guest room downstairs, and Danae and Alayna already connected with all the other LA Wolves wives and girlfriends for a meal train. There's nothing pressing he has to do, and I suspect the real reason he refuses to stop moving is because then he has to face his feelings about his brother.

"Do you want to talk about it?" I ask.

His shoulders sag. "No."

Disappointment hits me hard even though I know I don't deserve for him to open up to me—not after what I put him through. I look down at our daughter, my gaze tracing the lines of her sweet little face, wondering if we'll ever get back to that place where we had started to rely on each other.

He squeezes my hands. "It's not that I don't want to talk about it with you, Lex. It's just a big fucking mess."

If I'm really going to let down my walls, there's no time like now to start—to prove to him that I'm going to keep choosing him. "It scares me too."

His dark-brown gaze snaps to mine. "What does?"

"Opening up, sharing feelings, working through them." That last one might be the hardest of all to admit. "For the longest time, I thought if I just shoved it all down and locked it up tight, I could live my life with my head down. I would never be disappointed because I wouldn't really expect anything from anyone." I force myself to hold his gaze even if it frightens me to let someone see me be so vulnerable. I've never even been this honest with Blaire. "And then you came into my life, and suddenly I wanted something—something I didn't believe I deserved."

"Lex—"

"No, I need to say this, and you deserve to hear it. I got scared, Ty. Everything felt too good to be true, and in my experience, that was always when the rug got ripped out from under me. That day when the story blew up, when you asked if it was true, I felt judged. My brain immediately went to that place that says I'm not good enough and I don't deserve good things, so to protect myself, I lashed out and then shut down. And that wasn't fair to you. It wasn't fair to the relationship and trust we'd built, and I'm sorry. Clearly, I have a lot of issues I need to work through."

His hand slides into my hair, and he pulls my forehead to rest on his. "Lexi, I'll take you any way I can have you. I love you."

"I don't want to be this way." My voice is whisper soft. "I don't want to be waiting for the rug to be ripped out from under me all the time. I don't want to live my life expecting the worst. I don't want our daughter to grow up with a mom who hasn't learned how to conquer her demons."

"Can I make one request?"

"What?" I whisper, our foreheads still touching and our gazes locked.

"Let me fight them with you? Even if it's just standing on the sidelines cheering you on when you feel like you're about to lose, or throwing up a shield so you can take a breath. I don't want you to shut me out again."

I close the distance between our mouths, my eyes snapping shut, so all my other senses can heighten the experience of this man's love. I don't know what I did in life to deserve it—maybe he's my reward for surviving all the hard days up to this point—but I don't want to take him for granted.

When we pull away, both a little breathless, I say, "You can fight them with me."

His hands tighten in my hair, and he slips his tongue into my mouth, caressing mine with such care, my heart races as I melt into his kiss, his comfort, his love.

It's harder to break the kiss this time, but we both know it can't go anywhere—not for at least six weeks while I recover—and I want him to have some down time to himself.

He places a delicate kiss on my forehead before he gets up and heads to the shower while I stare down at our daughter who slept through her dad making me feel like the most important person in his life.

I run a finger over the thick, black hair at the top of her forehead, then over her round cheeks. She's so little, so delicate, and yet she's made such a huge impact on my life.

"I'm going to love you with every breath I breathe for the rest of my life, even when you're a moody teenager." Tears fill my eyes as those worst-case scenarios run through my mind, but I know all too well the possibility of growing up without a parent. "And if anything should happen to me when you're still young, I never want you to forget, bone deep in your soul, how loved you are. That you are worthy of every incredible thing that comes into your life. That you deserve the deepest love, the kind of love that makes you feel invincible and also scared shitless—because that's the kind of love you'll feel forever even if you lose it. I want you to feel brave enough to take risks, to spread your wings, to allow yourself to fall because you have faith you can get back up. You are the greatest gift I've ever been given. You are a miracle."

She turns her head, nuzzling against my chest, and then opens her eyes. They're still that grayish blue babies have when they're born, and I can't wait to see if she'll have my eye color or Ty's.

As we stare at each other, something inside me clicks into place, like a piece I never knew I was missing. And it's exactly what I needed to feel to know that no matter what happens, good or bad, this is the family I was always meant to have.

The journey was torture, but I ended up right where I always belonged, feeling more loved and cherished than I ever knew possible.

FORTY-TWO

Ty

It's amazing what a good night's sleep in your own bed can do for your mental state. Fortunately, Lana seems to be a good little sleeper. She wakes to eat, but doesn't cry much, and with Lexi and me switching off—I change Lana and then Lexi feeds her— we were both able to get a fair amount of rest. It was certainly better than any sleep I tried to get on that uncomfortable couch- cot-torture device the hospital had.

But with the dawning of a new day comes the realization that I can't freeze out my brother forever.

Or maybe it was just eavesdropping on Lexi while she thought I was in the shower and hearing her tell our daughter how loved she was.

I want Lexi to know endless love—and not just from me, but my family too. Unfortunately, that'll never happen unless my brother and I can work through the mess he made. It'll make holidays challenging, not to mention the strain I know it'll put on Lexi because somewhere deep down she'll believe it's her fault, and I refuse to let that happen.

So when I go downstairs to make Lexi breakfast, I ponder how best to approach the situation with Tanner. I'm staring at the scrambled eggs with ham while they finish cooking when Mom walks into the kitchen. She looks as tired as I should feel, like she's the one who got up several different times over the course of the night. She takes me in and arches a brow. "You look more refreshed than I expected you to be."

I throw a little cheese on the eggs and let it melt. "Lana's a good baby, and Lexi and I make a great team."

Her smile is soft as she hugs me from the side, and I move my arm to wrap around her shoulders, holding her close. "I'm so happy you two worked things out."

"Me too."

I break our embrace to plate Lexi's eggs. "I need to get these up to Lex, and then I was thinking about running an errand."

"I can take those up, and you can head out now if that would be helpful."

My gut tightens, not sure what'll come from what I'm about to do, but knowing I have to try. "Actually, I would appreciate you telling me where Tanner is staying."

Her eyes widen. "Ty..."

I hold up a hand, already seeing the concern on her face. "I'm not gonna kill him. But we do need to talk." I step closer, trying to implore with her to understand. "I can't live with this hanging over our heads. Lexi deserves the kind of family we had as kids, and I know she'll never get that until we resolve some of this."

Her gaze darts to mine. "He's staying at a hotel downtown. I'll get you the address."

"Thanks, Mom."

She shakes her head. "I love you both. He messed up, but I think if it's possible, he's punishing himself more than you ever could."

I don't know about that. But if he's willing to fix his mess,

I'm willing to let him. It'll be a start, although I don't know if our relationship will ever fully recover from what he did.

I knock twice and wait. When the door opens, Tanner doesn't look surprised to see me. "Mom call you?" I ask.

He nods and steps back, allowing me to enter. "She wanted to give me a heads-up in case you were planning to punch me in the face the second I opened the door."

"It would be justified."

He shuts the door behind me and spreads his arms out. "You're right. So, take your shot. I deserve it."

"Don't be a fucking martyr, Tan."

His arms drop to his sides and he lets out a heavy sigh. "I'm not trying to be a martyr, Ty." He sits on the bed, his whole body seeming to drop like a ten-ton stone. "I don't know what I was thinking. I guess I wasn't. All I kept thinking was this woman came out of nowhere and she was going to take advantage of my brother."

He leans forward, his elbows resting on his knees, and stares at his hands hanging lax between his legs. "She reminded me of Heather."

"Who's Heather?" I ask, confused.

He looks up at me, and there's a brokenness in his gaze I've never seen before. "Heather was a woman I met last year. I fell hard and fast, so swept up in her I couldn't see anything clearly."

"Why is this the first time you've mentioned her?"

He breaks my gaze, but his body is hunched in shame. "Because there was no time. She swept into my life like a tornado and left it just as destroyed. By the time I realized what was happening, I was too embarrassed to mention her to anyone." He runs his hands through his hair. "I bought a fucking $400,000 ring for her; that's how far gone I was. I thought she was the best thing to ever happen to me. Then a week after I proposed, she dumped me for another player on my team, one who'd gotten a better contract and made more money. When I asked for the ring back, she'd already sold it to fund her lavish lifestyle while she sank her claws into my teammate. He was such an arrogant prick about it that I didn't bother to tell him she was just using him the same way she used me. Then Lexi came into your life out of nowhere, and I couldn't stomach the thought of you getting conned like that, of you feeling even half as much of a fool as I felt after Heather's betrayal. It was wrong. *I* was wrong, and I can't ever begin to apologize enough for that. In my head, she was Heather, and I was so fucking bitter and angry...and hurt still, that I just kept seeing Heather's face whenever you'd mention Lexi."

"You should've told me."

His shoulders stay hunched. "I know," he says, his voice cracking.

"I'm still pissed at you." I can't let go of my anger that easily, even if I have a better understanding that the driving factor behind his actions had nothing to do with Lexi at all—but she still got hurt in all this.

"You have every right to be." When he looks up at me, his eyes are pleading. "I want to help fix this, Ty."

"Why did you give it to the press?" It would be much easier for him to fix things if he hadn't thrown her entire life out there for the whole world to see.

"I gave it to a friend of mine—someone I thought was a friend because she'd always written complimentary pieces about me. I guess I thought it was the only way for you to see what I'd learned. I knew you would likely blow me off if I tried to give it to you, but you couldn't ignore the press."

I lean forward. "Did you ever think about what this would do to Lexi?"

"Honestly, no. In my head, she was on the same level as Heather. I know that makes me a shitty person, but the only one I cared about was you."

"And you thought I deserved to find out that information by having it splashed all over the media where I couldn't control it?"

"It was stupid."

My voice rises. "No fucking shit, Tan. It was the stupidest thing you've ever done."

"It made sense in the moment," he replies, getting defensive. "How else was I supposed to get your attention?"

"I would've rather you showed up at my front door with the file than handing it off to a journalist."

We lock gazes, tension and animosity growing thick in the air.

He's the first to break the silence. "I don't know what else to say, Ty."

"How are you going to fix it?"

"I don't know," he says.

"Not good enough. We're not leaving this room until there's a plan in place. Lexi's dealt with enough shit in her life; I won't be cause for any more of it. This is getting fixed."

His face softens. "You really love her, don't you?"

"She's going to be my wife, Tan. I want to give her the family she always wanted, and I can't do that if we can't fix this for her. Not only will it affect her job, but I'll never forgive you as long as this is hanging over her head, which will mean no family holidays like we had growing up."

He swallows thickly and nods his head. "Okay, then let's figure out how to fix this."

FORTY-THREE

Lexi

Lana pulled a fast one on us. She was so sweet and innocent that first week, Ty and I were convinced we got lucky with a great sleeper. Apparently, she was just waiting until we'd let our guards down to really lose her shit.

I don't think I've slept more than two hours at a time—if that —in over a week. I've never been so exhausted in my entire life.

There's a knock on the door just as I finish pumping the excess milk Lana didn't finish before she passed out. I remove the flange from my breast and then cover up. "Come on in," I say, trying to keep my voice mostly normal so as not to startle Lana and wake her up.

The door opens and Ty's mom steps in. "Hey, honey, just checking on you."

I give her a soft, tired smile. "I'm hanging in there."

Sympathy fills her face. "You look exhausted."

"Gee, thanks," I mutter. I know she doesn't mean it badly, but I feel gross and tired, so I'm sure I look like I got hit by a bus.

She glances at the two filled bottles of milk I was able to pump. "Why don't you give those to me, and I'll put them in the fridge and take over watching Lana so you can get some rest. A decent nap will work wonders."

I nibble my lip, my gaze darting to my sweet little bundle of terror in her bassinet. She sleeps so peacefully, you'd have no idea she's wreaking havoc on her parents' sanity.

"A nap does sound nice."

She moves into the room, grabbing the two bottles of breast milk and tucking them into the corner of the bassinet that thankfully has wheels, so she can wheel Lana out of our room.

"Is Ty downstairs?" I ask with a yawn. He's been quiet the past week, ever since he went to see Tanner at his hotel. He hasn't talked to me about it, but I can tell it's on his mind. Whenever he thinks I'm not looking, he gets a faraway look in his eyes that I don't think is just caused by sleep deprivation. Guilt still eats away at me that I'm the cause of this rift, maybe not from my actions, but simply due to my existence in Ty's life.

Tina's already wheeling Lana out of the room when she turns back, her posture slightly stiff. "Uh, no. He said he had to run some errands."

It's not what she says but how she says it that has my nerves swirling in my belly. "Did he say what errands?"

She doesn't look at me, but continues to walk out of the room, only speaking when she turns around to close the door. "I don't think so, but don't you worry about a thing. Just get some rest and then take a nice, long, hot bath or shower. Okay?"

She doesn't wait for a response before the door clicks shut, and I'm left with blissful silence. No crying, no sounds from my pump. My brain tries to stay focused on wondering where Ty is and what errands he had to run, but exhaustion wraps around me like a warm, weighted blanket, and I sag against the bed, already asleep before my head even hits the pillow.

I wake up feeling like a brand-new person. Stretching my arms above my head, I stay relaxed in bed, allowing my body to wake up slowly instead of the jolt of concern I usually feel when Lana's cries wake me.

I sit up and reach for my phone, my hand stopping when I see the small tray on my nightstand with some fresh fruit, crackers, and nuts next to my favorite juice. A note says "Eat Me" with a smiley face. I recognize Ty's handwriting, and my cheeks instantly stretch into a smile as I pick up the note, tracing the letters and then holding it to my chest. Maybe it's silly, but his small acts of love always make me feel the most cherished. I don't need grand gestures as long as he keeps doing these little things that show he's thinking of me.

I eat a fresh strawberry and then notice a large box on the foot of Ty's side of the bed. Another note sits on top.

After your bath, put me on.

Putting down the rest of my strawberry, I pull the large rectangular box over and lift the lid. A gasp escapes as I see a gorgeous navy blue dress inside. A pair of silver heels are in a separate box.

My hormones have somewhat settled over the last few days, but at this sweet act, tears of happiness fill my eyes.

I don't know what he has planned, but I don't want to keep him waiting, so I throw off the blankets, steal another berry from the tray, and then make my way to the bathroom. When I walk in, another note greets me, and my smile is so wide at this point, my cheeks start to hurt.

Don't rush. Today is about relaxation. There's a lavender and mint bath bomb waiting to be used. Take your time, Precious. I love you.

I don't think my heart could feel any fuller if I tried.

Stripping out of my pajamas, I get the water running to fill the deep tub which has quickly become my favorite feature of this bathroom. While I wait for the steaming hot water to fill the tub, my gaze catches on my reflection in the mirror. I stare at my stomach and the scar from my C-section. My stomach has a small pooch it never had before, and a part of me struggles to see the changes of my body and stop the doubt from niggling in. Will Ty still find me attractive? Will my new insecurities about my body be another thing that gets in the way of our relationship? I nibble my bottom lip and wish I was strong enough to banish the negative self-talk as soon as it starts, but that's so much easier said than done.

It takes no effort at all to look away from my changed body and focus back on the water. Dropping the bath bomb, I watch it fizz and turn the water a light violet color before I slip in and turn off the water once it covers my shoulders. My muscles relax almost immediately from the heat of the bath combined with the lavender and mint essence. I stay in the water, letting my mind drift and my muscles relax until my body feels completely languid. I don't move until the water starts to get too cold, and then I finally get out and start getting ready for whatever Ty has planned.

I take the time to pump before I get dressed, knowing it'll buy me a few hours before I need to pump or breastfeed Lana again. I don't want achy or leaky breasts to interfere with whatever we're doing tonight. The dress slips on and fits loosely around my stomach so it doesn't add any pressure to my incision, while the heels are low and much more comfortable than I expected them to be. I keep my makeup simple and blow-dry my hair into soft waves, hanging loosely around my shoulders. I haven't worn my hair down since Lana was born because her little fingers love to find loose hair and pull hard while I'm nursing. Now wearing it up has become the norm—so wearing it down tonight feels luxurious.

When I walk downstairs, Ty is standing in the living room talking to his mom. I can't hear their conversation, but it ceases as soon as his gaze lands on mine. His mouth parts, and even from this distance, I can see the way his eyes fill with heat. His gaze coasts down my body like a smooth caress that has goose bumps rising across my arms. He moves around his mom, coming closer, and I finally get to see how his perfectly tailored navy blue suit hugs all his muscles, and my mouth waters at how good he looks.

He wraps his arms around me, pulling me close to his body —but gently because he knows my stomach still feels tender. "You look so beautiful, Precious."

My cheeks heat even as my gaze stays locked on his. "You look pretty handsome yourself. I feel like you've been holding out on me." My hands run down his thick arms. "You look very hot in a suit."

He tilts his head back, laughing, and it brings a smile to my face to see him looking so carefree after the stress of the last few weeks.

When he looks back down at me, his eyes are shining with love. His thumb brushes my cheek before he dips down and presses his lips enticingly against mine. A low rumble comes from his throat, and he pulls away but rests his forehead on mine. "You're too tempting."

He steps back but intertwines his fingers with mine. "Ready to go?"

"Where are we going?"

"It's a surprise. Do you trust me?"

The corners of my lips tilt up, and it feels good to answer so easily. "Yes."

FORTY-FOUR

Ty

My entire future rides on tonight.

Before Lexi, all I thought about was football. I lived and breathed the game until it was my whole identity, my whole purpose. Now, it's fallen to third place as Lexi takes first spot with Lana a close second. My family is my sun, my reason for living, and tonight will determine if I can convince Lexi to not only take my last name someday in the near future, but also accept a life with me in the spotlight—because the nature of my career means I'll never be completely free of the press, as much as I wish I could guarantee she'll never be harassed by them again.

So to say I'm nervous would be a bit of an understatement. But I'm hoping with what I've got planned, I can give her some reassurances and convince her to say yes.

Her brows furrow with confusion when I pull up outside the club where we first met. Unlike that night, there's no line down the block with people waiting to get in. But she doesn't ask; she just places her hand in mine when I open the door and lets me guide her inside. I can't begin to describe the thrill and joy that fill my body from her trust.

When we walk inside, she sucks in a sharp breath, her deep-blue eyes taking in every inch of the transformed space. It doesn't look like it did the night we met. The lights are soft and dim, and the only thing on the dance floor is a table with her favorite flowers and candles in the middle. When we get closer, she spots the two bottles in ice on the side—one sparkling cider and one champagne.

She turns to me with a quizzical brow. "I know how much you cherish those moments with Lana when you breastfeed, so I didn't want to presume you'd want to drink tonight. But if you want to pump and dump, then we've got champagne." I never thought in a million years the words "pump and dump" would come out of my mouth—or that I'd even know what they mean.

She wraps her hand around the back of my neck and drags my mouth down to hers, and I don't stop her because I'm dying for her lips. My hands instantly go to her hips, loving the baby weight she still carries. I know she's insecure about it, but I find her insanely sexy, especially knowing she looks this way because she carried my baby. Maybe that makes me a caveman, but I don't really care.

"Come on, let's eat," I say, reluctantly breaking our kiss. I scoot her chair in once she's in her seat and then move to mine. A waiter appears from the back with our first course—oven-roasted tomato mozzarella bruschetta.

Her eyes light up. "How did you make this happen?"

I watch her take a bite, her eyes closing as bliss washes over her face, and my pants get uncomfortably tight. "Being rich has its perks, and I wasn't lying the night we met when I said I was friends with the owner."

Her eyes practically sparkle, and her smile makes me feel a little breathless. Fuck, she's gorgeous.

"I hope you know you didn't have to go to all this trouble for me," she says softly.

And that right there is why I will always go to "all this trouble" for her. Because she's not with me for my money or the perks of my success. She's with me for me. Now it's time to give her the same reassurances.

I reach out and hold her hand. "This isn't any trouble, Lex. I'd do so much more to make you happy. And the fact you don't expect it just makes me love you more."

Her cheeks get a light-pink blush, just as the next course—a small Caesar salad—is delivered. By the time our entrée of bacon-wrapped filet mignon is brought out, her brows furrow slightly. "This is my favorite."

"I know."

Her gaze meets mine. "So was the last course."

"I know," I say, my voice going deep. She'll find all our courses tonight are her favorites, some of them things she never tried before we got together, but fell in love with instantly.

"But what about you?"

I rub my thumb over the smooth skin of her hand. "All I need is you, Lexi."

I shift so I'm closer to her. "I love you, Precious. And not because of the baby, although I'm in awe of how incredible a mother you are and the gift you've given me of being a father. You are the best thing that ever happened to me. I don't care about your baggage or the skeletons of your past—we all have them. Not a single one changes the way I feel about you."

She nibbles her lip, and I hate the doubt that crosses her eyes before she drops her gaze to stare at where my thumb is rubbing against her hand.

"Lexi," I urge, and I'm rewarded when she meets my gaze. "You're it for me. I've never been happier than when I've been with you. I want to spend the rest of my life with you."

Despair fills her eyes. "But I've caused a rift in your family."

I open my mouth to cut her off, but she holds her hand up and barrels through. "You said yourself your brothers were two of your best friends growing up and told me stories of how close the three of you were, and now you're not even talking to Tanner. I don't understand how you can fully love someone who's only brought turmoil to your life."

"Are you sure about that?" My gaze holds hers for a moment before it shifts behind her, and my smile grows as the last part of my plan falls into place. She spins around and lets out a gasp.

FORTY-FIVE

Lexi

I'm shocked as my brain tries to make sense of what I'm seeing. Ty's whole family walking toward us, Tina holding a sleeping Lana, Tim with his arm around Tina, Taron with a carefree grin on his face, and most surprising of all, Tanner with his hands in his pockets and his demeanor much more subdued than when I saw him at the hospital for the first time. Behind them are the other three members of the Fierce Four, along with Danae, Alayna, and Blaire. I have no idea what's going on or why all these people are here.

I stand as Tina moves closer, thinking maybe something is wrong with Lana, but she only smiles and wraps me in a hug with her free arm. She puts her mouth next to my ear. "We love you so much, Lexi. I always dreamed of having a daughter, but I never imagined I'd be so lucky to get one who's so strong, resilient, and caring. You are the best thing that could have ever happened to my son, and you've made our family more complete."

Her words heal a wound I've carried most of my life—the longing for a mother's unconditional love.

Tim is next. He wraps me up in a tight bear hug. "I'd be so proud to call you my daughter-in-law."

Taron follows behind his dad, giving me another hug—I don't think I've ever been hugged so much in one day before. "Welcome to the family, sis," he murmurs, his smile growing.

It doesn't seem to matter that Ty hasn't actually asked me anything yet.

Then he steps back, and I'm faced with Tanner. It's the first time I've seen him since the hospital when Tina escorted the boys out before I could ask him why he did it.

But I don't have to ask why anymore. I've had enough time to think about it, to realize he thought he was doing what he had to. It doesn't make it any easier to swallow, considering the fallout his actions brought.

Tanner's expression is filled with guilt and remorse which helps ease some of the awkwardness between us. "I'm so sorry, Lexi. Sorry will never be enough, but I'm hoping this will help."

He hands me his phone, and on the screen is an article with a video attached dated this morning. I scan the article, and my jaw drops as I look at him. "You did a sit-down interview to clear my name?"

"I took ownership of my mistake. I never should've violated your privacy that way. It was the worst kind of betrayal, and you did nothing to deserve it. This won't completely repair the damage, but it's shifted the narrative. If you go online, people are talking about me and Heather, not you anymore. Ty and I are working with our PR reps as well to clear things up the best we can. It's a start, and I promise I won't stop until I've cleaned up my mess. I truly am sorry, Lexi. I never should've assumed the worst about you. You'd be a great addition to our family." He leans closer and lowers his voice. "And I'm pretty sure the only way my brother will forgive me is if you say yes."

I'm overwhelmed by his apology. I turn to Ty for reassurance, only to find him down on one knee, an antique ring box open showing the most beautiful vintage diamond ring I've ever seen.

"You are so incredibly loved, Lexi, and not just by me, but by every single person in this room, including those from our chosen family," he says, glancing at our friends standing behind his family. Instant tears fall down my cheeks, probably ruining my makeup, but all I can focus on is the man of my dreams down on his knee, professing his love for me.

He looks back at me, his brown gaze intense and filled with love. "But no one will ever love you more than I do. It's not possible because what I feel for you is so strong, it's never-ending. My heart only beats for you. I want to be by your side for better, for worse, for always." He lifts the box a little, the lights hitting it just right to make it sparkle. "This ring was my grandmother's, and her grandmother's before her. It's always been passed down to the first daughter in the family. I'm really hoping you'll say yes and wear it with pride as the first daughter of the Russell family."

Tears fall unrelenting down my cheeks, and my heart feels so full of love it's like my body is struggling to contain it all.

"You really want me?"

He stands, his hands going to my cheeks to hold my face so I can't look away. "I want you more than my next breath. I want to hold your hand on your hard days and cheer for you on your best days. I want to love you more than you ever knew possible. I want to show you every day how special and cherished you are. Please, Lexi. Be my wife. Allow me to spend the rest of my life loving you with all my heart."

"Yes," I cry, nodding my head like a damn bobblehead doll. How could I say anything else when this man has made every dream of my heart come true?

He laughs, his eyes shining with pure happiness. "Yes?"

"Yes!"

His lips slam on mine in the sloppiest kiss we've ever shared because neither of us can stop smiling.

"Fuck, I love you," he murmurs against my mouth, right before we're surrounded by his family and our friends hugging us and celebrating with us.

For the first time in my life, surrounded by a family who loves me, I finally feel like I belong.

FORTY-SIX

Ty

TWO MONTHS LATER

My hands shake slightly, but not from nerves. My entire body is filled to the brim with excitement as I stand next to the floral arch we made for our backyard wedding and wait for my bride. Three rows of white folding chairs sit on each side, thirty in total. We didn't want a big wedding, just our closest friends and my family. There is no his and hers side because everyone in my life has fallen so in love with Lexi that I'm fairly certain they would've sat on her side even if they were my own relatives.

It's been two months since I proposed, and I would've dragged her straight to the courthouse to make it official then and there if I could've, but I want to give Lexi everything from her wildest dreams. But I also didn't want to wait, and once August hits, I'll be in full-on work mode prepping for next season. Thankfully, Lexi didn't want to wait either, and her "wildest dream" of a wedding included a backyard intimate wedding with only those who know us the best.

In the last two months, I've watched Lexi transform. She started seeing the therapist Danae recommended once a week.

Therapy days are hard on her emotionally, but each time, she comes out stronger. I've even gone to two sessions with her after she asked me to, so I can learn some tips and tricks to help support her. I want to be a partner to her in every sense of the word, and I love seeing her feel stronger as she slays her demons one at a time. She's only just gotten started, and she's already more confident. She says it's me—I make her feel brave and strong—but I know the truth; it's all Lexi. I knew it the minute I saw her in that club nearly a year ago.

She's a goddess.

And she's mine.

The music changes, and I lift my head from where I've been staring at my hands folded in front of me. Nothing—absolutely fucking nothing—could've prepared me to have the wind knocked out of me as my bride, a vision in white, comes walking down the aisle, my dad escorting her.

My eyes burn with tears as my smile grows so wide my cheeks already hurt. I can't believe I get to marry her. That she's really walking toward me right now, vowing to be my wife for the rest of our lives.

How the fuck did I get so damn lucky?

Lana squeals in my mom's arms as she catches sight of Lexi when she's only a foot away from her, and everyone laughs. Lexi pauses to press a quick kiss to our daughter's cheek before she looks back up at me, her smile wide and radiant, and her blue eyes shining with incandescent happiness.

I didn't think I could possibly love her more than I already did, but I was wrong. Because the only way to describe this feeling filling my chest and making my heart pulse rapidly is pure love.

Lexi says Lana was our miracle that brought us together, and while I don't disagree, she's forgetting one critical truth.

Lexi was my miracle before Lana ever existed. Lexi is my dream, my world, my everything.

When she finally reaches me, she breaks our eye contact to turn to my dad, who has tears in his eyes as he smiles down at her.

"Thank you," she whispers, her voice cracking with emotion.

He hugs her tight and whispers something in her ear I can't hear, but she hugs him tighter, and when she pulls away her smile is so wide, it fills her whole face.

He takes her hand and places it in my outstretched one and then winks at her. "And you tell me if this one is ever out of line."

That gets a chuckle from everyone watching. I shake my head at him, but still can't tear my eyes off my beautiful bride. I pull her against my body, wrapping one arm around her back as I nuzzle her ear.

"You are the most beautiful woman I've ever seen," I murmur, so low it's just for her.

Her cheeks are flushed, her eyes shining when I pull back. "I love you so much," she says, her voice watery.

"I love you more."

She shakes her head like it's not possible, but I don't think she has any idea the depth of my love for her. Maybe by the time we're old and gray, she'll understand.

The minister gets started on the service, but I can't focus on anything but her. The way the sun shines on her black hair which is in some intricate updo, making it look like there's almost a halo of light surrounding her. The way her eyes sparkle the longer we look at each other. The way her hand squeezes mine, and she arches a brow. The way her lips quirk with amusement, and I realize everyone's waiting on me.

"Uh, sorry, I was distracted," I admit, my own cheeks flushing and the back of my neck prickling with embarrassment. Everyone laughs, and the minister informs me it's time for me to say my vows.

I let go of one of Lexi's hands so I can dig in my breast pocket for the paper with my vows on it. I debated saying them off the cuff, but decided Lexi deserved my best and not just whatever I could think of in the heat of the moment.

It's harder to unfold it with one hand than I expected, but I refuse to stop touching her. Based on the sweet, bashful smile she gives me, she knows it, so she brings her free hand up and helps me unfold the paper. I give her a grateful smile and then take a breath, trying to tame the emotions stirring inside me and threatening to clog my throat.

"Precious, you might not know this, but you saved me. It wasn't obvious to anyone else—least of all me—that I was in need of salvation, but I was. I didn't know I was living in the dark until I met you, and it was like someone flipped a light switch on. Suddenly, I could see everything clearly. You illuminated my life and then disappeared just as quickly as you came into it. Those weeks without you were all I needed to learn I couldn't live without you, and that was before I knew everything about you."

A tear falls silently down her cheek.

"Through the highs and lows we've already been through, you have remained my light. You honor me with your love, and I want to honor you with these vows. I vow to love you through your hardest days. I vow to make you waffles whenever you're craving them." She laughs and my chest expands. "I vow to rub your legs and your back when you need to relax. I vow to take over midnight baby duty when you need more sleep." Another laugh, this time also from our friends and family. "I vow to always take care of my physical fitness so that your eyes get that heated look in them every time I take off my shirt." Now it's my turn to crack a smile as her eyes narrow, but her lips are tilted up in a grin so I know she's not really mad. Locking my gaze with hers, I don't need to look at my paper to know this last line. "But more than anything else, I vow to always choose you."

Keeping my gaze on hers, I fold the paper back up and tuck it in my pocket and then brush away her tears.

The minister turns to Lexi. "Lexi, are you ready for your vows?"

She nods and gives me a watery smile. "That's going to be a hard one to follow."

She slips her hand into the pocket of her dress—something she was so excited about when she bought it—and pulls out some notebook paper.

"I didn't believe in love when I met you. Happily ever afters only existed in books, but weren't something I ever expected to find. Then I found you, and you scared the crap out of me." Everyone around us laughs, but all I do is smile, not wanting to miss a single word out of her perfect mouth. "You made me feel things I didn't know were real. You made me believe in love and more importantly want it for myself, and that scared me most of all because I've only ever lost the people I loved, and I knew in my heart I'd never survive losing you."

I squeeze her hand, and another tear slips down her cheek. Before it makes it to her chin, my finger is there to catch it and wipe it away.

"Your love scares me because I want it so badly. It's like the rays of the sun warming my skin, and I never want to experience the arctic cold I lived in before I met you."

I'm already shaking my head. She'll never experience that again—not if I can help it.

"When I get scared, I vow to always choose you. To not run away, even if it's easier. I vow to let you in when I need help, and to always give you the love you deserve. I vow to stay by your side, fighting *with* you and *for* you for the rest of my life, no matter what comes our way. I will love you with every single breath I take for as long as I live."

She drops her hand with the paper, signaling she's done, and I don't wait for the minister before I surge forward and kiss her. It's too soon—we still have to exchange rings—but I can't *not* kiss her after that speech. The minister clears his throat, and I pull away just enough to tip my forehead to hers, her blue eyes shining into mine.

"I love you," I whisper against her lips.

"I love you too," she whispers back.

The minister clears his throat again and leans forward. "We're not quite done yet, you two." There's a chuckle in his voice. "She's almost yours, but let's get these rings exchanged first."

I turn to him with my smile wide. "You're wrong about that. She's already mine. Today's just about making it legal."

I don't bother keeping my voice down, and I hear the other members of the Fierce Four chuckling in the front row. They get it.

The rest of the ceremony goes by in a blink. We exchange rings, and then finally, I get to seal our marriage with a kiss. I hold her body close to mine, my tongue running across the seam of her lips until she parts them and lets me in. I don't care if it's indecent in front of our guests.

She's my wife now and I'll kiss her however I want.

Based on how she moans into my mouth and slides her fingers in my hair, I'm guessing she doesn't mind. Cheers and laughter, followed by hoots and hollers when we don't break the kiss right away, ring in my ears. When I finally pull away, I hold up our joined hands like I just won the Super Bowl.

But this feels better than any victory I've ever had on the field.

It feels like heaven.

Lexi

EPILOGUE

We didn't take a honeymoon after we got married last year because Lana was still so young, and neither of us really wanted to be away from her for any length of time, so for our one-year wedding anniversary, we decided to rent a villa in Hawaii while Lana stays with her grandparents. The last year has been a whirlwind.

Tanner's willingness to admit his faults went a long way in changing the narrative for the press. They immediately jumped on the "love" triangle story between Tanner, Heather, and his teammate and dug hard into the rumors surrounding Heather. Turns out, she'd done the same thing when she lived in Florida with other professional athletes. And while people stopped villainizing me on social media, the whole experience had showed me the true colors of the people I worked with. So, despite things shifting drastically after Tanner came forward with the press, I still decided not to return to my teaching job. As much as I loved my students, the politics had burned me out, and I wanted to do something that filled my cup instead of leaving me drained. Blaire also quit at the end of the school year to start the nonprofit she'd talked about. Together we help kids who've lost parents or guardians. We connect them with counseling, tutoring, and for older kids, helping them prepare for life on their own.

It's been fulfilling and challenging in ways I never would've expected, but I love it. More than that, I love not spending hours working once I get home. Days of grading on my couch for hours after a long day of work are over. For the most part, Blaire and I work hard to make sure our work stays at the office. When I come home, that's my time with my family.

Ty's eager to get me pregnant again. I tease him relentlessly that he has a breeding kink, something he doesn't deny. Since I'm not quite ready to put my body through that—and I'm a little scared after how my last pregnancy ended—we're enjoying practicing. We both want a big family, so it's just a matter of time before we have another baby. Right now, we're both loving our time watching Lana come into her own personality. She's curious and a little sassy. She's also the biggest daddy's girl even though she's the spitting image of me.

And as much as Ty pretends to be a tough guy sometimes, he's the biggest softie when it comes to our daughter. I even caught him playing dolls with her the other day when he thought I was still out running errands.

Not a day goes by where I'm not thankful that we ran into each other that night nearly two years ago. I had no idea then how much that man was going to change my life, but I don't regret it for a second. I'm a better person for having him in my life.

That's not to say I don't still have moments of weakness. I've done a lot of therapy over the last year, working on fighting my demons and healing the hurts of my childhood. It's not been easy, but true to our vows, Ty's been there every step of the way.

Every day we choose each other. We choose to love each other through the hard moments as much as the easy ones. I choose not to yell at him if he forgets to close the toilet seat, and he doesn't give me any grief when I'm sick and am surrounded by a mountain of Kleenex. We're both human—flaws and all—but we choose to love each other with our flaws.

It's better than the alternative of life without him. I've lived that life, and it wasn't anywhere near as full as what Ty and I have built together. What we have is real, one-of-a-kind love. It's the partnership of our dreams, and the deepest, purest love I've ever known.

I'm lying on my beach towel on the private beach where we're staying, my body relaxed and languid from the last few days of bliss in paradise, when Ty interrupts my reflection of the last year and how far we've come.

He drops down into the sand beside me and kisses my shoulder. "How are you, Wife?"

My lips tug up in a smile. As much as I love him calling me Precious, I think I love when he calls me his wife more.

"Wonderful," I murmur.

He hums and drops another kiss to my shoulder before he starts peppering kisses over my collarbone. "I wonder if I can make you feel even better," he mumbles against my skin.

"Mmm, I'm willing to see if you can rise to that challenge."

He chuckles, but doesn't stop kissing any inch of exposed skin he can find. My body starts to heat, and it has nothing to do with the sun. His hand slides down to my stomach then under my bikini bottoms until his long, thick fingers are swirling over my throbbing clit.

My back arches slightly from the pleasure while I place my

hands on his cheeks and pull his mouth to mine. He kisses me deeply, his tongue swirling inside my mouth as he owns me with his kiss.

He pulls back, panting. "I wanted to fuck you, but I'm not gonna lie, there's sand everywhere, and this was not how it was described in that smutty book you read."

I burst into laughter because he's not wrong. Sex on the beach is not nearly as romantic as it's implied in my books, and the last thing I want is sand in places sand has no business going. I sit up, kissing him with a smile on my lips, and then stand up.

"Race ya back to the villa?"

He grins. "Precious, I'm a professional athlete. You really think you can beat me?"

I smile salaciously and lean down to where he's still kneeling on the beach. My lips brush against his. "Winner gets the first orgasm." Then I spin around and race back to our lodging. I know he'll let me win because he always makes sure I come first, but I'm not expecting him to catch up to me so quickly and swoop me up in his arms and run back *carrying me*.

"Ty!" I squeal with laughter.

"We're both gonna be winners today, Wife."

He takes us straight to the outdoor shower and turns on the water. His eyes heat as he unties my bikini top, and I can't look away from him as he pulls the flimsy fabric off me before he gets down on his knees and slides my bottoms slowly down my legs. He brushes the remaining sand off, letting the water rinse away the remnants before he starts kissing my skin.

I have never had a man love eating my pussy as much as Ty does. I swear he gets cranky if he doesn't get to eat me out multiple times a week. But he'll hear no complaints from me, especially not when he slides my leg over his shoulder and sucks my clit into his mouth. I tilt my head back against the outdoor shower wall, my fingers plucking at my nipples as my core tightens.

"I'm so close," I whimper. I don't know how he always gets me there so quickly.

He growls against my skin, the vibrations ramping up my pleasure, but before I can topple over, he gently places my leg back down and stands up, pushing his swim trunks off in one smooth move. He steps forward, his body plastering mine to the wall as he grips my thighs and lifts me up. He holds my ass with one hand and guides his hard cock in with the other. He slides in slow, staying still once he's buried deep, only moving his hand to hold my hips with both hands as he starts guiding me up and down his steel length.

"Fuck, I will never get tired of the way your pussy squeezes me. You feel so damn good, Lex."

He buries his head in my neck, dropping kisses and sucking on that spot between my neck and shoulder that has my eyes rolling to the back of my head. His thrusts pick up until he's pounding me into the wall, my orgasm right on the edge.

My fingers grip his strong shoulders as my body tightens. "Ty," I beg, desperately needing him to push me over. He picks up his pace, his pelvis rubbing tantalizingly against my clit, and then he sucks hard at my neck, no doubt leaving a mark, and that's all I need to fall over the edge into pure bliss. With one more thrust, he comes inside me, his entire body shuddering with his release as he groans deep against my neck.

We stay locked like that for several minutes before he pulls back and kisses me reverently.

His eyes haven't quite lost their heat as he looks at me like I'm his entire world. "I love you, Wife."

My heart fills with so much joy it feels almost impossibly full. "I love you more, Husband."

He smiles. "Not a chance."

I'm okay with us spending our entire lives trying to out prove the other that we love each other more. Sounds like heaven to me.

Thank you for reading Closing the Distance! The final book in the LA Wolves Football series, Protecting the Boundary, is now available for preorder.

Ty

BONUS EPILOGUE

My stomach is so tied up in knots right now, you'd think I was the one getting drafted, not my oldest son, Troian. I'm seated next to him with Lexi on his other side, my arm draped across the back of the couch so I can touch her, since I know she's been a ball of nerves about this whole thing. My daughters, Lana and Taelyn are next to Lexi, while my other son, Landon, sits next to me. Surrounding us are my parents, my brothers and their families, and the members of the long defunct Fierce Four and their families—the honorary aunts, uncles, and cousins who've been there for every important milestone in my kids' lives just like I've been there for theirs.

It feels like Troian was born yesterday. Lana was three when he was born, and she adorably asked if we could return him for a little sister. When we brought Landon home two years later, she was a little more excited about another baby. Then three years after Landon, she finally got the little sister she wanted, and despite their eight-year age difference, Lana and Taelyn have always been very close.

But it's amazing how quickly time flies. As they say with kids, the nights are long, but the years are short. I swear I blinked and Troian was finishing up college. Now he's pursuing the same career I did. I squeeze Lexi's neck and catch her gaze when she glances at me. Her smile is soft, understanding. After twenty-five years together, we've learned how to communicate well without any words when it's necessary. But I hope she can see all the gratitude I have for her.

We never would've had this life without this woman by my side. Without her love, I would've never known what this kind of happiness felt like. I wouldn't have these four incredibly talented kids who make me so full of pride I feel like I could burst.

I remember my own draft day, although now it has the haze of a memory like it happened to someone else. Troian seems more calm and composed than I was on my draft day.

There's a small camera crew here filming because word is he's going in the second round and there's been a lot of hype since he's my son. Sure enough, his phone rings and the room goes silent as he answers.

"Hello?" he says.

I hold my breath, waiting.

Troian's head drops and he covers his eyes with his hand, but I can't miss his smile. "Yes, sir. I'm very excited. Thank you so much."

A pause as my heart beats so frantically in my chest I'm worried I might be having a heart attack for a second.

"I'm ready to get to work. Thank you again. Uh huh. Bye."

He puts his phone down and smiles at me. "I'm playing for the Wolves."

The room erupts in cheers as my eyes burn with unshed tears. Without a moment's hesitation, I wrap my arms around him, pulling him into a tight hug. "I'm so fucking proud of you," I murmur against his ear loud enough so he can hear it over everyone losing their damn minds. His arms tighten around me before we separate, and his mom pulls him into her arms for a hug. Not only is my son carrying on my legacy, but he's also playing for my old team.

I'm getting claps on the back by friends and family, but I can't look away from my kids and my wife. Of all the accolades I won as a pro athlete, none of them come anywhere close to filling me with the immeasurable pride of seeing my kids find their own success. They are my pride and joy, my greatest accomplishment. My greatest reward.

Everyone is standing now, surrounding Troian with hugs and cheers. Lexi moves to stand by me, threading our fingers together and leaning her head on my shoulder. Her black hair hangs loosely around her shoulders. It's not quite the same shade it was when we got married. She dyes it now to hide the gray—something she blames on me and our kids for making her worry. Even if she didn't color her hair, I'd still think she was the most beautiful woman in the world.

Dropping a kiss to her head, I squeeze her hand before loosening my fingers so I can wrap her up in a hug. Her arms wrap around my waist as she stares up at me, her gorgeous blue eyes shiny with happy tears, her infectious smile glued to her face. The same pride I'm feeling is reflected in her eyes. I place a small kiss on the side of her neck, right below her ear.

"Thank you," I say.

She pulls back just enough to look me in the eyes. "I feel like I should be the one thanking you."

Even after twenty-five years and a lot of therapy, she still has moments of vulnerability and fear that she'll lose everything we've built. It was the worst when the kids were little. Every worst-case scenario possible would run through her mind on repeat. But her therapist was amazing at helping ease her concerns and anxieties. And when her therapist couldn't, I would reassure her every chance I got.

"I think we can both be thankful for each other. How about that?"

Her smile still makes my stomach swirl the way it always has. "That sounds good to me."

Wrapping my hand in her hair, I kiss her plush pink lips, closing my eyes to soak up this moment with my wife. Not a single day goes by where I'm not grateful the condom failed all those years ago. The woman in my arms, the life we've built, our beautiful children, our friends and family—both blood and chosen—are all here because of that one moment in time.

And I wouldn't change a single thing.

AFTERWORD

I never thought I'd write a pregnancy book. Bear with me while I get pretty personal here for a minute.

In December 2017, I had my first miscarriage. We'd been trying for over a year, so when I got that positive pregnancy test, it was our own personal miracle. We were so excited. Overjoyed. We called it "Peanut" and I loved it from the second those two lines showed up on the test. And then I went to my first ultrasound appointment and I'll never forget the silence in the room for as long as I live. The way my heart dropped when I realized something was wrong. There was no heartbeat. To say I was devastated would be an understatement.

I never used the name Peanut again. I couldn't even say it for the longest time without tears forming.

Little did I know that wouldn't be the first time I didn't hear a heartbeat on an ultrasound. It happened two more times.

But this is not a sad story, I promise. After a second miscarriage and another year of fertility hurdles, I got my miracle baby. I held my breath the entire pregnancy, afraid to decorate or do anything to jinx it. I spent those nine months terrified of losing him. So terrified in fact, we probably wouldn't have even had a nursery if it wasn't for my mom. I can painfully relate to Lexi's fear of having the rug ripped out from under her. Of her happiness disappearing in the blink of an eye.

But then he arrived, healthy and perfect.

My third miscarriage came before my second miracle baby. My babies are my two rainbows after the storms and heartaches.

Why am I telling you all this deeply personal information? Because my personal experience made me worried I would never be able to write a pregnancy story. But then Ty and Lexi started talking to me and I knew exactly how their story would unfold. Did I cry while writing this? Definitely. But there was also something really cathartic about writing it. To use the name Peanut for the first time since December 2017. To give that baby I carried for only a few weeks life in little Lana. This book is for all the Peanuts that a mama somewhere is missing or holding in their arms with gratitude for their precious gift. It's for all the women who've felt unloved or scared of losing what's most precious to them.

All my fears of writing a pregnancy story were lost as I fell deeper into Ty and Lexi's story. I can say without fail this is my favorite story I've ever written and I hope you love them as much as I do.

I also want to thank several people who made this book possible.

To my beta readers, Alyse and Kelly. Thank you so much for your valuable feedback to make this book sparkle.

To my cover designer, Kate, for always making me incredible covers.

To my editors, Ann Suhs and Ann Riza. I would be absolutely lost without you ladies always making my books the strongest they can be. You have my endless thanks!

To my husband for always supporting this crazy dream of mine and making sure I have my writing time.

And to my two little miracles. You make every day brighter. You are my greatest accomplishment. I love you so much.

And last, but never least, to you, my reader. Thank you for coming on this journey (especially if you've read this far). I couldn't do this without you.

ABOUT THE AUTHOR

Cadence Keys is a bestselling steamy romance author. When she's not coming up with plots for her books, she's chasing her rambunctious toddlers around or cuddling with her husband. She loves writing heartfelt stories with relatable characters and a guaranteed happily ever after.

Learn more about her and her books on her website: www.cadencekeysauthor.com

facebook.com/cadencekeysauthor

x.com/cadencewrites

instagram.com/cadencekeysauthor

bookbub.com/profile/cadence-keys

goodreads.com/cadencekeysauthor

tiktok.com/@cadencekeysauthor

ALSO BY CADENCE KEYS

LA Wolves Football Series

In the Grasp

Across the Middle

Down by Contact

Taking the Handoff

Scorched Turf (Author Website Exclusive Novella)

Defending the Backfield

After the Snap

Closing the Distance

Protecting the Boundary

Rapturous Intent Rockstar Series

Noble Intent

Forbidden Intent

Devoted Intent

Promised Intent

Breaking the Rules Series

Only a Kiss

Just for Tonight

About Last Night

Printed in Dunstable, United Kingdom